A WILD RIDE

John Wilson cleared his throat and then sighed. "Well, Speedy," he said less enthusiastically. "I'm with you, if you say the word. We'll start now."

"Roll your blankets, then. Have you got a horse?"

"Yes, I've got a horse picketed out in the field behind the stable."

"Saddle it up, then. I'll be ready in ten minutes, and meet you in front of the cook house. Is that a go?"

"Only, Speedy, what's the terrible rush...and the night's like ice!"

"It's a long story, old man," Speedy said. "But the chief thing is that, if I don't keep lively on this trail, I'm likely to be dead on it. You understand?"

"You're followed?"

"Yes."

"By who?"

"Later on I'll tell you. Are you starting with me? Mind you, John, if you ride with me, the way may be a little rough. But if it's excitement you want..."

MAX BRAND®

Red Rock's Secret

LEISURE BOOKS NEW YORK CITY

A LEISURE BOOK®

January 2008

Published by special arrangement with Golden West Literary Agency.

Dorchester Publishing Co., Inc.
200 Madison Avenue
New York, NY 10016

ISBN 10: 0-8439-5874-X
ISBN 13: 978-0-8439-5874-4

Printed in the United States of America.

10 9 8 7 6 5 4 3 2 1

Visit us on the web at www.dorchesterpub.com.

Red Rock's Secret

TABLE OF CONTENTS

Cuttle's Hired Man

"Cuttle's Hired Man" was one of twenty-three short novels published in 1924 by Frederick Faust. It appeared under the Max Brand byline in the February 23rd issue of Street & Smith's *Western Story Magazine*. It is the tale of the testing of the friendship of Bill Warner and Chick Newton, two cowboys who wintered one year in the mountains of Montana, when, seven years later, they meet again in an Arizona desert town. This is its first appearance since its original publication.

I

No doubt there is a more mysterious poetry in the desert of the great Southwest than there is in the northern mountains, but there is nothing in the desert to compare with the brutal force of the mountain winters, and it is in those mountain storms that the friendships of men are discovered and made strong and then, at last, are welded together with a greater power than the power of steel.

Now, Bill Warner and Chick Newton had ridden together through only one season in Montana, but they had done for one another all that men can perform. Cut off from the rest of the world, fenced into a corner of the mountains, they had nothing but their wits and their hands and a small stock of food for themselves and the herd to rely upon. But they had played the game for four months and emerged lean of face, hollow of eye, sick with immense labors, but with a half-starved herd still able to stand and still able to graze. It was a great triumph, particularly keeping in mind that Chick Newton was new to that district and had to be broken in by Warner. However, Bill found an apt pupil. They worked to exhaustion every day; they slept until hunger wakened them in the dark of the winter mornings, and, when the winter was ended, each knew the other better, far better, than he could ever have known a brother.

Chick Newton had wandered south on a newly acquired horse. He got the animal by gift, not by purchase, as Chick sadly used to explain. But, having the luck against him one day, he had lost everything else, even to his watch, and finally he had offered his horse, although it was like parting with a limb. The horse went with the rest, of course, but, when it was discovered that he had no more resources, the winner staked him to a dollar and a horse. No words could describe that animal except the words of Chick Newton, who had just ridden the creature 1,000 miles, or thereabouts, and who therefore could be presumed to know it fairly well.

"They looked over the corral," said Chick in telling the tale, "and you could see 'em figure me down small. Look how I'd just stepped in and dropped eleven hundred in the pot besides a fine new pair of boots, a sombrero all done up in Mexican gold work, a saddle that had more carving on it than there is noise in a terrier pup, and the best steppin', wisest-headed cow hoss that ever made a yearlin' look plumb foolish. I'd dropped all that, and it sure looked like they could afford to stake me to a fair to middlin' hoss. I seen 'em pick over their gang with their eyes. And every one that they picked up to look at was worse'n the last. Finally they come to a yaller-haired, long-headed, short-legged, goat-eyed, Roman-nosed junk heap. And that was what they give me for a hoss! That was the stake that they handed me.

"Man, man, after that I jest nacherally can't help hatin' the whole state of Idaho . . . damn their ornery eyes. I climbed aboard that thing they called a hoss and sat down in a saddle that was nothin' but a wood frame . . . the rats had ate all the leather offen it a long time before. I sat down in the saddle and jabbed this hoss with my spurs. I call it a hoss, but you can see for yourself that it's a damned sight more like an old mountain goat than it is like any hoss you ever seen before. I thought it would sure bust apart and break down in the middle. But when it got a couple of jabs with the spurs, it begun to come to life and moved off. It had a movement like a grandfather's clock. It rattled all over every time it took a step. But it didn't fall to pieces. No, sir, it kept right on runnin', and it ain't rundown yet. It's a plumb queer hoss. It's got a gait like a rock breaker, and it looks like Methuselah's mule, but it sure don't stop goin'. It'll hit a jog in the morning and keep it up all the day. Don't make no difference how steep the slope is up or down, it keeps right on the same way. It's only got them two gaits. Never moves at no other pace . . . just the jog and the slowest damned trot that was ever invented."

It was upon this charger that Chick Newton arrived in the Arizona town in the blue ending of the long twilight, although there still was enough illumination to see and be seen easily across the width of the single street. But had they been half a mile away and that half mile composed of the thickest dark, Chick Newton would have sworn that he could not have failed to sense the nearness of his old bunkie.

He saw Billy Warner coming out of the door of an adobe shack. He saw Billy Warner with the cigarette carelessly in the corner of his mouth, as usual, and the hat upon the back of his head. He saw Billy Warner, long and lean and solemn of face.

Some one else was with Billy. Perhaps it was a woman, perhaps it was a man, but at least Chick did not pause to make sure. He emitted from the deeps of his lungs a yell that rasped the skin from his throat and brought men and women to their feet in every house in the town. Then he plunged across the street, shouting as he came. He had not been drinking, but it was seven years since he had laid eyes on this man to whom he had owed his life half a dozen times and who he had repaid by service in kind. He reached Billy Warner with a final whoop, but he stopped with his hands outstretched. Billy had not recognized him.

There could be no doubt about it. Through the door the light from the interior shone fully into his face. Billy might be a trifle in the shadow, but his own face was certainly well lighted for Billy's examination, and here was Billy Warner looking upon him with a sort of blank curiosity and unconcern.

"Bill," he said, "damn my soul, you ain't goin' to pass me up."

Bill Warner—for surely it was he, for God could not have created two men so like one another—shrugged his shoulders and began to roll another cigarette.

"Partner," he said, "you sure got me down wrong. My name ain't Bill."

Red blood poured through the face of Chick. He had been sure enough before, but he was mortally certain now. Seven years was a long time. They had been youngsters then, and in seven years the face altered, the lines grew deeper, the character was engraved more surely, so that it was barely possible that he could have been wrong about the face. But there was another method of recognizing a man, and that was through his voice. And by the voice, most assuredly, this man was Bill Warner. The fiber had grown a little rougher—otherwise it was identically the same.

"You ain't Bill Warner, then?" Chick said slowly.

"Sorry, partner."

"Is it the looks of my outfit that makes you give me the cold shoulder, Bill?" asked Chick sadly. "Have you gone and got stuck-up since you and me bucked the snow in Jackson Cañon that winter?"

He studied the face of the other with the most infinite caution, but there was not a shadow of doubt or of meaning in the eyes of this man who had the face and the voice of Bill Warner. And certainly, thought Chick, if this were indeed his man, such an appeal could not be resisted. A gleam must surely have come in the eye of this man if he were actually Bill Warner.

Yet the other now shook his head. "I dunno who you're drivin' to get at," he said with perfect kindness and good nature. "But the boys around here all know me. My name ain't Bill. My name is Joe Tucker. Come on along, Olivetta, or we'll be late as the deuce."

Chick Newton, falling back in utter bewilderment, saw a slender, olive-skinned, black-eyed girl supple as a whip stalk and light as its lash, and by the way the incarnation of Bill looked down to her, and by the way she looked up to him, with a flush in the hollow of her cheek and a light in her eyes, Chick knew perfectly well that there was something of great importance to these two young people between them. For his own part, he went back to the hotel.

"We got to have advance payment," said the proprietor, scanning the ragged attire of Chick and the absence of baggage.

A bone should not be shown to a hungry dog. Chick was literally starving for anything that would blot from his mind the rebuff that he had received a few moments before. All the devil in him, of which there was an ample measure, came up in his eyes.

"I don't pay in advance in a place like this," said Chick deliberately. "I got to see how I sleep, and from the looks of things I might be bothered here by . . . rats!"

The proprietor laid his hand on the gun that was always under the shelf that supported the register. Then he abruptly thought of his family and changed his mind. There was that in the face of Chick which made the proprietor see his own funeral procession with astonishing vividness. So he took Chick to the best room in the house and started to depart when Chick called him back.

"You know Joe Tucker?" asked Chick.

"I know Joe Tucker," said the other. "Everybody does."

"How long has he been around these parts?"

"He come down here the winter that Steve Monigle built his house. That was five years ago."

"Five years?"

"Lemme see. Monigle's kid is six . . . no, it was seven years back that Joe Tucker come to town."

Chick started. "That's all," he said finally, and, when the proprietor left, he sat down to think matters over.

It was just seven years since he had seen Bill Warner; it was just seven years since this Joe Tucker had arrived in the town. The similarity in date was too great to be idly passed over. Then he remembered a thing for which he should have searched the face of Tucker, if that were indeed his name. There was a little triangular scar on the right side of the jaw, the result of a kick received from a colt, according to Warner. If that scar were on the face of this Tucker, then Chick's mind could be made up.

With that, he turned in, fell instantly asleep, and did not awaken until the sun was high, for he had ridden sixty hard miles the day before. When he had finished his breakfast, he asked for Tucker's location, and he was told that the latter had a small ranch five miles out from the town, on the Middlebury Road.

Out on the Middlebury Road, therefore, he jogged the yellow mustang and came, in the course of an hour, within sight of the shack, a dreary little house put down in the middle of burned desert where only Arizona cattle could possibly find grass enough to make a living. He tapped on the door without dismounting, and the door was instantly opened by Tucker. The keen eyes of Chick fastened upon one thing only—a little triangular scar on the side of Tucker's jaw!

II

Tucker was at least the perfect master of his facial expression, and, if he felt either surprise or interest at the sight of his visitor, he controlled the emotions. "Manage to find out where your friend, Bill, was?" he asked pleasantly of Chick.

"Bill," said Chick, "is there anybody inside the house except you?"

"Look here," Tucker said, "you ain't gainin' nothin' by callin' me Bill. But if you aim to find out about the folks in the house, I'm free to say that I'm alone out here."

"Then," said Chick, "what'n the devil are you gainin' by lyin' to me. What's it mean to you? They ain't nobody to hear you tell the truth and that truth is that you're the same damn' Bill Warner that spent the winter with me in Jackson Cañon."

Tucker frowned. "I'm a considerable patient man," he said at last, "but I get tired of sayin' one thing over and over."

Chick sighed. For it seemed that Bill was determined even to make violent trouble rather than have his true identity fastened upon him. However, Chick's own temper was fast getting away with him. He fought against it, but he could not help the rush of blood to his head.

"Look here, Bill," he said. "I'm talkin' plumb soft an' easy. I'm hopin' that you ain't goin' to prove yourself no yaller dog that quits cold on his old friends as soon as he gets something to call his own . . . even the measly beginnin's of a ranch like this here one." And he gestured scornfully at the house.

"That house," said the other, scowling upon him, "is good enough for a better man than you, stranger, to live in. I made it myself!"

"I see," Chick said with mounting bitterness, "that you're a tolerable good cowpuncher, by the looks of the house."

"Meaning," said the other, "that it don't suit you?"

"Me?" Chick said lightly. "No, nor my dog. I wouldn't trust a good dog in there."

Tucker, or Warner, or whatever he might be, stepped boldly forth from the door, and spat upon the ground. "Say that over . . . slow," he said.

But when there was bloodshed in the immediate offing, Chick suddenly remembered that he was and that he always had been by far the better shot of the two. And, hand to hand, he was a stronger and a quicker man. There would be no doubt about the outcome of a battle with his old companion. And the sense of his own power melted him.

"Oh, Bill," he said quietly, "damn me if it don't make my heart sick to have you act up like this. My heavens, man, ain't you got no decency in you?"

"Bill?" cried the other. "What in the devil d'you mean by buttoning that fool name on me still?"

Chick pointed. "You got the brand on your face." he said. "There's the same little old scar. Had you forgot about that thing, Bill?"

The latter clapped a hand suddenly to his face and covered the very spot where the scar appeared. Very plainly he had forgotten that scar and the surety with which it identified him. Suddenly the color flooded his face. The red receded and left him spotted with purple. He looked down upon the ground miserably, and Chick, unwilling to take advantage of his confusion, looked sadly away across the great plains. For it was a hollow satisfaction, surely, to make an old companion understand that his falsity was well understood.

"Well," said Chick at last, very quietly, "now that I've seen you, I guess that I'll be driftin', Bill. So long . . . and good luck, partner."

He had turned the head of the yellow mustang to the west when he heard something like a sob behind him, and there was Bill Warner at his side, speaking in a voice broken and trembling as the voice of a child overcome with emotion.

"Chick, old-timer," he said, "for heaven's sake get off your hoss and set down with me. I figure out like a skunk in your eyes, and I don't blame you for it. But lemme have a chance to put myself right, will you?"

"You don't need to do no talkin'," said Chick gravely. "I ain't goin' to bother you none."

"Chick, I'm askin' your pardon, plumb humble."

The heart of Chick melted. He slipped from the back of the yellow mustang and faced his companion with the faint beginnings of a smile. "Why, Bill," he said, "there ain't no storm on the insides of me. But if you're down here in trouble, old-timer, why not lemme give you a hand? Ain't that right?"

Bill shook his head. "Nothin' this side of heaven could help me," he said gravely. "But if you'll listen, I'll tell you how come that I treated you this here way. It wasn't out of choice, old-timer, but from figuring that I didn't dare to take any chances with nobody in the world . . . not even you. Because if they knowed that my name was really Bill Warner, I wouldn't last five days down here or any place else in the world. Because Bill Warner has got to die . . .

and there ain't no way for me to keep on livin' than to let that name lie dead and to call myself Joe Tucker. That's what I am now. That's what I been for seven years. And the minute that I go back to my real name, I'm sure done for."

He made this strange statement with such a voice of solemn concern and with such a final tone of despair that Chick felt perspiration starting on his forehead.

"Bill," he said in a murmur, as though even in this place they might be spied upon, "if you done something that's made things bad for you, keep it to yourself. I don't want to know nothin' about it."

"You ain't been back around Jackson Cañon, then, all these here seven years?"

"Not once."

"That's why you don't know, then. If you'd been there, you couldn't help knowin'. Chick, they're set to finish me up if ever they can catch me."

"Are they right or wrong?"

"I don't know."

"What!" shouted Chick. "You don't know?"

"I don't."

"Whether you done something wrong or not?"

"That's it."

Chick stood back and regarded his old friend with a gloomy frown.

"I know," said the other huskily. "It sure sounds like I was stringin' you, old-timer. When a gent is accused of murder and has got to say that he dunno whether or not he done it . . . it sure sounds queer."

"It does," admitted Chick, still frowning.

"Shall I tell you the yarn?"

"D'you think that you'd better?"

"Chick," his old friend confided quietly, "I could

trust you a pile further than I could ever trust myself." And he began his narrative.

His tale started with his return to town after the bitter winter months spent in Jackson Cañon with Chick Newton. He had gone back to receive a fat little roll of bills for his pay for the four months, and, with that money in his pocket, he had begun a celebration upon broad and sweeping lines, part of which had been a campaign to drink, single-handed, all the redeye to be found in Montana.

In the midst of these brave efforts, he had encountered one of his oldest friends, Tom Cuttle, and Tom had willingly accompanied him on his expedition. How he could not tell, but he found himself one evening in a state of half-drunken stupor at the house of his rich old uncle, Henry P. Warner, more widely known throughout the district simply as Henry P. It was a name that suggested to the mountaineers infinite wealth, infinite cunning, and infinite integrity combined. He was so full of tricks that no one could dare to compete with him in the business game, but he was so honest that no one could blame him for his wily shifts. He took advantage of the breaks, to be sure, but he never forced them. He had built up a really fine fortune, perhaps of three or four millions, which was of course magnified into fifteen or twenty millions by the public rumor.

Old Henry P. had very little use for any young men, and he had no greater liking for his nephew, William, than he had for any other youth. In fact, he seemed always rather bitter over the fact that William, simply through an accident of birth, must be his heir. And he had often said that it was absurd for him to work, because the harder he labored, the more he was piling up for a young man who had never lifted his hand in order to enjoy all of the benefits that would be showered upon him. Naturally such talk as this did not make for good feeling, and, all his life, young Bill Warner had hated his uncle with a sedulous hatred, and his uncle had responded in kind.

Therefore it was extraordinary that he should have found himself in the big, rambling old house of Henry P. Warner in the midst of his party. It could only be accounted for on the understanding that a half-drunken whim had carried him there.

He was received by Henry P. without pleasure, but also without any rebuffs, which was the stranger because it was known that Henry P. was a most ardent opponent of the use of alcohol. He had only said on this occasion: "If you have to drink, my boy, stay to beer and leave whiskey to those who have stronger heads." Of this remark young Bill Warner was quite sure, for it had been spoken while he was in one of his clear intervals during the evening.

He remembered the dinner by fits and by starts. He remembered walking dizzily, after the meal ended, onto the porch that was Uncle Henry's favorite resting place after dinner—a lofty verandah looking down upon a narrow, swift-flowing tributary of the Mason River called Dulcy Creek. It was only a white streak rushing through the night far down below the level of the verandah, with the black pine trees climbing the farther shore. Here Henry P. took his nephew suddenly to task for the folly of his habits. Their words became hot, and the more violently they talked, the more dizzily the head of Bill Warner became, until finally his mind was lost in a swirl of darkness.

Bill recovered himself to find that he was lying flat

on his back on the verandah, with his companion, Tom Cuttle, shaking him violently by the shoulder and crying out: "Where's your uncle, Bill? For heaven's sake, what's happened? And what's the meaning of this?" He dragged Bill into a sitting posture and pointed to a section of the railing of the verandah that had been broken down and now hung swaying in the wind with a slight creaking noise. Bill, made almost sober by the grim suggestion of this thing, went to the gap in the rail and looked down. There was the white water of the creek just beneath him.

He had drawn back with an exclamation of horror and found the face of Cuttle very drawn and very white.

"What's happened?" cried Tom. "What has happened?"

"I don't know," said poor Bill Warner.

At that, Tom Cuttle drew back from him. "You don't know, eh?" he had said. "Well, Bill, it's too bad you didn't keep your eyes open. You might have seen some cowardly murderer throw your uncle over the verandah and into Dulcy Creek."

"What do you mean?" Bill had cried at him.

"Nothing," Tom Cuttle stated sneeringly. "Yet, after all, that murderer is not entirely an enemy of yours, I suppose. At least, his work gives you several millions, Bill."

There were no liquor fumes left now in the brain of Bill. He brought himself together at once and began a thorough search. But there was no trace of his uncle. The old Negro who had served their coffee on the verandah above the creek had remained close, ready to answer any call. He could swear that Mr. Henry P. Warner had not retired from the verandah by coming back through the house. He could also swear that he had heard voices raised very high on the porch and that he had thought it a shame that any young man should be permitted to speak to an older one as noisily as Bill Warner had to his uncle. He could swear, too, that he had heard a trampling on the verandah, and the voices of both men raised—then silence.

What it meant to Bill Warner was simply this: That in a drunken frenzy, irritated by the reproofs of his uncle and when he was by no means master of himself, he had attacked the older man—perhaps struck him down, and, in falling, Henry Warner had struck the rail of the veranda which had given under his weight and allowed him to fall into the stream far beneath. At the same moment the liquor fumes must have overcome his own brain.

In the meantime, however, such an explanation, bad as it was, would never have satisfied a jury that would have been convinced that he had attacked his uncle to remove Henry Warner and bring his wealth into his own hands as the legitimate heir. So Bill Warner fled before the morning and before the sheriff could arrive to make an arrest. He had spent a few months in Canada until the hue and cry after him had died down. Then he returned to the States, came south under a new name, and had lived as Joe Tucker ever since.

"Did they find the body," asked Chick Newton, when this grisly tale was completed.

"They found a skeleton with his coat and one of his shoes still on it . . . they were washed up on the bank of the Mason River some time later," said Bill.

"What became of the money? Who got that?" Chick asked.

"That was one of the queerest of the things. Seems that Uncle Henry had sold off most of his stocks and bonds not very long before. 'Most like he was getting ready to invest the cash over again, and, while he waited, perhaps he buried the money near the old house. Anyway, all that they found of his estate was not more'n half a million, and that was mostly all in real estate. The cash had plumb disappeared! I seen in the papers that they'd searched the old house from head to heel, but they never found nothing. They dug up all the ground all around the house. There wasn't no sign. The coin was hid too close for that."

"And what'll you do? Just keep on here, Bill?"

"Not me! They've heard you call me Bill Warner. Before they get to putting two and two together, I'm going to sell out and move on to old Mexico."

They went gloomily into the house and sat down.

"If I've brought you bad luck," said Chick, "I'll never rest easy so long as I live, Billy."

But Bill Warner shook his head slowly. "There never has been no rest for me," he said. "There never will be, I guess, until I find out the whole truth about what happened that night. They's been hell inside my mind ever since, and it won't come out."

They talked of other things after that for a full hour, half sad and half happy, until a sharp knock came at the door and then, without further warning, it was thrown wide open. There, in the doorway, stood a little gentleman with a narrow gray beard and very sharp eyes. He carried in his hand a naked revolver. And over each shoulder there loomed behind him a tall follower, one with a shotgun carried at the ready and the other with two Colts out for action.

Bill Warner turned very pale, but his voice was steady enough. "You got business with me, Sheriff?" he asked.

"Joe," said the sheriff, "dog-gone me if I ain't sorry to bother you, but I just been told that you're a ringer for a gent named Warner that's wanted plumb bad in Montana. It ain't what I want to do. It's what I'm told to do for the law. Y'understand?"

"Of course," Bill said almost cheerfully.

"Partner?" murmured Chick Newton. His voice was husky with emotion, filled with suggestion. His eyes burned against the face of Bill Warner, as though to say: *Give me the word and I shall undo the wrong that I have done you. We'll fight the three of them together.*

But Bill Warner merely shook his head and smiled. "It ain't you, Chick," he said. "But them sort of things will come out. Better to have it sooner than later. Only it'll be hard on poor Olivetta."

III

By the next morning the papers of every city carried the story. Age mellows crime as it does wine, and here was a crime that had ripened and matured without solution for seven years. At last the criminal was caught, and through the unconscious agency of the criminal's oldest and dearest friend, who would sooner have laid down his own life than have betrayed a friend. Of course the reporters could not overlook such an opportunity. In a few days Bill Warner would be on his way north, and for the brutal murder of seven years before he would pay the penalty. But, in the meantime, there were seven years of probity and hard work and good citizenship behind him. Did they count for nothing?

"For nothing!" said the men who read the story.

"For everything!" said the ladies.

And, cowering in her chair, weeping and trembling, Olivetta asked Chick Newton what would come of her lover. For surely the newspapers that spoke of the death penalty could not be right.

"And my own father," cried Olivetta, "has forbid me to ever again so much as mention Billy's name!"

"Well?" Chick said, watching her sadly and narrowly.

She threw up her head. "I'll marry Billy if I have to wait twenty years for him," she said. "But it isn't fair that they should take him now. No matter what he did seven years ago, he's a good man now."

Chick Newton got out of his chair.

"Oh," said the girl, "are even you against him?"

But Chick only smiled and went out into the sun. In half an hour he was on the yellow mustang. He had no money. The railroad was not for him. But the yellow horse jogged him north and north over the long trail. For a month he journeyed, and by the end of the month all was over. Sometimes he reached a big city and could read all the details of the trial. Sometimes he had nothing at all for days at a time. Sometimes it was a mere note in a village newspaper. But by the time he reached Dulcy Creek, all was over. Bill Warner had been brought north, the case had been tried, and Bill was found guilty of murder in the first degree. In five short days after Chick reached Dulcy Creek his old companion would be hanged by the neck until he was dead. So swift was justice when it had at last found its guilty man.

In the little town of Dulcy, Chick put up the yellow mustang, worn thin as a skeleton, with hardly vigor enough to kick at its master when he dragged the saddle off. Chick himself was hardly fatter. The long trail, the ceaseless anxiety, had drawn his face long and lean and withered the flesh from his body; his eye was a gleam beneath a deep shadow.

He looked like an invalid, and, accordingly, big Jeff Thomas thought that it would be safe enough to brush this hollow-cheeked stranger from his path through the door of the hotel, whereupon Jeff was caught deftly by one arm and thrown across the back of the stranger and into the thick dust of the street. He staggered to his feet in the center of a blinding white cloud and with a gun in either hand, but before he could fire, a long arm snaked its way through the mist of dust and a thin-fingered fist, hard as granite, tapped Jeff Thomas just to one side of the point of the chin. He sat down again, forgetful of his guns, which Chick now picked out of his hands and carried back to the hotel porch.

There he offered them for sale in the following fashion: "Gents," he said, "I was give these two guns by a friend of mine who said he didn't know how to use 'em real handy, so's they wasn't much use to him. What'm I bid for 'em?"

There were a dozen men lounging near, amazed at the sudden fall of Jeff Thomas, but not one of them dared to speak until it was seen that Jeff himself had risen at last out of the dust, flung himself upon his horse without striving to recover his lost weapons, and was now plunging down the street at the full speed of a very fast horse tortured by the thrusting spurs. Then, with laughter and with shouting, they started bidding. Before they had ended, Chick had stowed $50 in his pocket and had become an established factor in the town of Dulcy. They told over and over the tale of the downfall of big Jeff Thomas, and they clapped Chick upon his lean, bony shoulders and called him a fine fellow. Only one old cowpuncher drew him to the side.

"Take my advice, son," he said. "Climb on your hoss and start for the tall timber right *pronto*. Dulcy ain't no healthy place for you from now on."

"Why?" asked Chick.

"You've made a fool out of Jeff Thomas. The rest of the Thomas boys will be after you, and, what's worse than all, they'll have Tom Cuttle behind 'em."

"I've heard that name somewhere," Chick said. "Who's Tom Cuttle?"

"He's a young gent ranchin' out the Minaska Valley way, and he owns the most part of Dulcy. He even bought the haunted house, about a month back."

"What's that?"

"The old Warner house up above the creek. You've heard of the killin' of old Hen Warner?"

"Yes."

"His creditors been tryin' to sell the old house ever since. But they couldn't make no headway, partly because some folks said that the house was plumb unlucky and partly because it's said to be haunted by some."

"Creditors?" Chick said, holding fast to that part of the remark. "I thought that old Warner left half a million even with all of his cash hid away."

"He left half a million. He owed three times that much."

"Ah?" murmured Chick.

"He'd tried a flier in Wall Street and got trimmed.

Maybe that was why he turned his property into cash, so's he could pay them that he owed money to. But that skunk of a nephew of his stopped everything when he murdered the old man. Anyway, as I was sayin', young Tom Cuttle owns the old Warner house now and most of Dulcy besides. And if he wants to make things hot for you, he can do it easy."

"Why should he?"

"Well, Jeff is his foreman. That's the why of it. He likes to have a hard-handed gent to handle things for him. Tom is so plumb easy and good-natured that he likes to have a hard one do his work for him. He cottons to a gunfighter like a duck to water. That's why him and Thomas have got on so well together."

"Well," said Chick Newton, "here's thanking you kindly, partner. I'll aim to take care of myself while I'm in town."

"There's another thing," went on the other in the most good-natured manner, "but if I'm talkin' too much, you must give me the flag, will you?"

"Go on," Chick said. "I take this here talk uncommon friendly."

"Which I mean it so. But I took a likin' to you, son, when I seen you pitch that big chunk of beef and fat into the dust. And I took a bigger likin' when I seen you go up to that gun-fannin', man-murderin' skunk and tap him on the chin so hard he forgot his gats. Well, sir, the boys about these parts are goin' to do quite a bit of talkin' about you, for a spell, and the worst part of that is that, when a gent gets a reputation for bein' a fighter, they's always some damn' fools that ain't able to rest easy until they've took that reputation away from him."

"I understand," said Newton, smiling at this diplomatic attitude. "But I ain't a braggin', loud-talkin' fool, partner. I ain't a fighter, either. All I aim to do is to keep from bein' walked on."

"I know. But they's some of the boys around here that's mighty ambitious to walk everywhere. They might aim right for you. Since Jim Sawyer left these parts, you might say that there ain't no master around here."

It was, to be sure, seven years since Newton had ridden in that region, but the fame of Jim Sawyer was not confined to the small neighborhood of one or two sprawling mountain counties. His name and his repute had traveled north and south and east and west. He was one of those vague figures about whom men paused for an instant. That he was formidable all knew well enough.

"Sawyer," went on the cowpuncher, "was able to keep the young bloods in hand. They knew that he was too hard for 'em. But after he left, they's been a dozen of 'em tryin' to get a name as the hardest gent in Montana. Which they're apt to try themselves out on you, old son."

For that warning, Newton thanked him. He, on his part, was firmly resolved to keep out of trouble, rather from fear of what he could do than fear of what he could not do. For your true fighters fall into two classes. There are the men who know their power and are anxious to make a display of it; there are the men who, knowing their strength fully as well, are kept quiet by the very knowledge of the danger that is in them. Some pugilists by profession love nothing better than a brawl. But there are others who would rather run away than take advantage of their superiority over an ordinary antagonist. So it was with Chick Newton. He had been given by birth a steady hand and the ability to look straight at a mark; he had improved those natural advantages by constant practice, and, having come to the point when he was sure of himself, he assiduously avoided trouble until trouble had looked him out and cornered him. Besides, on this occasion, he had other and greater business on hand than brawling with fists or with guns.

He spent the remainder of that first day lounging about the town, seeing what he could see, hearing what he could hear. For he had not the slightest idea where he could begin or what he could do in order to help poor Bill Warner, and he was hunting desperately for an opening.

Dulcy itself lay on a shoulder of Dulcy Mountain, rolling huge and shapeless to the south. Clusters of the noble silver spruce grew in and about the town, mixed with great pine trees that in turn, farther up the mountainside, gave way to the scrambling, irregular ranks of the lodgepole pines that climbed toward the summit, dwindling out toward a timber line that left, above it, the big, bare head of the mountain, streaked with white in the crevices and already gathering a solid cap of snow at the very summit. Lesser peaks assembled around this monster in every direction, but to the north there was a narrow valley that had been eaten out in the course of some thousands of centuries by the labor of Dulcy Creek. That busy little stream ran under the northern edge of the plateau on which the town stood, and, although it was at some distance from the village itself and furthermore cut away by the lofty dimensions of the bluff that formed its southern bank, still there were times when the deep and rapid voice of the waters came grumbling through the town.

Dulcy itself consisted of a single street winding along close to the foot of the big mountain and thickly bordered with houses on either side. Every spring it wakened; every autumn, when the snows began to take the miners out of the mountains, Dulcy fell into a sleep again that lasted until the sun was once more warm and the sturdy prospectors came swarming up to make Dulcy headquarters for another year's campaign. It was a town built low and heavy to resist the winds and the cold of the winter. There was not a single building of any size in it. One had to walk nearly a mile from the village before one came to the single edifice that was worth seeing, and this was the ruined mansion of old Henry P. Warner, which stood on the bluff above the creek.

Toward it Newton sauntered that afternoon. A brick wall backed by a quadruple row of tall grown spruces bounded the grounds. But the wings of the huge wrought-iron gate had broken down their hinges and stood permanently ajar. Newton walked through them and up a driveway thick with grass and even with young shrubs. Plainly during the seven years since the old master disappeared, the estate had returned far toward a wilderness and nature was doing its rapid best to wipe out the traces of man's handiwork.

From the narrow forest that surrounded the place, Newton came out into a spacious series of lawns—now, of course, grown wild—interspersed with groups of trees and hedges that themselves had turned into packed rows of saplings. He passed a ruined orchard. He came upon a greenhouse whose interior was a jumbled mass of rank growth and whose roof had been smashed in a dozen places. Beyond was a great rose garden now quite without a vestige of roses. And beyond the roses stood the house itself. It was a rambling structure built according to the English style of cottages. It followed the curve of the bluff on which it stood, winding through the greater part of a letter S. It was built solidly of a fine limestone quarried not far away, and the white walls and the red-tiled roof made a brilliant picture with the blue of the sky arched behind and crossed with wind-blown wisps of cloud.

It seemed, at the first glance, in perfect condition and habited even now, but when he looked again, he noted a score of details of smashed windows, of broken and disarranged tiling, and of the untrained confusion in which the climbing vines had clambered up the sides of the building. He came closer and peered through a window into one of the rooms. A single glance was enough. For all was the most hideous confusion within—the flooring had been torn up and broken to bits; the walls had been smashed through here and there. For furniture there was a broken chair and a table whose legs on one side were gone. One would have thought that madmen or wild beasts had held high carnival here, but the simple truth, no doubt, was that most of this damage had been wrought by the creditors of the dead millionaire when they searched through the place to find the treasure that he was known to possess.

Newton was by no means an impressionable man, but from this scene of disaster he turned away sick at heart. Once, on a black day of his life, the leg of his favorite horse had been broken by stepping into a squirrel hole and Newton had had to kill the animal. He felt the same sick disgust with life when he turned away from the ruined home of Henry Warner. It was little wonder that the ghost of the dead owner was said to haunt the place, for if ever a spirit would return to the earth in wrath, the soul of Warner must come back to view the melancholy wreck that had been made of his dwelling.

So thinking, he took a hitch at his belt and wandered back toward the town. He had no sooner reached the hotel than his old cowpuncher friend sought him out.

"It's turning out the way I figured it," he said. "There's trouble ahead for you, partner. Tom Cuttle is in town looking for you!"

IV

It has been said that Newton was not a seeker after trouble, and ordinarily he would have avoided Tom Cuttle with the greatest care, but on this day he was in a strange frame of mind. He had come eagerly to the town of Dulcy hoping against hope that, once he arrived at the scene of that seven-year-old tragedy, he would be able to think of some manner in which he could help his friend, but nothing, so far, had come to his mind. A day had passed. Only four remained between poor Bill Warner and death, and Newton felt that he might as well have remained in Arizona. He had ridden an arduous 1,000 miles and gained nothing by his effort. So he almost welcomed an interview with Tom Cuttle, no matter what danger there might be in it. He would have welcomed, indeed, an interview with the archfiend. All that he wanted was something to fill his mind and take it from the brooding over the fate of Bill Warner.

Accordingly he went to the hotel desk and left word that he would be in his room, and that, if Tom Cuttle or any other man sought for him, he could be found there. To his room he went, spent a few moments looking to his pair of Colts, and then settled down to wait for whatever might happen.

The slant yellow light of the sun crept gradually across the rough pine boards that made the floor; the sweetness of the evergreens blew through the window, and a long, slow half hour passed before a rap came at his door. When he called out for the visitor to enter, there came in to him a handsome young fellow who announced himself as Tom Cuttle and requested a few moments of talk. So Newton sat on the bed and gave his visitor the one chair with which the chamber was furnished. He considered his guest narrowly the while. From the account of Bill Warner he gathered that the latter's old friend must now be very close to thirty, but he appeared at least five full years short of that age. There was no mark upon his face, no shadow beneath his eyes, no stoop of labor in his back. He walked as a child walks, lightly and carelessly. He sat as a child sits, slumping with utter abandon into his chair, his muscles completely relaxed. Yet, for all of his gay air, there was trouble behind his eyes.

"Mister Newton," he said, "being in a bad corner, I've come to you for aid."

Chick Newton, who liked directness more than he liked almost any other quality in a man, brightened a little. Moreover, this did not sound like an ultimatum that was to send him from the town of Dulcy.

"Keepin' out of trouble," Chick said, "is the game that I've always played. I got a long line of trumps to play in that hand, Mister Cuttle."

Tom Cuttle nodded hastily. "I'm a peaceful fellow myself," he said, "but sometimes trouble follows us around and tags us in spite of ourselves. As I said before, I need help, and I've come to you to get it."

Newton shook his head. "I'd mighty well like to oblige," he said, "but I'm full of my own business right now."

"What business?" snapped out the other eagerly, sitting up in his chair.

Chick Newton was silent. His dislike of questions was as great as his fondness for directness of speech.

"Oh," went on Cuttle impatiently, "I don't want to pry into your affairs, but tell me what this business of yours amounts to. I think that I can overbid for your time and services. It won't be a long job . . . I can promise you that."

"Money ain't what I'm after right now," admitted Newton warily. "But here's a town full of able-bodied men. You sure can pick a good substitute for me."

"Able-bodied men!" exclaimed Cuttle sneeringly, flushing in his anger. "I had the most able-bodied fellow of the lot, so I thought. A regular cock of the walk. From his way you would have thought him a tiger. But you turned that tiger inside out, tied a knot in him, and sent him home howling. The tiger, in short, turned out a cur. Don't tell me about the able-bodied men in Dulcy!"

Newton eyed him again. There was nothing, he told himself, that could possibly make him take an instant of his time from the pursuit of his work for Bill Warner. There was nothing that could do that, to be sure. Not millions in gold could pay him. And yet—there was something in the manner of the young rancher that promised infinite excitement.

"How far away is this here business of yours?" asked Newton.

"My ranch is only a step from town."

"You want me there?"

"I do, and I intend to have you, Newton. Now, I say, cut the preliminaries short and tell me in a word what your time is worth to you?"

"What sort of a job?" asked Newton. Then he recalled that his fame as a horsebreaker was not unknown in certain sections of the West. He had done little of that work in this region, but perhaps his reputation had spread even as far as this. He went on: "Maybe you got some fine-blooded hosses that you want broke, and you've heard that I handle 'em with kindness, instead of spurs. Is that it?"

"Horses? Damn horses!" snapped out Cuttle. "What matter to me whether they're broken with a whip in three days or kindness in three months so long as they answer the reins and don't spend all their strength bucking?"

A shadow fell over the face of Chick Newton, and he leaned back against the head of the bed. Some of the curiosity passed out of his eyes, and a great deal of the eagerness. One would have said that he had come to know his visitor in the short time they had been together.

"It don't make no difference to some," Chick admitted quietly. "The only difference is in the insides of the hoss. Well, if it ain't hosses you want me to handle, what is it?"

"Men!" said Cuttle.

"Eh? Got some raw 'punchers workin' for you? Well, sir, I don't aim to be no straw boss on a cow ranch. I can do my part with a rope and a hoss. But I ain't no expert."

"The devil, man!" cried Cuttle. "Wake up and listen to what I have to say. I need you because I am afraid of certain men. Do you understand?" His face blanched with his emotion, and, starting from his chair, he glided a long step nearer to his new acquaintance. "Newton," he whispered, his eyes roving from window to door as though he expected death itself to look in upon him at any instant, "I am living in constant fear of murder. God knows. At this very moment I may be no better than a murdered man. You . . . you . . . may be the very man who has been hired for that purpose."

As this idea came borne to him, he shrank away and staggered back until he leaned against the wall, gasping for breath, whiter than the dingy spread that covered the bed. Newton did not know whether to despise or to pity him most.

"You not bein' a gunfighter?" he asked as gently as possible.

His query seemed to reassure Cuttle, who stood forth again, wiping his forehead with a trembling hand.

"Guns?" he said, shuddering. "I know nothing about them. They're only toys to me . . . things to be used in hunting a few times a year. But there are men here in the mountains who spend hours every day in the manipulation of their weapons. They burn up pounds and pounds of powder and of lead in order to make themselves ready for fighting with other men. Perhaps the chance will never come to them. But if it does come, they're ready. They talk of new ways of drawing a revolver from its holster as a mining engineer might talk about a new method of drawing the gold out of the rock. They lie awake nights conceiving new ways of making that draw smooth, so that for all their speed their hands may be steady as they fire the shot. They are, in fact, murderers in the making . . . every one of them." His face wrinkled and blackened with rage and with disgust.

"Well," said Newton rather guiltily, "they's a pile of interest in a little ol' Colt." He could not keep his fingers from the butts of his guns as he spoke.

"I know!" Cuttle said, brightening at once. "You're like the others. You love the fine points of a gun play as an artist loves the fine points of an oil painting. Well, Newton, the chance has come for you to use your skill."

"I ain't said that I'm for sale," said Chick Newton.

"No matter what you say, I shall have you. I must have you. The more I see of you and your quiet ways, Newton, the more clearly I understand that you are the only man who can help me. And yet even you, no matter how you handled Thomas, may be afraid of the very name of the other."

"What other?"

"The man who has been hired to murder me," Cuttle declared, the perspiration pouring down his face. "A hired assassin, Newton!"

Newton set his teeth. "That's damn' black," he said. "I've knowed of skunks that would do things like that for money. I've never seen one. And if I did, I wouldn't fear him none. The biggest and most dangerousest crook in the world has got one bad weak spot in him and that's because he ain't honest. I'd be more scared of a lad at a plow if he was square than a killer that was crooked. And a bought killer is sure a low dog." He smashed his fist against the palm of his other hand as he spoke, and his voice raised until Cuttle rushed at him with hands uplifted.

"Be quiet, for heaven's sake!" gasped out Cuttle.

"What's wrong?"

"They may hear you."

"Who?"

"Anybody. Everybody. You never can tell who has been bought by that fiend."

"What fiend?"

"Never mind," Cuttle broke in hastily, his color altering a little again. "What's important just now is not the man who's behind the mischief, but he who has come here to do the work. Newton, I know that you're a brave man . . . a thousand times braver than I could ever be. But still you may have your blood turned to water by the name of the fellow who is coming to hunt me down."

"Try me," said Newton, perhaps a little too confidently.

"Jim Sawyer," said the rancher, staring at Newton fixedly.

Although Newton was like one set and prepared for the shock of a heavy blow, yet he quivered now as though its fall had half stunned him. He was ready for any other man in the world, but the thought of Jim Sawyer, in fact, half turned his blood to water. It was only the weakness of a moment, however, then his blood ran warm again and his eye looked steadily out upon Cuttle.

"I knew it!" Cuttle cried softly, but in a sort of ecstasy of happiness. "I knew that the luck was with me when I heard what you had done to Jeff Thomas. By heavens, I would wager a thousand to one at this moment that you will not be afraid to take the job of protecting me against that man-killer."

Newton hesitated. If he recoiled now, it would look very much like fear, to be sure, and it had never yet been said that he feared any man. Yet it was not the thought of the formidable Sawyer that made him hold back. It was another and a far more important thing. How could he leave his work for Bill Warner? Still, he had not yet been able to do so much as conceive a means of helping poor Bill, and, working for the rancher, he would at least be near the town.

"Well," he said, "just what's the job?"

"Good," breathed Cuttle. "What a brave fellow you are. The job is simply to stay with me day and night until . . . until Sawyer is no longer at large."

"You're dead certain that Sawyer is really after you?"

"Do you think that I'd be making these efforts if I were not? No, my information is from a source that cannot have made an error."

"Well," pondered Chick Newton, "it still sort of beats me."

"In what way?"

"There's a tolerable good sheriff in this county, ain't there?"

"No, no!" Cuttle exclaimed. "The last thing I'd dream of is to carry this to the law. That would never do. There's no purpose in that, I tell you, and whatever happens while you're with me, must be kept from the law. You understand? This affair is entirely between me and the man who hired Jim Sawyer."

"I suppose I got to understand it that way . . . if you want me to."

"And now for the terms, Newton?"

"What terms?"

"What do you want for this work? Make it anything in reason . . . or even a little out of reason, if you wish. I know that this is extraordinary business and that you'll be risking your life if you do your duty for me."

"Why," said Newton, "I guess twenty a week wouldn't be too much, then?"

"Twenty a week!" gasped out the rancher.

"Or make it fifteen, if you want."

"Fifteen? Good heavens, man, I'll pay you a flat bonus of a thousand dollars if I'm saved, and fifty dollars a day until Jim Sawyer has. . . ."

Newton held up a forbidding hand. "I dunno how it is," he commented, "but I sure hate to rob a man. My time ain't ever been worth more'n fifteen a week before this. I guess that it ain't worth more'n twenty right now."

"Very good . . . very honest, of course. But you've never done this sort of thing before."

"You cotton to this right here and now," said Newton. "It ain't the money in sight that's buyin' me. It's the fun of this here game, Cuttle."

And Cuttle, struck dumb with amazement, stared blankly at his new-found hired man.

V

They started for the ranch at once—Newton on his ragged yellow mustang, and Cuttle on a dancing thoroughbred that he managed with surprising grace. Certainly he had never seemed more like a child than he did on this day. The terror that had fallen upon him when he talked with Newton about

his enemy, Jim Sawyer, had now utterly disappeared, as if, having hired a man for the purpose of
protecting him, it did not enter his mind that the
man might fail. He was as gay as a lark now,
whistling and singing as he rode along, and making
a mock of the yellow mustang.

"Slow and steady," Chick Newton stated, grinning, "is my motto. You could dance rings around
me on that there hoss for a five-day trip, Mister Cuttle. But if it come to a three weeks' drive through the
hills . . . I dunno but that I'd wear you down."

"A three weeks' drive!" exclaimed Cuttle. "Do
you ever make such trips?"

"Now and ag'in'," Chick answered shortly.

Here Cuttle stopped to pass a word with a veteran
cowman who was perched on the high seat of a
buckboard. He had jammed on the brakes at the
sight of Cuttle and stopped his pair of mustangs so
short that the collars were shoved almost to their
ears. Now he hung a leg over the side of his rig and
pushed back his hat—a sign that he wished to talk.

"I seen you last night, Tom!" he called to Cuttle.

"Too late for a youngster like you to be up, Dan,"
said Tom. "You should have been in bed."

Old Dan chuckled and shifted his quid. "I didn't
say what time o' night it was," he continued. "But the
moon was high enough for me to see pretty well.
Looked like she didn't hate you none, Tommy."

"The moon?" Tom said, laughing with perfect
good nature. "No, the moon has seen enough of me
to get acquainted, I suppose."

"The moon I mean wore skirts," Dan said. "Well,
Tommy, here's wishin' you miles an' miles of luck
with her. I've knowed her daddy and her grand-

daddy. I've knowed her ma and her ma's ma. They was all white folks. But Judy is a sweet gal, Tom. She's the best and the finest of the whole lot."

This frank opinion of his lady, even though expressed before a stranger, did not at all upset Tom Cuttle. He nodded and laughed in turn.

"If you got half as much to say about me as you have about her, take a trip to see her and tell her what you know, Dan."

They rode on, leaving old Dan laughing and nodding behind them. Everyone knew Tom Cuttle. Everyone seemed to like him. The trail, presently, wound close to the creek until they could hear its big, sullen voice and see the front wall of the old Henry Warner place.

"I took a stroll over to see the old house today," said Chick Newton. "It sure looks like a wreck . . . like a ghost of a house, eh?"

The joy fled from the face of Tom Cuttle. He turned with a shudder toward the Warner estate, and then cursed beneath his breath. "Let ghosts lie," he said gloomily. "And the wisest thing for you and everybody else is to keep away from the Warner house. Let me tell you that."

"Why?" asked Chick.

"Because it's full of bad luck. There's a curse on that place . . . a black curse. If you come within a mile of it, the stain of it will come off on you." With that, he touched his horse with the spurs and went on at such a round pace that Chick Newton had his hands full urging his horse on to follow. So gloomy had the young rancher become after the remark about the Warner house that he did not utter another word from that moment until they were safely at the ranch itself. There, in front of the big stable, they dismounted.

It was a big, ramshackle stable, near a house of similar sprawling design. Even Chick Newton, who was no expert in architecture, could see that it had been built according to no definite plan from the beginning. It had simply grown up like a child's dream of what a house should be. To a central core, various sprawling wings had been added, and it was indiscriminately reared of adobe, brick, and wood. Yet it had, in spite of these peculiar contradictions, or perhaps because of them, a singular charm. One guessed at rooms of twenty-odd sizes in the interior, of strangeness, comfort, and foolish attention to personal whims. It was a house with a personality, or, rather, with half a dozen personalities.

The horse of the master was taken by a Negro stable boy. But Chick Newton, unused to such services, preferred to see his own animal put up by his own hands. He unsaddled and fed his mustang, dodged the flying heels of the ugly brute, and escaped rather breathlessly while the Negro groom, who had been assigned to his horse, looked on in fear and gratitude that he himself had not been forced to encounter such perils. Newton took advantage of such an admirable opening for conversation with the man.

"How many families have lived in that there house, George?" he asked.

"Just one," said the other.

"A big one, then," said Newton.

"Tolerable big, sah," said the Negro.

"How many, then?"

"Just Mistah Cuttle, sah. How many he counts for I dunno. But he sure counts for a lot."

"D'you mean to tell me that only one man lives in that house?" asked Newton, astonished.

"Yes, sah."

"And built it?"

"He shohly did, sah."

Newton broke into a laugh in which he was heartily accompanied. After all, it was exactly what such a boyish, reckless chap as young Tom Cuttle would have done. He had built the house for amusement, not to live in. This was the result, in which half a dozen families could have been accommodated.

"Then he's made a pile of money ranchin'," suggested Newton.

"Him?" The Negro broke into still louder laughter. "Mistah Cuttle can't make no money ranchin'," he informed Newton. "They's grease on all the money that comes his way. It jest slips away from him, boss."

"Where does he get the coin to build such houses, then, and ride such hosses?"

"Ah dunno how come," he admitted at length. "Ah done heard a white man say that Mistah Cuttle must be a spec'lator on Wall Street. Ah guess that's how he makes it."

So Newton went on toward the house, but slowly and thoughtfully. What Wall Street exactly represented he could hardly have said. But he had a vague idea that it was a place where men gambled with huge sums of money, took vast chances, and sometimes won hugely, sometimes were ruined in a day. After all, it exactly fitted in with his idea of Tom Cuttle that that worthy should be such a speculator. He would have gambled with a million as readily as another gambled with a hundred. Out of the very recklessness of his methods he might have wrested his success. If he were a Wall Street millionaire, however, how did it happen that he remained in the West, so far from the scene of his financial operations?

That girl who had been mentioned by old Dan—that same Judy might be the cause of his lingering west of the Rockies. And Newton conjured up a lovely, laughing face that would have been enough reason for another Antonius to have thrown away another world.

When he arrived at the house, he found that his new employer was eagerly waiting for him. He was escorted at once by Cuttle to the bedroom of the latter and shown into a neighboring apartment. "This is your sleeping quarters," said Cuttle. "It will be at night," he added, lowering his voice. "Something tells me that it will be at night that Sawyer will make his attempt. He works in that way. He wants the dark. The devil seems to be able to see in it like a cat."

These words raised a picture for Newton of glowing eyes, and a shadowy man's body beneath them, stealing toward him through the darkness.

"Perhaps," Tom Cuttle added sharply, "he may make his try this very night."

"You know that he's tolerable close to you right now?"

"He may be, for all that I know, behind that very wall at this very moment."

In spite of himself, Newton could not help cringing a little.

"But if he stepped out?" queried Tom Cuttle, clasping his hands together in a most feminine gesture of alarm.

"I'll take my chances," said Chick Newton, "with any gent that was ever born, so long as I got my Colt with me. They ain't nobody in the world that can be more'n a hundredth part of a second faster'n me, and that much time ain't too big a handicap to take on even if I was doin' this job for fun."

Tom Cuttle nodded with a wan smile, and then he left his bodyguard to his own devices for a few moments to make himself at home. Those seconds were busily employed by Newton. He examined not only the environs of his own room but those of the rooms adjoining his and his employer's. He found that the very first request that he would have to make would be that Tom Cuttle should move his sleeping quarters to some less accessible portion of the house. For, as Newton found, it would have taken a dozen men, standing guard constantly, to defend this suite of sleeping chambers properly. Several huge trees grew just outside from which the windows could be easily reached. In addition, there was a long upper story verandah or balcony running along that face of the house, and from the inside two separate stairways led from the lower story of the building to the upper. There were twenty turns, therefore, from which the sleeping quarters might be attacked.

Now there was a shrill whistle, an obvious signal, which sounded from the outside, and Newton, half fearing that the assault had already taken place or was about to fall upon Tom Cuttle, jumped to the window. It was only the boyish figure of a young girl dressed in riding togs and sitting on a restless big chestnut mare that sidled back and forth, tossing foam from her bit. The rider controlled these maneuvers with a careless hand upon the reins and, with her head raised, surveyed the house. She whistled again. And now, from beneath, Tom Cuttle ran into the picture until, standing beside the rider, he caught both her hands.

There was no shadow of a doubt but that this was the lady of his heart. For the whole body of poor Tom trembled with delight and excitement, and the face that he turned up to her was transformed. He was asking her in, but she resolutely was refusing and at the same time dexterously withdrawing her hands.

She's baitin' him on, decided Chick Newton from the window above. *She's a young devil. Besides, she's too pretty to be good.* But, in spite of that sage conclusion, he sat down on the window sill in order that he might watch them more closely. The girl—it was the Judy of whom Dan had spoken; he could see the lips of Tom Cuttle framing the name in the distance—now leaned lightly in the saddle and chatted very amiably and with some excitement. Whatever it was that she said, it struck Tom Cuttle dumb and white. His head fell, and she, at the same time, gathering her reins and drawing back her horse, prepared to depart in high dudgeon.

A flirt, by heaven, thought Chick Newton. And yet she was so lovely that he still kept hoping against hope that he might be wrong.

Tom Cuttle, in the meantime, recovering from his first shock, hurried after her, caught her horse by the bridle, and now began to plead.

He's askin' her, thought Chick Newton, *to please let him throw his head away.*

But she, oh, subtle minx, was not to be persuaded at once. She shook her head; she frowned upon the ground; she waved him away, and still he recaptured the very hand that strove half heartedly to dismiss him, and pleaded again. At last she seemed to melt. And if her reluctance had been feigned, at least her next change of mind was so sudden that it had all the ring of reality. One instant she was pouting and frowning in the saddle. The next, she had stooped as a bird stoops, kissed him squarely on the lips, and then wheeled her horse rapidly away. The last that Newton saw of her was the blue flash of her eyes as she turned, and the gleaming of the red hair that was coiled smoothly beneath the deep shadow of her hat. Then her galloping horse passed outside the picture that he could view from his window, and he stepped back with a sigh. He felt strangely giddy and light-headed, with an ache at his heart. Truly he should not have stood to view that scene so long.

VI

Whatever the assent was which the girl had wrung from young Tom Cuttle, it plunged him into the deepest gloom and kept him almost mute during the dinner. He and Chick Newton sat down alone at a great table. While they ate, Newton made his suggestion that the sleeping quarters be changed, and he pointed out his manifold reasons. The answer was most surprising. Of all timid men in the world, Tom Cuttle was surely the most reckless.

"What difference does it make?" he said. "If I'm to be murdered in my bed," he added with a shudder, "nothing will save me from it. If I'm to die by night with a bullet in my back ... then I'll die by night. Nothing I can do will change what's bound to happen."

"You put me on a job," Chick said, a little angry, "and I tell you the best way it can be done. But if you want to gamble, it ain't for me to dictate. Still, if Jim Sawyer turns out a sneak and wants to steal up on you, you're in a trap in that room of yours. He's got three doors and four windows to come at you. That's enough to satisfy any fool . . . let alone a gent like Sawyer."

"There's no need for him to sneak up on me," Cuttle stated bitterly. "I've put my head into the noose of my own free will. Newton, knowing what I know, nevertheless, I've agreed to take a long ride tonight through the open."

"What made you do that?" Newton asked, frowning. "There's going to be a full moon. It'll be made to order for Sawyer."

The rancher threw out his hands, palm up, in a rather Gæalic gesture. "It was fate . . . I could not resist," he answered. He added a little later, after they had sat in silence: "Newton, I'm taking a girl ten miles across country to a dance. Do you understand?"

Newton, remembering the blue of the eyes and the dimpling smile, understood only too well.

"I want you to ride behind us. Keep out of sight if you can. It'll be a hard thing for you to do, but I want you to ride near enough to protect me if you can and yet well enough hidden to attract no notice from her. If she should suspect. . . ." He did not finish his sentence but continued for a time to stare before him with a most speaking glance. Plainly he felt that he had hidden his greatest weakness from the attention of the girl.

Indeed, from what Newton could observe and hear, no one in the district regarded Tom Cuttle as a coward. Perhaps his careless, reckless air shielded him from discovery, while his real good nature and apparent open-heartedness kept him out of actual trouble. And certainly he could hardly have confessed to others what he had been forced by the very terms of his application to Newton to confess to the latter. If the girl should guess such a thing concerning him, therefore, he was a lost man. This could be very well believed by Chick Newton. For, of such a nature of whimsy and reckless impulse as he believed the girl to be, she must hate physical timidity worse than a plague.

Therefore, after dinner, they both mounted. The yellow mustang would not do on this occasion.

"She rides like a madwoman," said Cuttle. "The best blood I have in my stable will hardly keep up with her . . . she's such a lightweight."

Accordingly Chick Newton was given his choice among a dozen fine animals, each such a glorious specimen that his eye lingered fondly. What he chose, however, was not a showy creature. It was a tall gelding with huge bones and rather overlarge hoofs, a gaunt neck and a big head hung on the end of it. But he had the barrel of a Hercules and the well-let-down hocks were the sign of a runner. Tom Cuttle, who knew a horse if he knew nothing else, nodded approvingly at such a choice.

"Old Mixer will still run a bit," he said. "The old devil needs a master . . . that's all. Better try a leg up on him and see if you can manage him."

There was no trouble about that. Mixer, in the capable hands of Chick, became a lamb, and so the two galloped across country to the house of Judy Hern. When they approached the thickly clustered trees that surrounded the ranch house, Chick drew off down the road. He dared not go far, for Tom Cuttle had begged him to stay as close as possible. Sawyer, the rancher was sure, would be abroad on this night. It would ideally suit his nature and if he, Tom Cuttle, lived until the morning, it must be owing to the exertions of Newton. So, despising his employer for his cowardice and yet admiring him for the willpower that was able to drive him ahead in spite of that fear, Chick Newton waited down the road. The particular point to this ride was that Judy had been forbidden by a stern parent to go to this dance and his denial of permission had apparently made the dance a highly desirable thing.

The two came from the ranch house presently, and certainly Judy was riding like a madwoman, as Cuttle had said. Newton had only a glimpse of her as she flashed by with her head thrown up to the moonlight sky, and her laughter trailing behind her. They covered a dozen miles across country with Judy sweeping across short cut, over barbed-wire fences, and through tangles of brush, which, it seemed to Chick Newton, must surely tear her clothes to pieces. Yet, when she arrived at the schoolhouse where the dance was given, and, when Chick from the distance saw her come into the light of the open door, he could see that she was as neat and precise in her costume as though she had merely stepped from a comfortable carriage. Chick, having tethered his own mount in the horse shed, climbed shamelessly up to a window where he had to press in between two barelegged youngsters who had clambered there for the same purpose. They greeted him with snickers, and yet they gave him a place from which he could sweep the hall and see Tom Cuttle stepping into the next dance with Judy Hern.

In his two previous glimpses of her, he had not really seen her. Of that Chick could now make sure, and with the lamplight turning the red of her hair to gold, she seemed to him now so lovely a creature that he hardly dared watch her closely. Rather he looked at her as she was reflected in the faces of those she passed. They seemed to Chick like shadows that the moon casts, or moths near a flame, and how the whole world could keep from the worship of her, he could hardly understand. For a brief and glorious half hour he watched her. There was no doubt about the democracy of her spirit. She danced with whoever first asked her, and Chick Newton would have sold his soul for the sake of five minutes of dancing skill. Alas, that was an art that was denied to him.

It was only the half hour—no more. After that, she left the building with Tom, and Newton had barely time to regain his horse in time to fall in behind them, for she was leading the way back across country and by a quite different route. They had gone through a tangle of woods before, and it had been comparatively easy to keep them in view without being himself seen. The new route was far different. It was a more roundabout way in which she kept to the open country. Twice he found himself forced to follow recklessly without shelter from a backward glance. The third time he saw them draw rein, and the girl turned back. He could think of nothing better to do than to ride straight on down the trail. It would be foolish to attempt to dodge out of sight behind the next clump of trees after he had been seen. It would only needlessly alarm the girl.

He took Mixer in hand, therefore, and cantered casually on. As he drew near, he raised his hand and gave them a "Howd'ye, folks!" and then swept by. But her call came tingling after.

"Wait a moment! Hello!"

He hesitated, then he drew rein and waited until the pair came up with him. He dared not look at the face of poor Tom Cuttle, which he knew was black. But the girl came straight up to him and drew rein. There she sat her saddle with one hand dropped on her hip and the other strongly controlling her horse that had been pricked with the spurs often enough to keep it full of pepper. She went straight to the mark.

"Seems to me that you've been following us?" she queried.

"Me?" Chick Newton said mildly. "I'm just driftin' along toward Dulcy."

She pointed to the heaving sides and the sweat-darkened flanks of Mixer. "D'you call that drifting?" she asked.

"This dog-gone hoss," Chick said, "gets blowed doin' nothin'. He ain't had work enough."

"No?" she questioned sharply. "He looks to me as if he were in the prime of condition. Don't you think so, Tom?"

Tom coughed a politely indistinct answer.

"Besides," went on the girl, "Dulcy lies over yonder."

She pointed across country, and Chick, damning his bad fortune, wondered what answer he could make. She gave him no time for thought.

"Also, I think that I know that horse. And it seems to me, Tom, that you ought to know it still better."

Here Chick looked across to Tom, and he saw the face of the latter stricken with the direst pain and confusion. He could think of nothing but a partial confession.

"I'll tell you the whole truth, Judy," said Cuttle. "I was afraid that your father might find you gone and start out to trail us. I had a rear guard follow along to give us a warning."

"Then why didn't you tell me?" cried Judy.

He could only answer that he had not wished to bother her. But she shook her head and continued to look from one to the other.

"There's something more in this," she said, "and I'll never rest until I find out what it is. Who are you?"

"Name is Chick Newton."

"Ah," she said, "you're the man who beat Jeff Thomas. I'm glad to know you for that. I always hated that bully, Tom. But . . . are you working steadily for Mister Cuttle?"

Chick admitted that he was, and she wished to know at once in what capacity he was serving.

"Just a general hand and 'puncher," said Chick.

At this she looked him up and down and finally laughed. "Men don't keep bull terriers as sheep dogs," she said not obscurely. "Tom, what is it all about? Is there trouble? Did you need a guard? Is that why he's here?"

The red flamed into the face of Tom Cuttle. There was no denying the scorn that was in her voice.

"At least," she added with unnecessary cruelty, so Chick Newton thought, "I'm surprised that you're afraid of *me*, Tom!" And with that she touched her horse with the spurs and flew away like mad.

Chick had barely time to notice the grief-stricken face of his employer. Then the horse of Cuttle, which was a slow beginner, dropped behind. But big Mixer was off like a greyhound after a hare. And Chick

Newton jockeyed his mount with all of his skill. Just what he could do even if he succeeded in overtaking the girl he did not know, but he was consumed with red anger against her. She held him even for a breathless half mile, for her horse was a racer and her weight was light. But behind her, big Mixer labored like the honest veteran he was, and what Newton lacked as a weight handicap, he made up by the consummate mastery of horsemanship. She was too excited, apparently, to keep her mount running straight, but Chick made Mixer cleave to a straight line, and at the end of that half mile the long, ugly head of Mixer was at the hip of the mare. With this, Judy Hern gave up the race as quickly as she had begun it. She reined in short and cried to Chick: "What d'you mean, sir?"

He glared back at her, wondering at his own anger. "Is it square to pay him back like this?" asked Chick. "He's been tryin' to take care of you. And now you want to lose me my job and break poor Cuttle's heart!"

He saw her lips quiver apart in the white moonshine with a fierce retort, but at once the anger left her and she smiled so suddenly that Chick Newton was staggered.

"I like you," Judy Hern said. "Whatever you are, you're all right. I've acted like a spoiled baby, and I'm sorry."

"Tell Cuttle that."

"I shall. But . . . I'd give a thousand to know why you're working for him."

"Money," Chick answered. He felt her eyes search him again, and she shook her head.

"That's not it. There's still something behind."

Then Cuttle came up, and Chick Newton fell to

the rear. She was as good as her word. The rest of the way back to her father's house she chatted blithely with her escort and gave him the cheeriest of good nights at the time of their parting.

"But," she said suddenly as a final word, "if I'm ever in trouble, will you lend me Chick Newton, Tom?"

VII

They rode slowly back toward Cuttle's place. "What did you do to her?" asked Cuttle. "She left me like a shot . . . you stopped her as though she'd struck a stone wall. I thought that she'd want you horse-whipped. But instead, she spent the rest of the ride telling me how much she liked you."

"I told her half of what I thought," explained Chick, "which it looks to me, Cuttle, like she was interested in the truth."

"Truth the devil!" said the young rancher bitterly. "She's interested in the way that truth comes wrapped up. She likes the man that the truth is inside of or she doesn't like him. But the devil take my luck with her. She always sees through me, Newton, and what she finds inside is devilish small."

He fell into the blues again, and they continued the ride in silence until, long after midnight, they reached the ranch house. As for the fear of Jim Sawyer that had so whipped and driven Cuttle during the day and the evening before, it seemed to have left him entirely. The problem of Judy Hern had blocked all lesser things from his mind.

But that was not true of Chick Newton. Let Judy

be as lovely as God permitted. Nevertheless his own work must be done, and he went about it with singular care. If he were to protect his employer, it was ridiculous to think that he could sleep in the adjoining chamber. Since he could not budge Cuttle to a safer room, he had the rancher secure from the housekeeper some very thin, very strong cotton thread, and this he strung six inches from the floor level, passing in front of the windows and the doors. If anyone entered the room and advanced toward the bed where Cuttle was sleeping, there were few chances that he could avoid striking one of those threads, and, if he did so, the pull of the thread would immediately snap on an electric light. The click of the lights and the flood of their radiance must be trusted by Chick Newton to waken him in case he fell asleep at his post. For that post he arranged an easy chair in a far corner of the room, facing toward the bed, and, when Cuttle had retired, he took up his post in it, wrapped a blanket around him, gripped a revolver in his lap, and waited.

It had been a busy day. There had been both mental and physical strains, and in half an hour the soothing darkness closed his eyes. He dreamed of Bill Warner facing the judge who pronounced the death sentence; of a stealthy figure moving in darkness with the shadowy outlines of a man's body and the glowing eyes of a cat; of a self-willed girl who would break her father's command and ride far across the countryside in order to spend half an hour at a dance. But in his dream, she danced with him, and Tom Cuttle moped in a corner, watching and envying.

From the golden heart of that dream he was wakened by a snapping sound and a flood of strong light against his eyelids. They opened upon a view of a tall man standing in the very center of the room with a revolver in his hand, a tall, masked man who had leaped back when the light flooded upon him and now swept the room with a hasty glance to see from what point danger threatened him. He saw the figure in the chair at the same instant, and snapped up his gun—all of this in a fraction of a breathing space. But Chick Newton had been able to twitch up the muzzle of his own weapon, and the two guns went off almost as one. Something hummed briefly at the ear of Chick and crashed into the stout wall behind him. Then he was on his feet facing Tom Cuttle, who sat up in the bed, a staring ghost, looking down at the long body of the man who lay prostrate on the floor with a seam along his head.

Footsteps began to sound at once. Someone was rattling the locked door and shouting out even as Chick leaned above his victim. It was not death. He was mortally glad of that, for he had never before killed a human being, although battles had more than once come his way. It was only a glancing blow along the head, and, after the first thin penciling of blood, it flowed steadily from only one short, deep gash just above the temple. He twitched the mask from the senseless man and exposed a broad, brutal face. Even now the mouth was writhed back in a murderous snarl.

"Jim Sawyer!" gasped out Tom Cuttle, and then he cried with exultation in his voice: "It's all right, lads! I'm safe! My automatic went off. Nothing else."

There was a muttering of relief from the hall, then many footsteps stole away.

"Tie his hands, for heaven's sake. Tie his hands quickly," Cuttle was stammering.

Newton obeyed. He still could hardly believe that this thing was true and that his own hand had beaten the famous fighter. He hastened to do as Cuttle bade him, for Jim Sawyer was one who had been known to take victory out of the very teeth of defeat. But to steal into the chamber of a sleeping man with a gun ready for the secret murder this was too foul for credence.

He stood back when Sawyer was secured, and stared down in detestation at the man-killer who now opened his eyes and sat up slowly. There was one twitch at the bonds that controlled his wrists. Then with no show of shame for the dastardly crime that he had attempted, with neither remorse nor fear, he turned his head slowly from one to the other and looked Cuttle fully in the face, and then regarded his conqueror. They were like the great, brutal, impersonal eyes of a lion, staring behind the bars of his cage, helpless, but filled with undying hatred of all humans. Newton found that gaze to shake him like a strong hand upon his shoulder. Well was it for him, he felt, that he had not met this destroyer by full daylight so that he could see the ferocious face and meet the strange eyes.

Cuttle was asking him to leave the room. "I have a few questions to ask Jim Sawyer," he said. "Leave me alone with him, Newton. You've done a job here that's worth almost more than my life to me. It's worth . . . but I'll give you my thanks later and in something better than words, Newton."

Seated in his own room, Chick Newton reviewed the scene carefully. It had come so swiftly upon him that he hardly realized what he had done. It was not all mere good luck, for Jim Sawyer had seen him as quickly as he had seen Jim. If he had the advantage of being seated where his arm would be steadier, Jim Sawyer had the advantage of not having been suddenly awakened. Sawyer was warned and alert for danger. And, take it all in all, this had been a fair fight in which he had conquered. It was as though he had found himself capable of lifting a mountain. He could hardly believe that these hands of his had accomplished the fall of such a man, and that this forefinger had pulled the trigger that brought down Jim Sawyer.

There were other ramifications. When the story was out and told abroad, he could not help but become known throughout the West as a gunfighter with all that title suggested. He would be sought by men who had desperate affairs that needed mending. He would be bribed to undertake foul work. Law-abiding men would look askance upon him. It would be impossible for him to hold down any ordinary position. He could know nothing, hereafter, except fight. And a fighter's life was apt to be very short indeed. He brooded over this, but he brooded also upon the glory that would be his. The children would run out to stare at him. The men would give him place. He had made himself, at a stroke, a hero. It was a strange mixture of sweet and sour, therefore, that he was turning in his mouth when he heard the first sound from the bedroom of Tom Cuttle.

He could not believe it at first, although it brought him out of his chair with his hair bristling and his flesh crawling. But in a moment it was repeated, and this time there could be no mistake. It was the groan of a man suffering the direst agony. In an instant a leap had carried Chick to the door and his shoulder was against it. But the knob would not turn.

"Open up!" he called, controlling his voice as well as he could. "Open the door, Cuttle!"

"Keep out of this!" returned Cuttle in a strained tone. "You're not wanted."

"Open the door!" repeated Chick Newton. "Otherwise, damned if I don't shoot out the lock and come through anyway."

"Wait a minute. . . ."

"Not a second!"

There was an oath, then the key turned and the door opened. Cuttle blocked the way, his face white, his eyes blazing. Newton had never seen a man so transformed, or so horrible to look upon.

"Keep out of this," Cuttle warned him. "I don't need you now. If you hear anything, shut your ears . . . go for a walk!"

But Newton, with a wordless exclamation of disgust and anger, brushed the other from his path with one sinewy arm and stepped through the doorway. What he saw was Jim Sawyer lashed into a chair, his brutal eyes bulging from his head, his face dripping perspiration, and both thumbs swollen and blackened.

Then all the wrath and horror that had been piling high in the heart of Newton since he first heard that groan of the tortured man broke out in words. He turned upon Tom Cuttle and drove him back against the wall with short, savage oaths like blows of a fist.

"You snake!" he concluded. "Too yaller to fight your own fights and like a devil when somebody else has won one for you!"

"Newton," stammered the rancher, "you're throwing away your reward."

"D'you think," said the cowpuncher, "that I'd take a reward from you? Your money ain't no good to me, Cuttle. I've a mind to cut Sawyer loose and let him take his chance with you!"

"No!" screamed Cuttle, his knees sagging. "No!"

From that exhibition of cowardice, following so closely on the heels of such a display of cruelty, Newton shrank back.

"It's a rotten mess from one end to the other," he said at last. "I'm through with it all. But I'll tell you this, Cuttle . . . if any harm comes to Sawyer, I'll finish up what he started to do. Except that I won't use no night to sneak up to you by. I'll do my work in the daylight and I'll stand a trial for it, and no jury in these parts would ever hang me for puttin' an end to a skunk like you."

He turned upon Sawyer. "Sawyer," he said, "if you was anything but a coyote, I'd turn you loose. But you're as bad as Cuttle. Only different. If I set you free, you'd go gunnin' for him first, and then for me. You'll stay put." He backed to the door. "Remember, Cuttle!" was his last warning.

"Stranger," broke in Sawyer, "if you got a heart in you, don't leave me here with this hound dog. Dyin' I don't mind . . . but bein' wore away bit by bit." He groaned and tugged at his bonds.

"There'll be no more of that," Cuttle said, still shaking with his recent fear. "I know what I want to know now."

"And if you use what I've told you," said Sawyer, "by the eternal, the ghost'll turn you into stone."

Chick Newton waited to hear no more, but hastened from the house.

VIII

He saddled the yellow mustang in the stable and rode back for the town of Dulcy feeling that he had just passed through a nightmare converted into earthly fact. He was so sick at heart by what he had seen; he was so stirred by the groan of the tortured man, that he dared not let his mind linger upon those things. He wanted to wash his brain clean with a long sleep. So he went to the hotel, found that he could have his old room, went to it at once, and dove into the covers.

He did not waken again until midday. Then he sat up with a heavy head like one who had been ill and wakens from a delirium. He ate a dinner of noble proportions, then, over a cigarette, he digested the odd events with which he had been mixed during the past day.

Still stranger things were about to happen near Dulcy—of that he was convinced. All that he had done had been to scratch the surface of the mystery, but of all the things that moved at the heart of this affair he had small idea. Who, for instance, had hired Jim Sawyer and sent him on this murder mission? Who could it be of whom Tom Cuttle dared not inform the police? What held back Cuttle? What was the thing that he dreaded like death but dared not fight openly? Again, what was the secret that Cuttle had extorted from poor Jim Sawyer by means of torture? And what was the "ghost" concerning which that answer had apparently dealt?

At this point in his reflection, Newton started and grew so excited that he broke in two the cigarette that he was rolling. There was at least one proper setting for the appearance of a ghost near Dulcy, and that was the old Warner house. More than that, he remembered the strange detestation with which Cuttle had viewed the old mansion. Of course, these were tenuous ideas to cling to, but they meant a great deal to Newton. He could hardly tell why, but, while his conscious mind moved slowly forward, from step to step, his subconscious mind was leaping off among the heights, topping range after range of shadowy presumptions and possibilities that he hardly dared name to himself.

But, in the meantime, exciting as all of this was, it did not advance the welfare of poor Bill Warner, waiting in jail for the execution of his sentence. Dulcy was big enough to support one tiny newspaper, so that Chick bought that day's issue and found the case of his friend upon the front page. The last hope has been lost for Bill. The appeal that had been made to the governor for his pardon had been based upon several grounds. He had been asked to consider that the crime for which Bill had been convicted had been committed seven years before, that it had been done, if at all, under the influence of liquor, and that since the day of the murder Bill Warner had proved to the world that he could make a peaceful, law-abiding citizen. His whole career in the south showed this. He had been able to give up the hopes of a great inheritance and carve out his happiness with the labor of his hands. Such a man was entitled to a real chance. Laws were meant, it was held, to reform rather than merely to punish crime.

To this the governor replied most sternly. Time

had never been held to make the awful crime of murder less worthy of punishment. As for liquor, the part it played in the affair simply served to make the whole tale more ghastly. As for the good conduct of the man during the past seven years, it was well enough to shut the trap, but of what use was it after the game had slipped away? He felt that the sentence of death was richly deserved, and he would not be budged from his position.

Over this statement, Chick Newton pondered long and sadly. He could not but admit the justice of the governor's language. And yet he felt that something more gentle might have been done or said. For his own part, he had no doubt of Bill's guilt. In any other man he would have shunned and detested such a brutal slayer of a helpless old man. But Bill, having once been his friend, was kept in a magic circle in the heart of Chick Newton. And every word and every blow aimed against the former struck the latter almost as sharply.

His own impotence in the matter maddened Chick. He could not sit quietly to smoke, so he went out behind the village for a brisk walk to quiet his nerves, and it was on the northern trail that he came upon Judy Hern, riding in to town. He had been stubbing along with his head down when her cheery call made him look up. There she was before him, laughing and nodding and as gay as you please. No one could have suspected her, ever, of a midnight ride. She was as fresh as the dew. And although the black horse she rode was streaked with crusts of salt here and there where his sweat had dried, and although his eye was dead with weariness, his rider was poised as lightly in the saddle as though she had but just started on a canter.

"They're talking about you, Chick Newton," she told him.

"Who talks?" Chick asked, his hat now dangling in his fingers.

"Everyone. They say that you've left your dear friend, Tom Cuttle."

"Him and me fell out," Chick said, watching her face with a sigh of delight.

She was nodding again. "I thought you would fall out. You think too much to suit Tommy. He likes to have people about who jump when he pulls the strings. When did you get up this morning?"

"Noon."

"Are you getting ready for another ride to Dulcy?" she inquired laughingly.

"Are you?" he answered, with an implication that made her blush a little.

"I am," she said frankly. "I've taken a bet that I can spend the night alone in the haunted house."

"The haunted house!" exclaimed Chick.

She drew the quirt through her hands and shrugged her shoulders. "I'm already frightened to death about it," she told him. "And this is broad day. What will I do in the dark?"

"Don't go," he urged her eagerly. "Don't do it!"

"Why not? They'll call me a coward."

"Let them call you what they please . . . but somebody might be there."

"Do you believe in such stuff as ghosts?"

"No. But someone who knows about your bet might go there to play a trick on you. That would be as bad as a ghost."

"I've got to take the chance. I won't quit. They dared me, and then they made a bet. They'd never stop teasing me if I didn't go."

He thought of the ruined interior of that house. It would be an ideal place for tramps to jungle up. The idea turned him cold. "Let me go with you, then. If your friends are watching, I'll sneak in so's they'll never know that I'm there."

"You are a kind fellow," the girl said, smiling down to him. "But I can't do that. It wouldn't be playing fair."

She went on down the trail toward Dulcy, while Chick Newton turned about and stared helplessly after her. She rode jauntily, gaily as ever, and the sway of her body in the saddle reminded him of nothing so much as the lightness of a bird, half afloat on a branch.

But she was to spend the night in the old Warner house, and that meant to Chick, whether she wished it or not, that he was to spend the night in the same place. He rambled on aimlessly, turning the thought of her back and forth in his mind as one turns some delightful memory out of childhood. For she was like that, he thought—like a child, and yet all of a woman—brave and reckless as a child and sweet and gentle as a woman. He drew so great a sigh, presently, that he was forced to stop.

I'm plumb winded, Chick said to himself, *or else I'm turned lovesick. Jiminy, Chick, but you're a fool, and an old fool. She ain't for the likes of you. Not her!* Such a sober reflection, however, did not help the strange and delicious sorrow that had spread through his mind. It lingered there all the afternoon. He found himself looking toward the night with a leaping heart, for that night, unless she lost her courage, he would be near to her. And she was not one who would lose courage.

He went back to Dulcy in the late afternoon.

There was a letter waiting for him at the hotel, and, when he opened it in his room, he drew out a check for $500 and a note. The note was very brief and very much to the point. It read:

Dear Newton: You have been very foolish. Otherwise this check would be for several times $500. But, after all, $500 isn't bad for a day's work, is it? My advice to you, in all friendliness, is to ride to the nearest railroad station and buy a ticket. It doesn't matter where you go so long as you go away. If you stay here, I believe that you may be in danger. Perhaps you will be able to guess that I myself am not threatening you. And I believe that you will be sensible enough to take my advice.

My best wishes to you,
Thomas Cuttle

Friendly, Chick said to himself, *but too damned friendly to be true*. For, as he argued with himself, after a man had been talked to as he had talked to Tom Cuttle, there could be nothing but hatred for him in the heart of the other. Friendship and friendly advice argued a largeness of heart much greater than that which he attributed to Cuttle. As to the character of the latter he had quite made up his mind. The charm of Cuttle was his boyishness. And his boyishness was simply his lack of responsibility. Under that gay exterior lay all the darkness of cowardice and cruelty such as Newton had witnessed.

No, most certainly he would not take that "friendly" advice. No doubt Cuttle wished to have him out of his way. He would then be free to dispose of Jim Sawyer as he saw fit, but Newton was not at all inclined to go back on the guarantee that he had given to the gunfighter. Even a cold-blooded murderer, he felt, was preferable to such a creature as Tom Cuttle.

With those conclusions, he dismissed from his mind everything connected with either Cuttle or Sawyer except one thing, and that was the last remark that he had heard the gunman make. He had warned Cuttle against the ghost. And, in the range of possibility, that ghost might have something to do with the Warner house—with that very night—with the vigil of foolish Judy Hern.

IX

To view the house of Henry Warner by day was one thing, but to steal through the tangled thickets that surrounded it and come upon it in the white of the moon was quite another. Even the steady nerves of Chick Newton were shaken when he came out from the shadows and saw the twisting front of the old mansion, the limestone glistening except where the black masses of the climbing vines washed up its front, and the empty windows staring forth like dead eyes.

There was no sight of the girl about to enter. He had hung in the neighborhood all the latter part of the afternoon, waiting and hoping to catch a glimpse of her as she stole toward the old building, for he had thought that she might attempt to enter the house while the sun was still shining, so that she might be able to accustom herself to the place before the mystery of the night began. But he had been unable to see her, and now he had determined to enter the building and begin a search for her, for the night had already set in, the last of the sunset color had died in the horizon, the mountains had melted into the earth-wide shadows, and finally the moon had climbed up among the branches of the trees, floated a moment on the ridge of the woodland, and then cast itself adrift in the upper spaces. So in that lonely time he came to the house.

Now that he was before it, he must enter unobserved. That was most necessary, for the girl, above all, must not dream that he was near to protect her, neither must any others see him enter. For he had no doubt that those of her friends who had made the bet with her would be on hand with a few practical jests to frighten her out of her wits and out of her dare if they could. They must not be able to detect his entrance. Therefore he chose a place where the new-grown shrubbery marched up to the side of the house, and, crawling among these, he gained the wall, reasonably sure that he could not have been spied upon, either from the front or from behind.

At the edge of the shrubbery he reached a window and through this he swung himself as quickly as possible. He lowered himself into a dark room and there he crouched upon the flooring, trying to accustom his eyes to the darkness, and loosening his revolver in its holster.

A broken bit of the moonlight dropped through the window and gave him enough light, eventually, to make out that he was in a small chamber with a door opening on the farther side. Through this he adventured, and, keeping close to the wall always, moving by inches, aware of the broken flooring that had been torn up in the treasure hunt, he worked his way down the hall that lay outside the first room. As he came to doorways upon either hand, he peered into the chambers. There was no need of going through the noisy process of opening doors. They had all been broken from their hinges long before, for, being movable, they were also salable. Each of these apartments he examined in this fashion, and yet he found nothing, and, when he paused now and again, he heard nothing. Certainly the very wind and air of emptiness was breathing through that house.

He told himself, at the last, that there could be no possibility that the girl had dared to venture into the place. He had searched, finally, nearly the entire ground floor of the place and found nothing whatever that lived. And so, coming to the rear of the building, and beginning to give up all hopes, he saw through a window the shadow of a man.

The heart of Chick Newton jumped into his throat. It has been said that his nerves were steady, but still they quaked now like the nerves of a frightened child. Crouched there by the window, he watched. The figure was moving in the thick darkness under the rear wall of the house, but now it stepped out toward the open of what had once been a garden and Chick heard the slight grating of a stone underfoot.

In all of his life he thought that he had never heard a sound so musical, so delightful. For all of his ghostly fears were that minute vanquished. It was a man in the flesh who walked yonder, and he feared nothing of the earth.

The unknown now approached the wreckage of a pool. There had been a statue once to grace it, but now there remained on the central pedestal that stood in the pool only the mutilated legs of the bronze. The stranger stepped into the weed-grown bowl of the pool. There he leaned—there was a slight noise of stone gritting against stone—and the unknown sank out of sight.

But once more the heart of Chick had leaped within him. They had searched the grounds of the house from one end to the other, but who would have thought of looking beneath the fountain pool for the wealth of Henry Warner?

He was through the window in an instant, and, running noiselessly to the place, he saw that one of the huge flagstones of which the bottom of the pool was formed had been lifted and exposed a deep hole, quite wide enough for the passage of a man's body.

That sight was enough for Chick, and, hearing now something that stirred in the depths, he hastened back and regained the house in time to see the shadowy form reissue and come back toward the building. It entered through one of the broken doors and passed down a hallway not unattended now, for Chick was slipping in the rear, cat-like, feeling his way with his hands, crouching low to the floor. He had even forgotten Judith Hern for the instant.

He saw the stranger turn into a room, at last, and from the darkened doorway he observed the other draw something from his pocket and then throw the flash of an electric pocket lantern across the window once, twice, and again. Having done this, he of the shadows sat down on the floor and was still.

There could be no doubt but that this was a signal. Perhaps, after all, this was one of those practical jesters who was about to make merry at the expense of poor Judy Hern, and this was the signal that informed his fellows that the coast was clear and that they might advance. But there was a solemn slowness in the gait of the unknown that hardly went with the movements of a young man, no matter how cautiously the latter might be stepping. And there was the passage under the fountain, down which he had disappeared.

In all cases, the place for Chick Newton was here where he could observe what next was accomplished by this night wanderer in the Warner house.

For his own part, he drew back into the opposite room and dropped upon one knee close to the wall to wait. In his excitement time dragged on slowly, slowly, and yet it was not long before, without a sound made, he saw a figure loom in the hallway, and then another. Both turned into the opposite chamber where the first man waited, and now Chick could hear their voices.

"Here's the old bird," said one.

"But where's the old bird's cash?" grunted the second. "That's what I want to know before I take any more trouble."

"The fee for your services I have in my pocket," said the voice of an older man, and Chick knew instinctively that it must be he who he had first observed. "I have it ready here in cash for you."

"We'll have a peep at it, then."

Chick slipped from his place and lay prone on the floor of the hall. Peering through the doorway, he had no trouble to make out the three figures. There were two wide-shouldered fellows; the third member of the group was obviously much older, and, although his back was turned to the doorway so that

Chick could not see his face, yet the observer would have guessed his age as sixty, at the least. Some of the resonance had left his voice, and some of the sprightliness had also left him. An electric torch was now being held by one of the two newcomers, and the older man counted forth in his hand from a thick wallet, bill after bill.

"There you are," he said at length. "Twenty-five hundred apiece. That is five hundred apiece more than I agreed. But I never wish to underpay. To me, your work will be worth that much."

"It may be worth the stretchin' of our necks," said one of the two. "But give me the iron boys."

The older man returned the wallet deliberately to his pocket. "I pay upon the receipt of services," he said quietly. "I never pay in advance. It is against all of my business principles."

"Your business principles be damned. I say, I get my share or I don't step in the job."

"Very well. One man is really enough to do the work, and he shall have the double pay."

"Not me. What goes for Sam goes for me, too. You can count on that, cap."

"Very well," said the man with the money. "Then we cannot do business, and it is useless to waste our time any further. Good night, gentlemen."

"You damned old four-flusher!" exclaimed one of the pair snarlingly. "What holds us up from tapping you on the napper and grabbing the stuff?"

"The fear of death keeps you from it," said the older man with his same unshaken and unhurried gravity. "I am armed, as you see." A long revolver glimmered in his hand as he drew it from a coat pocket. "And though the two of you would be sure to dispose of me, yet I shall be sure to account for one of you first. You may trust me for that, although, of course, I cannot tell which one of you would fall, and which one would take the five thousand."

The two cursed fluently. They circled to either side, but the other, putting his back to the wall, held a steady face to them and they dared not press home their attack. The very moral force of his calmness was sufficient to press them back from him.

They tried to egg one another on to begin the attack, but each lacked the nerve to make the first move, making certain that it would be he who would receive the bullet from that leveled gun.

"You see," said the older man at length, "that you can take nothing from me. You get not a cent until the work is done. But if the work is done, and if you bring back to me a certain locket that he wears around his neck, then I shall accept that as proof. The moment I see it, the money is yours. Consider, my boys. I know your records. You have tried a hundred times, but neither of you has ever made as much as twenty-five hundred at a haul . . . nor half that amount."

There was a groan of assent from one, but the other muttered: "I've done well enough. But murder ain't been my line before."

"Be off with you," said the employer. "Be off and do the job at once. Come straight back here. It is your safest course. They will never think of searching this place for you. I almost think that they would be afraid to." And he chuckled softly.

"Will this Cuttle put up a fight?"

"Not a stroke. He'll be paralyzed when he sees the danger coming. He'll die like a dog, whimpering."

X

The two made off at once. With all his heart Chick Newton wished to stay here to follow the mystery of this evil old man who knew so much and was willing to work so much harm. Here, perhaps, was the secret of the ghost that haunted the house of Henry Warner. This sly rascal had discovered the treasure chamber of the millionaire and had appropriated it to his use. Doubtless there was far too much in it to be carried off in random trips from time to time. He had come again and again. Finally, this trip, he was probably making his final looting and with a part of it he was paying off his two hired murderers.

Here was the man, then, who must have hired Jim Sawyer, just as he was now hiring two to accomplish what he had entrusted to one before. There was this temptation to remain; there was the temptation, too, to stay near to protect the girl from any eventualities. But, deeply as he despised and distrusted Tom Cuttle, he could not very well stand by and see an innocent man destroyed.

He left the house at once, therefore, gritting his teeth with impatience. By the time he returned, no doubt the hirer of the two would be gone. Having secured the death of Cuttle, which he desired, he would make away. Why should he throw away $5,000 on two such rascals if it were possible to succeed without any expenditure? So for the sake of Cuttle, Newton was throwing away a clue that might lead—to what? He hardly dared to name what was beginning to be formed in his thoughts. Yet there remained a hope that the older man might actually remain in the house according to his promise, to pay the two miscreants when they returned from their ill deed.

In five minutes Chick had reached the yellow mustang in the cluster of saplings just beyond the wall of the estate where he had left the horse. That resolute philosopher had lain down to enjoy a nap, but Chick kicked it to its feet, flung himself into the saddle, and sped away down the slope.

Fortune helped him then. He had not gone a quarter of a mile when he reached the western trail out of Dulcy, and he had hardly swung into the trail when he heard the clatter of hoofs approaching swiftly behind him. He looked back and made out a single horseman coming at a round gallop. He wheeled about and held up his hand.

"What the . . . ?" began the stranger, alarmed.

"Friend," said Chick, "you can save a man's life if you'll ride to the ranch of Tom Cuttle. Ride hard, in heaven's name. Tell Tom to watch himself . . . the attempt will be made on him tonight by two men. . . ."

"Who are you?" cried the man from Dulcy, amazed quite naturally by such a salutation and such a tale.

"A man with no time on his hands. There's other work. Partner, take it from me, this is straight talk. Tom Cuttle . . . warn him . . . ride hard." He did not wait, but wheeled the yellow mustang about and dashed back up the slope. He, who he had stopped, paused for a moment in the trail. Perhaps he doubted what his ears had heard; perhaps he put it down as a practical jest. At any rate he was not long in this hesitation, for soon Chick heard the sudden rattle of the hoofs begin again, and, glancing over his shoulder, he saw the stranger bent low along the neck of his horse, flying at full spur-driven speed up the trail and toward Tom Cuttle.

So Cuttle was saved again, he said to himself, and, wondering at the fortune of that rascal, he rushed the yellow mustang back toward the Warner house. Something told him that this delay would be fatal to his success, but, delay or not, he would make the effort to find that same elderly gentleman of the polite voice and the unscrupulous mind again.

He put the yellow horse in the same clump of saplings. Then he raced for the house, shifted swiftly through the trees, doubled over, and sped among the shrubbery, and finally swung into the house again by the same window through which he had entered once before that night.

He started again on his progress through the building. He pulled off his boots so that he might move more noiselessly and more surely. So he advanced with hardly as much caution as before, for he was desperate at the thought that he might have missed his man.

Perhaps he had gone half the length of the long and winding corridor. Twice he had stumbled and made a slight noise. Twice he had ground his teeth at the thought that he might have betrayed his approach by those sounds. Then came a thing that turned him to stone and brought the happy face of Judy Hern brilliantly before his eyes. For, somewhere in the house, a woman screamed—a gun exploded—the long, dull echoes wandered up and down the corridor, and then the house was all in silence again—a listening silence more terrible than the wildest confusion.

Straight on sped Chick Newton now, regardless of

the noise he made, regardless of everything saving that he must reach Judy Hern, for the wild cry that he had heard came, he knew, from her lips. There was only one place to which he could instinctively go in the hope of reaching her. That was the room in which he had seen the three confer upon the killing of Tom Cuttle. To that chamber he raced. He veered through the doorway with his gun in one hand, ready to fire—and fell headlong over a soft form that lay on the floor.

He sprang up with a groan of fear lest it should be as he most feared. An electric torch lay on the floor of the room and, striking the wall in a broad half circle, cast a reflected light over the rest of the place. By that light he saw a dead man lying near the doorway with his arms thrown wide and his face turned to the ceiling. In the very center of his forehead was a great purple spot.

But after the first shock of horror—and of relief—it was not the fact of death so much as the face of the dead man that startled him. He caught up the light and played it fully on the glazed eyes and on the features of death. He had thought even at the first glance that he recognized it. Now, when he cast the full glare of the electric light upon it, he knew it, for he had seen the photograph many times in the daily papers of late. And the title under the photographs had been: *HENRY P. WARNER, the murdered man.*

But Henry P. Warner had died seven years ago, and another man was about to die for that crime. Henry P. Warner was dead seven years before and only his bones could remain, washed white in the lower reaches of the Mason River. Yet here he lay, freshly slain! It was more horribly bewildering than any appearance of a ghost. The brain of Newton reeled with it. Then, steadying himself, he examined the face more in careful detail. It was the same as that of the photographs, except that it was a little more deeply lined, thinner of cheek, the head more bald, the hair more gray. Between fifty-three and sixty the face does not greatly change, but the passage of seven years might well have accounted for every difference that he saw. There was even that detail of the left brow being raised slightly above the level of the right, which had always given the face of Henry P. Warner the singularly whimsical look for which he was known.

Then the truth broke wildly upon the mind of Chick Newton. The millionaire had not been murdered on that other day. Instead, he had lived and lived in hiding, unknown to the rest of the world. He had allowed his nephew to lie under the imputation of his assassination. He had allowed the poor fellow to be brought to trial and condemned to death. He would have allowed the death sentence to be exacted from the innocent man. It was a profundity of crime that staggered Newton, newly come as he was from a scene of matchless villainy.

He knew, in a trice, who it had been who hired Jim Sawyer to dispose of Tom Cuttle. And it was Henry Warner, again, who had this very night dispatched two miscreants to attempt Cuttle again. But what was the relation between the two? He could recall that the name of Cuttle had appeared only once in the narrative of the disappearance of Warner that he had heard from poor Bill. Cuttle had been the friend who accompanied him to the house of his uncle on that fatal day seven years before.

There remained, for the moment, to find the girl who had cried out. She, too, perhaps, had become the victim of the murderer. Newton, dizzy with that thought, reeled out of the room and stood in the hallway, trying to make up his mind. By that time the guilty man might have been fleeing from the house with all his speed. No doubt that was exactly what he was doing. In that case, it would be wise to follow to the open at once. But where was Judy Hern? What could have happened to her?

Something led him through the opposite doorway into the chamber where he himself had hidden not so many minutes before, and, as he crossed the threshold, a light leaped before him, and the *boom* of a gun smote against his ears.

XI

He felt, rather than heard, the whisper of the bullet past his face, and he jumped to the side as the gun spoke a second time. Then he heard a voice—God be praised that it was indeed the voice of Judy— crying out—heard a struggle, and his straining eyes made out two dim figures in the corner.

He was at them in an instant, found his hold, and crashed his man down against the floor, his fingers biting deeply into the soft flesh of the throat. His thumb found the hollow of the neck—a wicked old Canadian lumberman had once taught him the proper principles of throttling with a single grip. Before that grip was pressed home the groan of the man gave him pause, and the girl was crying: "Don't kill him! Don't kill him, Chick!"

"Who?" he asked her savagely.

"Tom Cuttle," was the amazing response, and, with an exclamation, he turned the half senseless man on his face, and then secured his hands tightly behind him.

They could hear Cuttle gasping and sobbing to regain his breath, then groaning in misery of body and soul. In the meantime, Newton had snapped out his demand for a quick recital of what she had seen and heard.

She told him quickly, and it was a simple story. She had lingered outside the house waiting until the night closed in, and then she had prevailed upon herself and entered cautiously. She had stolen as silently as possible from room to room, trying to find one into which the moonshine fell as brightly as possible, in order that it might make her some sort of a poor substitute for the companionable cheerfulness of the sunshine. In this fashion she had gone on until she had heard voices and footsteps approaching, and she had turned into the first chamber that was at hand. There she crouched in the farthest corner, but she was no sooner settled there than the two men who she had heard in the distance hulked big in the doorway. One was Tom Cuttle, her lover. One was, to her utter amazement and terror, Henry P. Warner himself. They were in the hottest sort of a debate.

"I have kept you in your foolishness for seven years," Warner had said.

"How much have I cost you?" asked Cuttle.

"Four hundred thousand dollars in cold cash!"

"Very well. You've made a whole million off your crooked deal! I need only fifty thousand dollars more, and, upon my word of honor, that is the last call I'll make upon you."

"How can I believe that?"

"This is on my honor, I tell you. I've never pledged you that before?"

"You lie!"

"Don't be ugly. I tell you, I have to clear up my debts. Then I'll straighten the ranch out. I'll put it in charge of an overseer who'll handle all the details. I'll have the income only."

"Until you happen to want more money."

"The income will be big enough for all of my wants. As soon as I marry, I'm moving East with my wife."

"Are you married?"

"I shall be soon."

"God pity the girl. She's marrying a rat and doesn't know it."

"You old scoundrel. I've come here for money, not for abuse."

"You can't have it, Cuttle. I'm through with you."

"You sent Jim Sawyer to finish the job, I know."

"I did not."

"You lie like a dog. I made him confess."

"He did? Nothing could make Jim talk."

"I found a way." And Cuttle had chuckled.

"At any rate, Tom, this is our last interview."

"I hope so. But I have to have the money. If I don't get it, you know what happens?"

"You tell what you know about me?"

"I tell them that you're alive, while you let your nephew hang for your murder. That's the beginning of what I tell them about you."

"What light will you appear in?"

"I'm a young man. I can change my name and live in some other place. Don't worry about me."

"Thank you, I shall not. But now, Cuttle, let me tell you another side of it. I shall not give you another penny, and, if you dare to attempt to inform against me, I shall immediately send word to Miss Judith Hern that you are. . . ."

"You devil!" cried Cuttle.

"Why, young fool, don't you think that I've watched every step you have made? I tell you, Cuttle, I have you in my hands, and I have had ever since you found a human being you cared for more than you care for yourself. Do you understand?"

There was a wail from Cuttle. "Then, damn you," he cried, "no one else shall have what I can't have myself!"

"What do you mean, Tom?"

"This!" answered Cuttle, and whipped out a gun.

From Judy, in the corner, the sight of the gun tore a shriek of terror. Old Warner caught the arm of Cuttle and tried to master the gun, but the other tore himself away and shot his man down. Then he wheeled upon Judy, discovered who she was, and wildly caught her in his arms and tried to explain—tried vainly, stupidly, of course, until they heard the approaching footsteps of Chick Newton, when Cuttle had carried her into the opposite room, dragged her to the floor, and, with his hand at her throat, promised to throttle her if she tried to make a sound. There she had lain, daring not to move, until the tall, lean form of Newton appeared and entered the other room.

"It's fate," she heard Cuttle whisper then. "He was born to be the ruin of me. It's Newton."

Then followed the entrance of Newton to their own room and the brief fight in which, as Cuttle fired, she had knocked up his arm and then thrown herself at him. Such was the story she told, and then Newton, boiling with fury, took Cuttle by the nape of the neck and dragged him from the house as one might drag a cur. With the girl beside him, he marched his victim through the grounds of the Warner place and brought him to the place where he had left the yellow mustang. On the horse they placed Cuttle, tied his feet beneath the animal, and led him down toward Dulcy.

There was no rebellion left in the coward. He had been through enough on that night to unnerve him completely, but, as they went down the hill toward the lights of Dulcy, twisted at the foot of the mountain, he broke into pitiful lamentations, begging for the liberty that meant life to him. He was met with silence until he stopped his complaints. After that, unasked, he began the miserable relation of his crime.

He had come to know Henry Warner rather intimately, in the old days, because of a debt into which he had fallen. From Warner he had borrowed the money to repay it, at an extravagant rate of interest. So, when he was unable to repay the sum, he had fallen completely under the influence of the rich man.

In this fashion it was possible for Warner to open to him his plan for dodging certain debts that he had himself accumulated, simulating death, placing the blame for his murder on another man, and rewarding Cuttle for his complicity in the matter by giving him a round sum of money—$100,000 was the first estimate.

The bait was far too huge for Cuttle to resist it. He accepted the proposal. When his friend, the nephew of Warner, was proposed by that malicious old man as the victim, Cuttle had feebly expostulated, and his objections had been brutally overruled.

So, waiting for an opportune moment, Cuttle had found young Bill Warner newly returned from a winter's work, already more than three sheets to the wind, and amiable for any proposal. In this condition he had led him to the Warner house. There, after supper, he was brought, as arranged, to the balcony overlooking the Dulcy creek far beneath them. A small portion of a drug in his next drink served to turn the trick. He succumbed to deep sleep. Then Warner broke down a corner of the railing as already prepared and lowered himself on a long rope to the bank of the creek. When he reached this, he gave the signal by jerking at the rope, which was at once cast loose by Cuttle. The latter then roused Bill Warner and accused him of the murder, as Chick Newton had heard from Bill's own lips.

That was only the beginning of the story. Having received his money, Cuttle proceeded to spend it like a foolish child. Finally he was forced to call upon Warner for fresh supplies, for Warner all this time, under a new name and with his habits grown into those of a carefree man of the world, was living in Honolulu. Warner had met the first two or three demands. He had warned Cuttle not to make fresh calls upon him for supplies, and finally, when Cuttle continued to drain him of funds, old Warner had returned to the site of his crime to commit another and remove from the earth the only man who was a witness of his villainy.

Such was the story of Cuttle, strung out with laments and groans as they entered Dulcy. Such was the story that made Bill Warner a free man and the heir to the remnant of his uncle's fortune. For that fortune they found invested in Honolulu properties under a different name. As to the secret passage under the foundation, it was simply the hiding place of Warner when he returned to the house. It had never been used to secrete his treasure. That treasure, in large bills and in negotiable stocks, he had carried with him in a small satchel. The skeleton with the shoe and coat that were found on the bank of the Mason River, had been purposely thrown into Dulcy Creek by him, and had been washed on into the river as had been expected. No one ever knew where he got the skeleton.

The rest of the story is short. Bill Warner became a rancher on a large scale in Arizona and married the girl of his heart. But he was not unconscious that Cuttle had been sent to the gallows in his stead solely through the intervention of his old friend, Chick Newton.

He would have rewarded Chick handsomely with as much cash as Chick could have named without blushing, but the girl who married Chick Newton refused to allow him to accept charity. She was a firm believer that he could do anything in the world that he wanted to do, and that he should be beholden to no one but his own magnificent self for his successes. The name of that girl, of course, was Judy.

The Girl They Left Behind Them

It was in the June 21, 1924 issue of Street & Smith's *Western Story Magazine* that "The Girl They Left Behind Them" first appeared. It was published under one of Faust's many pseudonyms, in this case John Frederick. In this story, it is the enmity of two men—Jack Innis and Miles Ogden—that provides the conflict of the story as these two larger-than-life men vie for the attention and love of Stella Cornish, the sheriff's daughter. This is the first time the story has appeared since its original publication.

I

His real name was Jack Innis, although that name was usually rarely used. People preferred to call him Blondy or Big Blondy, or even Freckles, on account of the array of auburn spots that were strewn liberally across his nose and the upper parts of his cheeks. He was marked out almost from the beginning for a career of excitement. He was born, said rumor, with white hair on his head, and teeth already glittering through his gums. He walked at a time when most infants are unable to sit up without aid. And he talked six months before the normal time. At two years he could speak the vernacular fluently. That is to say, he could discourse like a trooper or a mule driver, which is a superlative in its own way.

When he was eight, he could sit any horse down

whose shoulders his legs could stretch far enough to give him a grip with his knees. When he was ten, he could make a long sixty-foot rope become a living thing in the air, darting like a snake and settling like a swooping bird that stoops from a height. At the same time he received his first lesson in gun play from a certain hardy gentleman who had already served two terms because of his too great facility with powder and lead. A few weeks later his boxing lessons were begun by the blacksmith, who had been a runner-up for the middle-weight championship some twelve years before and who still had the art in his mind even though he could not telegraph instructions into his old hands quite fast enough.

With such happy beginnings what could have been expected for Jack Innis, alias Blondy, alias Freckles? Either that he should become a knightly hero or else a hopeless ruffian. About the result, opinions were divided. There were some who swore that Jack was a true knightly hero. There were more, it must be admitted, who declared up and down that he was a ruffian of the blackest dye. And the vast majority declared that Blondy was a hopelessly irresponsible fellow with some good in him but a great deal more weight of evil.

He led a traveler's life. These travels were involuntarily undertaken. As he continually vowed, there was nothing of which he was really fond in this world except a home and a settled life. He used to talk fondly of the day when he could settle down with his own chickens in his own back yard and his own life in his own kitchen. Such was the ideal of Blondy.

But, alas, conditions were never favorable. As a

matter of fact, he was rarely in the same town more than from three to six months at a stretch. He had a way of making friends who would swear by him, but he also had a way of making enemies who would have thought nothing of pistoling him at the first opportunity, so that some wise-headed officer of the law usually dropped around, on a day, and rounded a secret in the ear of Jack, with advice that he wander on to some more pleasant place on the range.

This had happened when he was a cowpuncher, a miner, a lumberman, and even when he had been herding sheep.

Once he said to a sheriff, who was a man of noted wisdom: "Sheriff, what the devil is wrong with me? Why can't I get on with folks?"

"Because," said the sheriff without hesitation, "you love one thing more than you can love a friend."

"What's that?" asked Freckles.

"A fight," said the sheriff.

This, after all, was the bitter truth and the inward secret of the life of Jack Innis. When he looked at a man, he could not help judging his weight in pounds and temper; he could not help selecting vital spots for attack.

As for the methods of the assault, he was quite indifferent. He had learned, in the long process of the years, as many ways as there are weapons. But, in his heart of hearts, he preferred the might of his bared hands to all other things. The other things were many and various. It happened that on a time, while sundry officers of the law were searching for Jack Innis, and while it was unknown whether or not a certain former friend of Jack's would recover from a fractured skull and internal injuries, Jack himself decided to give the law and all its votaries a wide berth, so he traveled out to the Far West and took a sailing ship through the Golden Gate. It was bound for Australia via Honolulu and half a dozen ports in the East Indies.

In that huge steel frigate, during the next two years, more things happened than would have made stirring history had they been spread thin over the entire great West of the States. During that time he was on the inside and the outside of two mutinies, marooned among savages, adrift in a small open boat without sails or oars, and, having passed through red hell for two years—with some very blue glimpses of heaven thrown in between, here and there—Freckles, that is to say, Jack Innis came back to the country of the cow waddy with a somewhat rolling gait, a leathery brown of hand and face and neck, and a discourse flavored with the salt of sea terms liberally applied.

Such expressions, being in the great West almost as rare as white blackbirds, caused some smiles among those who did not know of Jack Innis and his ways. When they had stopped smiling and their wounds had been bandaged, they were willing to listen more quietly to the strange lingo of the cowpuncher-sailor. That is to say, they either listened or else put their hands together and gave him a swift start for the regions beyond that particular town.

It was after such a flying start from a village that Jack Innis arrived at the town of Oakwood, so called from a grove that had been cut down fifty years before and that had never risen from the hot soil again, and, as he jogged his horse down the main street of the little town, he saw Stella Cornish standing on the verandah of the hotel-general merchandise store, swinging her straw hat by its ribbons and talking coyly to a dapper little fellow who, as she departed with her bundle, tipped his hat to her so politely that big Jack Innis felt his heart stabbed with a pang of envy.

He flung himself from his horse. He tossed the reins over the head of that well-trained mustang, and in a stride he was beside pretty Stella Cornish. She looked up at him through the open work on the brim of her hat, but all that he could see of her was her chin and her mouth which was smiling delightfully. Jack Innis began to take deep breaths of pain and joy commingled.

"I'll take this here bundle along for you," said Jack Innis.

"Do I know you?" said the gentle voice of Stella.

"You're goin' to know me dog-gone' well," said Jack Innis. And he strode on at her side talking of various things, his head in a mad whirl and his heart, also. At the front gate, Stella would have left him, but he spied a stern-faced gentleman sitting on the verandah and wished to know about him.

"That's my father . . . he's the sheriff," Stella said proudly.

"Take me in and introduce me," Jack Innis requested. "Sheriffs is my favorite meat. Raw, with salt is the way I like 'em."

At this, she blinked a little. "I don't even know your name," said Stella.

"Jack Innis is my name," he said.

"Oh!" said Stella.

"Have you heard about me?" Innis asked.

She only answered obliquely: "Are you sure that you want to meet Dad?"

"Of course I do," Jack Innis replied. "Lay a course aboard the sheriff and I'll speak to him."

She could not do anything else. She tried to find arguments and persuasive words, but there was something about the chin of Jack Innis, lean and square and big of bone, like the prow of a ram, that made her decide that mere words could never have much influence over this fellow.

So she took her new acquaintance to the verandah and introduced him. Her father said, by way of acknowledging the introduction: "I see that things is looking up with you, Stella. Looks like you've found a man at last."

"Dad!" Stella cried, and flew through the front door, and then she dropped back to the open side of the screen to hold her breath and listen to every word.

"You're the Jack Innis that busted up things in Shawneytown?" asked the sheriff.

"Sure," Jack answered. "I'm him. That was a fine large-sized party over in Shawneytown."

"That was where you killed Dud Oliver?"

"No. Dud Oliver got so sore, because he'd been licked, that he crawled into a corner and drank himself to death in ten days, tryin' to forget. I didn't do nothin' to him more'n break his nose and a couple of ribs."

"Oh," said the sheriff, "was that all? I understood that you beat him up pretty bad."

"Some folks talk a devil of a lot about what they don't know nothing about," said Jack Innis. He paused, rather bewildered by the bad grammar of his own sentence.

"What you aim to do in this here town?" asked the sheriff, puffing strenuously on his pipe.

"I dunno that there's anything here worthwhile,"

answered Jack Innis, "except your daughter, and I guess I'll stay here and get acquainted with her."

The sheriff said not a word.

"If you ain't got no objections," Jack Innis added.

"The devil . . . no," said the sheriff. "It'll be good for her, but it might be sort of bad for you, old son."

"I dunno what you mean," Jack Innis said.

"Sure you don't," remarked the sheriff. "But if you hang around, you'll learn."

"About what?" Jack Innis asked.

"Life," said the sheriff, and knocked the cinders out of his pipe. He added suddenly: "How old are you, Jack?"

"Twenty-two."

The sheriff sighed. "Thank the Lord," he said, "that fool time of life is done with, as far as I'm concerned. But maybe you'll weather it through. How much d'you weigh, Jack?"

"Two hundred and twenty," Jack Innis informed him. "I got sort of thin with the grippe last month."

"Well," said the sheriff, "maybe you're sort of wore down, but I reckon that you might pull through right enough. Are you goin' to the dance tonight?"

"If they's a dance, I aim to go. Is they anybody takin' Stella?"

"I dunno," the sheriff said. "I think young Tom Powell is takin' her."

"Where might Tom Powell live?" asked the ex-sailor through a yawn.

The sheriff grinned, and then covered and banished the grin by coughing loudly. "Tom lives down to the end of the town in an old house that was white once. It looks sort of gray now."

"Well," Jack Innis stated, "I'll be payin' off before the wind, I guess. So long, Sheriff."

The sheriff rose from his chair and sauntered out to the gate. "Listen to me, Jack," he said. "This here Tom Powell is a gunfightin', man-killin' son-of-a-gun."

Jack Innis turned his bright blue eyes pleasantly upon the sheriff. "I dunno what you mean, Sheriff," he said. "I sure avoid them dangerous men. You never can tell. They might out and hurt you quick as a wink. They got no conscience." With this, he went off down the street—toward the end of town.

The sheriff, returning to his chair on the front porch, rocked himself back and forth in it, chuckling to himself and even breaking from time to time into loud laughter.

His daughter came out and sat on the verandah rail before him. "Dad," she said, "what's it all about?"

Her father looked at her with a joyous eye. "Set still and wait," he said. "You been playin' around with boys up to now. Now you're goin' to have a chance to play around with a real man. He's in love with you, Stella."

"Him?" Stella sneered. "He's got freckles across his nose. Besides, he ain't seen me more than once."

"And even then," said the sheriff "he didn't look very deep inside of you. Run along and help your ma get lunch ready."

II

Early that afternoon the giant returned to the Cornish home. His thundering rap brought Mrs. Cornish in frightened haste, wiping her hands on her apron anxiously.

"Are you Missus Cornish?" said the giant.

"I am," she said. "Is there anything wrong?"

"There is," said the giant. "Send out your daughter to me."

Mrs. Cornish went hastily back to the dining room and whispered in the ear of her man.

"Dog-gone it, Mamie," said the sheriff, "that ain't nothing. That's only this here Innis beginnin' to act up. Go and see him, Stella."

She tossed her head. "I don't like him much," said Stella. "His voice is too loud."

The sheriff smote the table with his fist; his eyes were wild. "He's too good for you!" he thundered. "Get out there quick or I'll. . . ."

Stella vanished.

"Harry, Harry!" The poor wife sighed. "How you do talk to your own child."

"Mamie," said the sheriff, "you dunno the half that's in her. You dunno the half. This Innis . . . he's a man. I know one when I see him."

"Ain't my Stella a lady?" cried the mother angrily.

The sheriff sank lower in his chair and raised his coffee cup. "Sure," he said. "Sure."

At the door Jack Innis leaned above the girl, his vast gloved hand resting against the wall at a level with her fluffy head. "I come here with a message from Tom Powell," he said.

"Oh, do you know Tom?" she asked more brightly.

"Sure," said Innis.

"He's a wonderful dancer," Stella commented with enthusiasm.

"Sure he is," murmured Innis. "But right now he's took bad with . . . er . . . chilblains. He says that doggone him if he can shift around and dance tonight."

The girl stared at the big man in the deepest wonder. "Does he really . . . but what do you mean? Chilblains in summer?"

"Some gents are took funny that way," Innis explained sadly. "I knowed a gent in San Francisco that got the chilblains in his blood like that. Doggone me if he didn't suffer the whole year 'round."

"*Humph!*" said the girl.

"So I thought I'd slide up here out of friendship to Tom and ask you to the dance with me."

She eyed him with a sudden dark suspicion. "I'll have to hear right from Tom."

"Tom thought about that," said the big man. "He sent you up this note."

She opened the envelope, which was not sealed, and read:

Dear Stella: I'm all laid up. I'll tell you about it when I see you. I can't go to the dance. I'll tell you why when we meet up.

                                        Tom Powell

So the girl went to that dance with big Jack Innis. When she reached the hall, she learned the truth about Tom and his chilblains. Jack Innis had descended upon Tom in the middle of the day. There had been a brief and awful affray, after which Jack Innis took the other into his house, put him to bed, and forced him to write the note.

"He's gonna make you love him, Stella!" giggled her friends at the dance that night.

But no one dared to laugh at Jack Innis. He had about him the air of one who possesses. And when he swept the crowd with his bright blue eyes, there were few who dared to meet his glance. Certainly there were none among the men.

Two reckless fellows, the very next night, waited for Jack Innis as he left the house of the sheriff. They made a valiant assault and fought with all their might, and, since they were heavy-handed men themselves, the battle was strung out for the better part of half a minute. At the end of that time, Jack Innis carried them, one by one, to the house of the doctor that was fortunately close by.

After that, Jack led a lazy life in Oakwood. No one cared to interfere with him, and certainly no one cared to interfere with his affairs of the heart. They let him strictly alone, which was all well enough from the viewpoint of Stella, but they let Stella alone, also, and that was not at all to her liking.

She rather enjoyed the situation for the first week or so. It made her stared at and talked about and tickled her vanity from her pretty head of yellow hair to the bottoms of her little feet. But, alas, by the time ten days had passed, she was mortally weary of talking with one young man only, of dancing with one man only, of walking with him, of sitting on the verandah with him.

Sometimes she told herself that, if his nose had been a little longer and a little straighter, she might be able to love him, or if his mouth, even, were a little smaller. Other girls, she knew, considered him a handsome fellow. But Stella insisted that he was not "smart" enough. He didn't have a "way" with his clothes. There was about his conversation none of that cool and superior air that means so much.

And Stella, being born with a pretty face, had enjoyed much variety in the shape of men even from her adolescence upward. She was accustomed to having them flock about her. The arrival of big Jack Innis put a stop to the flood. She endured him for a week; she shrugged her shoulders at him for three more days, and then she began to hate him with all the poison in her soul.

She began to detest his very face, and one day, when he called, she told him everything she thought about him, frankly, eloquently, at length.

"You can't talk," said Stella bitterly. "You can't walk, you can't dance. What can you do to amuse anybody?"

"I dunno," Jack Innis said. "I figured that out a long time ago."

"Then why do you stay near me?" cried the girl.

"I thought," Jack said with perfect good humor, "that you'd get used to me."

"Bah!" shrilled Stella. "I hate you."

"Well," Jack Innis said, grinning broadly at her, "I aim to state that you're the kind that's got to marry."

"I had rather die than marry you!" she cried.

"Suppose they ain't nobody else to choose from, Stella?" Innis asked.

"What d'you mean?"

"Well, they don't seem mighty anxious to bother me none while I'm talkin' to you, Stella. Suppose. . . ."

"Could you marry a girl if you knew she hated you?"

"I'll take a chance on the hate," Innis said, and smiled again.

At that moment, if God had given her the power, she would have blasted Innis to a crisp with a lightning stroke, but that speech gave her a clue to a solution for the trouble that was weighing her down, and that solution was simply to cast about her until she found a champion able and willing to stand up to the blond giant who had stepped into her life and now threatened either to marry her or make her die an old maid.

As for appealing to her father, he merely laughed in her face and told her that this was what she or any other flirt deserved, and in the end, said the sheriff, he knew that she would find some way to torment big Jack Innis far more than he had ever tormented her.

It was shortly after this that she heard of Miles Ogden. The reputation of Miles Ogden was proceeding toward the north and west from the south and east. He was a man of huge size, of unmatched strength, and full of the ferocity of a wild animal.

This unpleasant description filled Stella with joy to the very tips of her fingers, which trembled when she sat down and wrote her letter. A wild, romantic thing to do, she told herself, and the thought of her sad plight here in Oakwood, held as she was by a giant, so to speak, made the tears run into her eyes. She mailed the letter at once, having addressed it to the town to which rumor had now most lately linked the famous Miles Ogden. Then she sat down to wait. She had not long to wait, for the letter was indeed most pathetic, and it might have stirred even a grimmer heart than the heart of Miles Ogden.

Jack Innis had paid his accustomed and hated evening call. Every night, when she said good bye to him, she swore that it was the last time she would permit herself to lay eyes upon him, and every night, when the evening drew near, she remembered the long day of loneliness that was behind her and sighed for any male society—even that of the wooer she despised.

Jack Innis, then, had gone back to his room in the hotel, and she was walking disconsolately back and forth through the garden. There was no living thing near her, saving the dull red, slow pulsing of the pipe of her father, who was lost in the distant blackness of the verandah. Then, through the night, a slow and heavy step approached. A monster loomed before the gate, and a great voice rumbled toward her.

"I'm lookin' for Stella Cornish. Does she hang out in this place?"

So she knew that it was her rescuing hero. She had been half prepared to fall in love with this gallant gentleman when she thought of him in the abstract. But seeing him in the concrete, she saw instantly that he would never do at all. In fact, he was quite impossible. Oh, quite!

Mrs. Callum's window was open and sent a shaft of light that fell on the big man and illumined, particularly, his face. She could see a nose, huge and hooked like the nose of a hawk. She could see a swarthy complexion, dark as the skin of a Mexican. She could see bird-like eyes, small, cruelly bright, and long, out-thrusting chin. All of this was interesting, but the sheer bulk of the man meant more than his face. His face told her, at once, that he would never do for an affair of the heart. Certainly he would never do for one of her affairs. Therefore, he had only the significance of a warrior who must be amused, urged on to the battle, and then allowed to reward himself with the battle itself and with nothing more substantial than praise, say.

But the body of Miles Ogden was all she could have wished. He was a full inch and a half taller than Jack Innis. That is to say, he bulked not a whit less than six feet and some four inches in height. Neither was his build more lean than that of Jack Innis. It was larger. It was much larger. She guessed his weight at, perhaps, 250 pounds. In short, he was a colossus. Jack Innis was big, powerful, formidable, but, compared to this machine of destruction, he was nothing. One wondered, looking at Innis, if he did not find it difficult to get a horse that could endure his weight over long journeys through the mountains, but considering the gigantic thews of Miles Ogden, one felt that horses were out of the question. He must travel on foot, and those powerful legs—would they not carry him forward as far and as fast as any horse?

She came closer to him. It was like entering the presence of a great beast in a zoo—like stepping into the shadow of the elephant. Coming nearer, she could see the revolver at his left hip; she could see the revolver at his right hip. And her heart swelled in her with music. She could have sung, saying that her soul was really too filled. Not only was this monster a Hercules, but he was also a two-gun man. That, she felt, ended all the argument and all the doubt. There was no question. Jack Innis must perish when he encountered this terrible foe. In fact, a vague stir of pity for poor Jack entered her breast. After all, his greatest crime had simply been that he loved her too well.

"I am Stella Cornish," she said in her gentlest and most practiced childish voice. "Are you Miles Ogden?"

The sombrero was taken from his head. He bowed above the gate. "Madam," he said, "I have your letter. Accordingly I am here at your service."

Stella Cornish listened and hardly believed her ears. These words—this enunciation—before her in the physical guise of a giant and a destroyer of men was a cultured gentleman.

III

The swimming pool, which was a scene of rioting carnival every afternoon at nine minutes past three—for it took the older boys from the school just nine minutes to race through the fields, tearing off their clothes as they ran, and then dive into the water—was in the middle of the day a drowsy place where the doves *cooed* up the stream, their voices more than half lost in the wind that stirred among the willows and the squat oaks. And when the doves and the wind were silent, one could hear the water lisping gently over the dam.

Blondy Innis, having thrown off his clothes, stood for a moment on the bank and looked at his reflection in the still water. His face, his neck, his hands were all dusk as an Indian, but the sun striking on the rest of his body set it flaming and flashing like semi-translucent stone of the purest white. Then he dived in, felt the ripple curl over his feet, touched the bottom with his hands, and swam on strongly toward the head of the pool until the current that entered at that point began to slow his progress. Then he came to the surface, snorted out a great breath, threw his arms wide, and with just a little play of his hands kept afloat in the cool water. So he began to drift by dim degrees down toward the dam, his eyes fixed ever upward through the screening limbs of the trees upon the rich blue of the sky above him.

The heat of the day passed out from his body. The heat of the day passed out from his brain. There remained only the dream-like beauty of Stella Cornish, her yellow head and her mild blue eyes afloat somewhere between his gaze and the eternal sky overhead. She was his! He reached the conclusion of the problem easily. It was *reductio ad absurdum.* Someday she must marry someone. If she were not permitted to marry anyone else, she would have to marry him. That this was rankest tyranny did not bother Jack Innis. For, once he possessed her, he would make her love him. That was another problem. When one wanted a horse, the first thing was to buy it. After that one could break it at leisure and teach it the proper paces. He had, he felt, already "bought" Stella. The men of her town would as soon have tampered with fire as go near her while Jack Innis was in the offing. She was his! And at that, exulting, he whirled over on his face and began to swim around the pool with a slashing, long crawl stroke, driving his hands swiftly and noiselessly through the water and churning the pool behind him with his feet. He swam around it and around. He was like a great, glistening white seal in a zoo's pond, fully as soundless and almost as supple and swift.

There was nothing like swimming to Jack Innis. There was nothing in which he could use every muscle and fiber in his big body as he used it in swimming, At last, contented, he floated again on the surface, breathing deeply, his eyes half shut, smilingly aware of his prodigious might of limbs, forgetful in that delight even of the vision of Stella.

"How's the water?" boomed a voice from the bank.

He turned his head and saw, standing in a gap among the trees, one hand leaned against the trunk of a willow, the hugest man he had ever laid eyes upon in all his life of battles, a giant among giants, beside whom he sensed his own smallness with a little shudder.

"The water's fine!" Jack Innis called back. He turned on his side and began to swim in leisurely fashion toward the head of the pool, at the same time beholding the stranger as the latter undressed. Clothes are to the body what a mask is to the face. Many a wide pair of shoulders appears, in the raw, covered with a padding of flabby fat. Expectantly Jack Innis watched.

The face of the stranger was a face of war. His great, hooked nose and his glittering black eyes made Innis think of the face of a bird of prey. His neck was the neck of a wrestler. Now, by degrees, he emerged from his togs and stood on the edge of the water, wrapped in his arms and squeezing the ooze of the margin of the pool between his toes. There were no flaws. With a jealous and an expert eye big Blondy Innis made his estimate of the stranger.

He was a dark bronze. Face and hands were hardly more weathered than the body of the man. It was not the effect of a mixture of colored blood. This fellow was all white, beyond a doubt. One could see that in his eyes and his nose and something clean-clipped about his head, his face, his very body. But that deeply stained skin gave him an effect of the strength of metal. He was in the very pink of condition. The blood shone dimly through the dark skin. There was no superfluous fat; his belly sank sharply in beneath the high, strong arch of his ribs, and all the stomach was as corrugated with muscles as a Greek statue of an athlete. He was such a statue, a cast in bronze rubbed smooth by the careful hand of the artist.

So much for the general survey, but a general survey was not enough. No matter how strong the engine may be, if its force is not applied skillfully, by means of levers, by means of gears, that engine may labor and grind forever and yet accomplish small results. Many a man of Herculean build is little more than a beast fit to heave and haul; how many such have stepped into the prize ring, confident in their padding masses of muscle, in their crushing strength, only to see a champion of half their bulk gliding smoothly about the ring, almost in grasp, and yet away, just brushing beyond reach of the fingertips, snapping home accurate blows at the vital points of assault—stinging as the wasp stings. Many such a giant had Jack Innis encountered in his wanderings. He had no fear of them.

But here was another matter. Here was a man finished as Innis himself was finished, tapering to long, bony hands and feet, bulky but graceful, immense but alert. The striking muscles along the arms of Jack Innis began to harden; his fingers began to curl. As a dog takes the scent of a fox, so Innis scented a battle in the offing more terrible than any combat in his arduous past.

The stranger dived. The great body slid into the water with an oily smoothness. Behind his feet the water clapped together with a soft spat, and the big man came up on the farther side of the pool. He began to swim with a leisurely long stroke, like a glistening shadow in the water.

They found themselves side-by-side at the lower end of the pool. They gave one another a single glance, like race horses at the post, then they kicked themselves away from the dam and fought through the pool to the upper end. At the same instant their hands touched the ridge of rock that marked the upper boundary over which the stream trickled. There they lay a moment, breathing deeply, consciously avoiding the eyes of one another, each astonished that he had met his equal.

Innis went ashore and, whipping the water from his body, dressed; the stranger followed that example.

"A little too chilly . . . this water," he explained.

They sat in the shade on the bank. There was a darkness on the brow of Innis, for he estimated that the handicap that he must overcome was fully twenty pounds of bone and brawn. In the stranger he felt the presence of an equal self-confidence due to that same knowledge. However, what are a few extra pounds save in battles hand to hand? Skill is the thing that counts where weapons enter the question. He took out his heavy-handled hunting knife and juggled it in his hand.

"Ever made a cruise in Mexico?" asked Innis.

"I have," the big man said.

"They have a way with a knife," said Innis.

"They have," said his companion.

"Like this," Innis said, and flicked the knife from his hand. It turned into a shooting ray of light that went out in the trunk of a narrow sapling ten feet away. The knife stuck there, quivering and humming. Then, from the corner of his eye, he watched the stranger take out a knife of his own.

"I learned the same trick," he said, and instantly his weapon was buried in the trunk two inches below the hunting knife of Innis.

The jaw of Blondy thrust out a little. He knew, without turning his head, that his newfound companion was grinning to himself, enjoying his triumph.

"It was a greaser," said the dark man, "who taught me how to shoot from the hip. Same fellow, in fact, who taught me how to handle a knife."

"A lot of gents," Innis said, "can shoot from the hip, but few can hit anything."

"That comes with practice, my friend," said the stranger.

Innis felt that he was being quietly talked down. "Lemme see some of your practice," he said. "They's a rock, yonder. You see? With a white spot on it. . . ."

The rest of the words were torn off short at his lips, so to speak. Blue light winked in the hand of the big man, and, as the gun exploded, half of the white spot was blown away. Now he looked squarely at his companion. For here, in fact, was a dexterity that could not be greatly exceeded, no matter who attempted it. But, watching the faint, sneering smile on the thin lips of the dark man, his heart swelled with anger.

"Pretty smooth," Innis observed, "but a little slow, I think." He jerked out his own gun and fired; the rest of the white spot was blown away, and he had

pile about the part of the country I come from. You might figure out my name from that."

"Go on," said Ogden.

"Well, sir, it's a range where they got some queer ways."

"I believe it," Ogden agreed heartily.

Innis started and set his teeth. He had not intended to leave so wide an opening.

"Education," said Innis, "in a school, they don't bother so much about."

"So I guessed," Ogden broke in smoothly.

Once more Innis gritted his teeth. "But manners," Innis continued, "is what they make a point of."

"Really?" said Ogden. "You surprise me more and more."

"Why . . . ," began Innis, but he checked himself and went on: "Manners is what they like the most and the worst sort of manners in that neck of the woods is to lay aboard a stranger and ask questions. Questions ain't popular around my home town."

"Ah," Miles Ogden said. "A very primitive people, eh?"

"A very which people?" Innis echoed, conscious that he was getting much the worst of this foolish war of words.

"You wouldn't understand," Miles Ogden declared.

"I dunno," said Innis, "that I like the way you say that."

"I don't know," Miles Ogden said, "that I expected you to."

"Speakin' of manners . . . ," began Innis.

"Let us talk," said Ogden, "of something which we are both familiar with."

"I'm mighty sorry that I been talkin' over your head," Innis said.

"Damnation!" exploded Miles Ogden.

"What's wrong with you now?" Innis asked.

"You infernal puppy," said Ogden, "stand up and let me see what manner of man you may be."

"Son," said Jack Innis, "if I stand up, you'll be wantin' me to sit down ag'in mighty quick."

The face of Miles Ogden was purple. "There," he said, pointing to an open space among the trees at the head of the bank, "is a place where we can talk a little more to the point. Stand up, Innis, or I'll take you by the neck and kick you into the pond!"

"Son," Innis said, rising, "you talk like a battleship. Damn me if I don't show you that you ain't no more'n a tramp freighter."

They climbed the bank side-by-side like amiable friends; in the clearing they squared off at one another, and the instant Jack Innis surveyed the pose of the other, he knew that all his fears were about to be realized. Here was a foe of fistic science as well as fistic might.

"Innis," Miles Ogden said, "are you ready?"

"Ready and fit."

"Then start in."

"Ain't you big enough, Ogden, to think for yourself?"

"Very well," Ogden hissed through his teeth, and led.

He struck as straight as though his fist were a thrown ball, with all of his bulky body driving behind it. His long right leg, his stalwart back, his shoulder were in a line behind that smashing fist. Jack Innis blocked. It was like raising one's hand to check a landslide. The blow crashed through his raised guard and glanced along the side of his head. He staggered back half a dozen paces. Certainly here was the battle of his life upon his hands. Here was a man who struck with his left hand as though it were a club. What would his right be?

He learned an instant later. Big Miles Ogden came gliding in with a thoughtful, cruel look in his eyes and ripped a right-hander into the ribs of Jack. It felt to Jack as though a heavy man had jumped with both heels and full weight upon his side. He could feel the ribs spring. The breath was jammed out of his body. A shooting pain flashed like a flame up the center of his breast. That blow fairly lifted him and set him back on his heels, and he saw the glare of triumph already in the eyes of his enemy.

So, all at sea, groggy, a red-flecked mist before his eyes and barely breath in his body to serve for speech, he gasped: "You got science . . . you know how to box a little, Ogden, but you ain't got no punch."

"The devil!" Ogden said. "I'll tear you in two." And, closing his eyes in his fury, he rushed like a bull.

When a man tries too hard, he tops a golf ball. When a fighter tries too hard, he hits short. Miles Ogden drove his fist through the air hard enough to tear the head from the shoulders of his enemy. But it merely fanned the chin of Innis as it sailed by. He, in turn, struck the huge man on the very point of the jaw with his bony right, and Ogden, with a foolish look, swayed backward, walking on his heels.

It was a lucky punch. Even as he delivered it, Innis knew it was lucky. He had all his force behind that blow, and it landed squarely upon the proverbial button that usually brings down the curtain of darkness over the most stubborn brain. Moreover, the huge bulk of Ogden was swaying in at the moment of impact. The jar turned the arm of Innis numb to the shoulder. For the first time in his life he had struck with all his might and that might had landed on a vulnerable spot in the human frame. What he expected was that the jaw of Ogden would be smashed like brittle glass. Instead, he had barely succeeded in staggering his man.

He was too astonished for a moment to take advantage of the temporarily helpless mark in front of him. Then he leaped in, ducked a loosely swinging arm, and smote with all his might a second time, and a second time he landed on the mark. Miles Ogden began to fall, but he fell as a great forest tree topples. There was time to strike half a dozen times while he was still on his feet, and Jack Innis did not waste that time.

The colossus crashed to the ground and rolled to his back. It was done, then, and, with trembling arms hanging at his side, Innis stared down, wondering at his work. But, no, that great bulk continued to turn, lay face down, thrust itself up on long arms, and suddenly with a bellow like the roar of a wounded bull charged at Innis again!

It was a miracle of instinct. The eyes of Miles Ogden were still dull and staring; the blows he struck were wildly swinging, but their power was like the power of a flail of iron. The battle that big Jack Innis thought over had barely commenced.

He blocked two roundabout blows, but their swinging force knocked him off balance, then a plunging overhand thrust landed cleanly on his forehead and picked him cleanly off his feet. Before he could rise, the giant had plunged upon him.

"Foul!" Jack Innis cried.

"I'll tear your throat out!" gasped out Ogden, and buried his talons in the neck of the fallen man.

It would have been the last moment on earth for almost any other man. But a trained wrestler is even more at home on the ground than on his feet. Innis flung up his legs into the air and turned his whole body over, using the head as the pivotal point. That broke the grip, but the tearing fingers scraped the skin from his throat like five files.

He fell on top of Miles Ogden, shot his right hand under the shoulder of the big man, and clamped it down on the back of his head. It was a perfect half-nelson, but, having obtained the hold, it was like trying to turn over a loaded cart. Ogden was an invincible mountain. He shifted the hold like lightning, therefore. A second later he had the toe and the heel of his enemy and began to jerk the foot violently around—a toehold as perfect as the half-nelson had been. But it was like trying to hold the leg of a kicking horse. In a moment they were on their feet again.

All of this was in the beginning, the mild prelude, as it were, of what was to follow. What followed occupied not more, perhaps, than ten minutes, but ten such minutes as might never before have been seen on earth. Ten long eternities to both the struggling men. Standing toe to toe, they smashed at one another with their iron-hard fists. Grappling close, they crashed to the ground and caught for painful holds that would have snapped the bones or broken the backs of ordinary antagonists in an instant.

They grew feebler. The noise of their breathing was like the noise of a storm wind through trees. Their clothes were ripped to shreds. Crimson spattered their half-naked bodies. Their eyes were expressionless, except for a look of brute suffering and a certain indefinable light that meant that the soul was still alive and unconquered.

Then, locked in a last fatal embrace, they staggered to the edge of the bank of the stream. There they tripped and rolled rapidly down to the edge of the water. A projecting stone stopped them. It struck the head of Miles Ogden and jarred them to a halt. And Jack Innis, rising to his knees, saw a senseless, helpless bulk before him.

V

What he felt first of all was the liberty of a man freed suddenly from the grip of a tornado. Then he looked about him blankly and drank in the scene about him as though he were looking upon it for the first time. The trees seemed small, the pool a dirty mud hole, the sky a blue-gray rag stretched closely over the tops of the trees. There was nothing in the world of importance close on the heels of this conflict. He began to feel a thousand aches and pains through every inch of his big frame. And what of Miles Ogden?

When he raised the head of the giant, it fell back again limply so that a sudden fear ran into his soul. What if that rock had pierced to the brain? What if this were death? He pressed his ear to the breast of Ogden and then he heard the beating of the heart. At that, he ran with sagging legs to the edge of the water. When he looked down into it, he did not recognize his own face, so swollen and deformed was it by the battering that he had received. But he had no time to waste in sympathy for himself. He filled a hat with water and hurried back. To climb the slope was now a huge labor. His knees were trembling and threatened every instant to give way beneath him, and the effort sent a mist of darkness across his eyes.

But when he dashed the water into the face of Miles Ogden, he had his reward at once. The giant groaned and blinked, opened his eyes. Then he propped himself up on his long arms and stared at the other.

"Innis," he mumbled, "you beat me."

It was the vastest temptation that had ever come to Jack Innis, for he knew that his bare word would be accepted now. Here lay a man recovered from unconsciousness, still with a cloud of blackness hanging near his brain, and there stood he, Jack Innis, upon his two feet above the fallen. But something told him, moreover, that the knowledge of defeat would crush the soul of big Miles Ogden even as his body had been crushed in the battle.

Already the premonition of the truth was heavy in his face. His eyes bulged with the horror of it; his lips sagged drunkenly; his whole bulk was loose with shame and despair. And if the lie were spoken, it would be the blow of a club, beating down his pride forever. But if the whole truth were to be spoken, Innis knew that he would have to attribute his victory more than half to chance. The lucky position of that rock and the chance that it had struck the head of his antagonist, instead of his own, had ended the fight—not his own prowess of hand. As for the struggle itself, he had felt to the end the overwhelming might of Miles Ogden, crushing his own strength, annihilating him. It had been like a struggle with a bear.

The truth he would not tell; the whole lie he could not tell. "Ogden," he said, "it sort of looks to me like this was a draw. I dunno how it would've turned out. But rollin' down this here bank, your head hit that stone . . . that was how you went black. It wasn't my fist that slugged you cold."

It was a magic word to Ogden. Jack Innis could see his enemy's strength of soul return as though sent from heaven. His head rose; his chest arched again; his features grew composed, and the old, indomitable sparkle came into his eyes. "I might have known that," he said. And he rose to his feet. To the horror of Jack Innis, the giant was as light in his step and his carriage, well-nigh, as though the battle had never been fought. But Ogden in the meantime was looking over his foe from head to foot with an equal curiosity and horror.

"Where do you get it?" Ogden asked at last. "It isn't your size, heaven knows. I have twenty pounds on you"

"I'm big enough, son," Jack Innis said sullenly. "I'm big enough, and you can lay to that."

The other nodded. He even was able to smile as he gestured his assent. "Personally," he said almost lightly, "I'm glad that there was no one here to see this fight. Of course, if there were any audience, I'd have to try to finish you. And finishing a bulldog like you means killing you. . . ."

"Or being killed!" snarled out Innis.

"Exactly! However, since no one is looking on, I'm glad to say, Innis, that I've never met your equal. I've never met a man who could stand to me for three minutes before today."

It was such an honest tribute that it warmed the heart of Jack Innis. A twisted smile, in turn, came upon his battered mouth. "Old-timer"—Innis grinned—"I'll say that much and more. I've fought for business and I've fought for fun ever since I been able to stand up and cuss like a man . . . which was damn' early. But I never yet met up with a two-fisted batterin'-ram like you that looks like a man and fights like a damn' grizzly. That's a fact!"

Behind the swarthy lips of Ogden the white teeth flashed again in acknowledgment. Each had crowned the other with a wreath, so to speak. Half the sores of the battles were salved at that instant. They began to look upon each other with new eyes.

"Suppose that we shake hands?" suggested Miles Ogden.

Innis shook his head. "Lemme get at the bottom of this here," he said. "I just want to find out who sent you out after me?"

"Nobody," Ogden said, scowling suddenly again.

"Wait a minute," said Innis, "there ain't no use in us playin' wild and loose and rambunctious to each other. Cap'n, they's only one way that I could settle you, and that's by bein' settled myself. And if you go after me, you could get me, but you'd be dropped yourself. Ain't that logical?"

Ogden sighed. It was a bitter admission, but, staring into the keen, undimmed eyes of the other, he was forced to admit the truth. "We seem to be equally matched," he said, "with fist and hand and gun and knife . . . damned if we aren't mates, Innis!"

"That's a true thing for you. Well, Ogden, lemme have the straight of it. Once I understand, I'll shake hands free and willin'. But you know more'n I know. Who sent you out here?"

"It's a private matter," said Ogden slowly, frowning upon the ground.

The other cleared his throat with a growl.

"However," Ogden said suddenly, "there's no reason why you shouldn't hear it from me as well as from anyone else. It's unpleasant, but I think we know a bit too much of each other now, Innis, to split hairs about a little excess information. You'll bear me no grudge for this, if I tell you honestly what I believe to be the truth?"

"Old son," said the cowpuncher-miner-sailor-lumberman, "if I was to pick out a brother for a side-kicker, the cut of his jib would be the cut of yours. He'd be like you fore and aft and abeam. Talk right out. If I don't like what you're sayin', I'll give you a hail."

They sat down again. Each, tentatively, from time to time, touched some sore place on head or body. Wherever those giant fists had alighted, they had bruised the flesh against the bone.

"I have to begin this in a way that may make you think me a conceited ass," said Miles Ogden.

"They's a pile of you to be thought about," Innis declared. "Make sail, partner, and let's have your course."

"I have to tell you the first part of it, or else the second part would seem too odd to you. You see, Innis, no man can understand what a girl sees in other men."

"Right," breathed Innis with the heartiest assent. "I've seen damned beggarly craft making fine harbors with their flags flyin', while honest men couldn't show canvas around the same waters without bein' laughed at and sent home."

Over this odd lingo Miles Ogden thought a moment, smiling, but, having made out the meaning, he went on: "That's what you'll say of me. A fellow with my face, Innis, you might say would be as good as a scarecrow to most girls."

Innis surveyed the huge hooked nose, the small, overbright black eyes, like the eyes of a bird, the prominent cheek bones, the cruelly projecting chin of his companion. And he suppressed a smile. "I wouldn't get on as fast as that," he said. "Matter of fact, Ogden, you never can tell with calico which way it'll blow."

"That's it." Ogden sighed. "I've had very little luck with the ladies, to tell you the truth. There's something about my face that doesn't please them." He shook his head gloomily. "But they say that there's one woman in the world for every man in it. By Jove, I used to doubt that. And I never believed, either, in such a thing as love at first sight. You understand?"

"Sure," said Innis. "Fairy-tale stuff. But speakin' personal, I believe in such things. I know." He thought of Stella Cornish and how his heart had swelled when he first saw her.

"Well, Innis, last night I found out that I was wrong all the way through. There is such a thing as love at first sight. I tell you, my friend, that I heard a girl's voice in the dusk and could barely make out the outlines of her face. But I loved her. And before we had been talking half an hour, by heaven, Innis, I had certain proof that she loved me."

"*Hmm*," Innis said. "Maybe you better drop anchor right there, old-timer, while we find out what you mean by certain proof. Maybe you mean . . . she told you so?"

"Ah, no." The big man sighed, lifting his ugly face to the blue heavens, while a smile illumined his battered features. "I know that words may often lie. But acts can't lie, my friend. Will you believe it? She came close to me and lifted her face to me. And I kissed her, Innis . . . tenderly . . . it was a sacred moment to me. And to her. She told me then that she loved me. It would have been sacrilege to have lied at that instant. She could not have lied to me."

"Well," said Innis, "you bein' fixed up like that, and already to get married, you start out celebratin' by pickin' a fight with me as soon as you can find me? Is that it?"

"You don't understand. She could not promise to marry me. There was one obstacle in the way."

"The old man couldn't see you, eh?"

"Not her father. Her lover."

"What? She had a lover?"

"Unwillingly, you see? A fellow had forced himself on her. She did not love him, but she did not dare to pay any attention to another man while he was around."

Jack Innis rose to his feet. "Ogden," he said darkly, "maybe you better make sail ag'in and hunt for another port. Looks to me like you anchored in an open sea with a storm comin' up."

The other rose, also. "You're right, Innis," he said quietly. "Heaven knows I'm sorry for this. I confess it's as you suspect. She told me that, if she could be sure that you were no longer near enough to interfere and to make trouble, she'd marry me in a minute. That's why I hunted you out."

Fury stormed into the brain of Blondy Innis. He choked it back, panting. "Now, Ogden, lemme get this right . . . this here Stella . . . she kissed you, you say?"

"She did, Jack."

"And told you that she was . . . fond of you?"

"More than that. She said. . . ."

"Damn the rest. What I mean is . . . well, Ogden, you been actin' the part of a fool."

The big brown hand of Miles Ogden stole back to his gun.

"Wait a minute," Innis went on, seeing that eloquent and smooth gesture. "Because we don't agree, do we have to murder each other?"

The hand came away again. "Look here," explained Ogden. "You'll admit that a woman has a right to select her own husband?"

"I don't admit nothin'. Except that you've had the wool pulled over your eyes. Her . . . why, she ain't that kind. She ain't the sort that gets excited easy. She's as cold as ice, Ogden. I know. I've tried to melt her. And all she wanted to do, when she seen you, was to use you to shovel me out of the way."

"*Hmm*," murmured the larger man sternly, his anger growing during this explanation. "It looks to me, Innis, as though we should have kept on to the finish."

"If I'd kept on to the finish," Innis stated truthfully, "you'd be at the bottom of that pool long ago."

Ogden set his teeth. Then he nodded. "My friend," he said, "I give you my word of honor that I put a higher value on you than on any man I've ever met in my life. But about Stella Cornish . . . she belongs to me, and there's an end of it."

"Old son," said Jack Innis, "damned if you ain't the closest imitation of a real man that I ever seen, but when it comes to that girl . . . she belongs to me. I seen her first, Ogden!"

They stood glowering.

"Look here," broke in Innis with a sudden light falling on his mind. "Suppose that you make a test. If you win, I'll vamoose. If you lose . . . you slide out. Does that go?"

"Let me hear the idea."

"Go to Stella and tell her that you've cleaned me up. Y'understand. You've broke me up fine and kicked me out of the country. Then you just ask her to name the day for the weddin' and see what she does."

The other started. "If she asked me for proof?"

"Here's proof. She knows my guns. She knows that I love 'em, them bein' old friends. Take this here Colt and show it to her. If you got that, she'll know that I'm dead or worse'n dead."

The other handled the gun solemnly. "You're confident, Innis," he said sadly.

"Sure," said Jack Innis. "About her, I'm a prophet, damn my hide!"

VI

In the telltale light of the day, big Miles Ogden dared not advance into the town of Oakwood. But with the earliest coming of the dusk, he approached the house of Harry Cornish and found that the sheriff was already on the porch enjoying his pipe before dinner. The night was cool, for the autumn days were shortening rapidly, and already some of the loftier peaks of the northern mountains were turning white, things of perfect beauty in the clear blue of the horizon. But the sheriff would not give up that after-dinner pipe beneath the stars no matter how cold the weather turned. This was his moment of peace, his daily breath of larger thoughts and solemn quiet.

He said to the man in the dark, the huge bulk that

stalked like a shadow down the garden path: "Who might you be, stranger?"

"I'm a friend of Stella's," said the deep organ tone of Ogden.

"She's got more friends," said the sheriff, "than a buzz saw has got teeth. What particular tooth might you be?"

"My name is Ogden."

"I've heard tell of that name. I've heard tell . . . why, man, you ain't the Miles Ogden who . . . ?"

"My name is Miles Ogden."

"Set down here beside me and rest your feet. So you're Miles Ogden?"

"I'm glad to know you, Sheriff."

"There ain't one chance in ten of that bein' the truth. Them that like Stella ain't got much use for her dad. And I suppose that you're with the crowd, Ogden?"

"With what crowd, sir?"

"Them that make fools of themselves about that girl."

"I . . . I . . . ," Miles Ogden stammered, and then found that he had no words for the completion of his sentence.

"Suppose that she was to wear a mask," said the sheriff. "I wonder how many would pick out Stella?"

"You are very frank," Ogden said haughtily.

"I am," said the sheriff. "I been to school in my house long enough to know a little about some things. I ain't talkin' because I hope to be changin' your mind. Mind of a young man can't be changed about a girl until he's got her. The way to marry off a girl is to put up a fence around her with a big pad-lock on the gate. The young gents will think that they're in love with the girl inside the fence. Matter of fact, all they're in love with is the trouble of bustin' through that particular padlock or else maybe breakin' down that there fence. Oh, I know you young fools." The tone of the sheriff was one of genial amusement, not of anger. "Look at Stella," he continued. "I can't spoil her good time. When I tell you that she ain't good-nachered, patient, lovin', kind, nor true . . . when I say that she can't cook, that she can't make her own clothes, that she likes to stay up all night and sleep all the day, that don't make no difference to you, of course. Sure you're above thinkin' of them things. What's sewin' or bakin' to a gent under thirty that's in love? But, young man, what a difference it makes to a gent over thirty that's married to a wife and her kids and anchored to the job of findin' the bread for 'em! Well, I say, put a mask on Stella, and who'd pick her out? Her figger ain't better'n the figgers of other girls in this here town. Her hands and her feet ain't no prettier. But because God took time off on the rest of her body an' soul and put it in on her face, she's follered by young gents like you thick as bees. What you want? To marry a pretty face? That there face is the first part of her that'll grow old."

"Sir," said the younger man, "I cannot argue with you. In fact, I don't care to."

"I ain't arguin'," said the sheriff. "I'm judgin'. I ain't a lawyer. I'm a jury, right now. I'm twelve honest men tellin' you the truth, Ogden. But when you see her tonight, you just figger what she'll be ten years from now. Now I guess I've said enough to make you go right in and tell her that you want to marry her tomorrow." He raised his voice: "Stella!"

There was no answer.

"She takes her time about doin' anything," said the sheriff, "includin' comin' when she's called. Stella!"

"Well, Dad?" drawled the voice of Stella from the screen door.

"Have you heard what I been sayin'?"

"Of course not!"

"You have, though, and you're swearin' mad at me. Here's another young idiot that wants to marry you. Go on in and chin with her, Ogden."

Ogden waited for no further bidding. He passed through the screen door and stood before the lady of his heart.

She was dressed in pale blue. Let the fashion makers from Paris and Manhattan with their jaded tastes and their eyes craving stimulus turn their backs on all gentle colors, still, there is nothing that quite takes the place of blue. Stella, living in a little village where the stern currents of fashion drifted only in magazines twice or thrice a year, had chosen her color and was content with it. To the man who stood before her, she seemed a chosen bit of heaven. And she knew his thought.

She was in a towering passion. "Did you hear what he said?" she gasped out at him. "Oh, you heard! You heard! But did you believe? Did you believe? You aren't going to trust what he says about me? Oh, why did God have to give me such a father? There is no love in him. Miles Ogden . . . sometimes I . . . I. . . ."

She was about to say *hate*, perhaps, but something warned her to go no further. The shadow of the disapproval of Miles Ogden extended like a shadow to her very feet. And she, peering up at him, as he stood in the dark, with only his big hands illumined by the low-shaded lamp, finally saw that his face itself was altered—very materially. At this, she grew a little pale. He had not said a word, not a syllable since he entered, and that silence was more terrible than any speech. It promised everything that she had desired.

"You . . . you found him, Miles?" she whispered.

He nodded, and she drew him into a secret corner of the room. Still her bright, guilty eyes roved past him, searching the rest of the chamber against an eavesdropper. Pulling him into the light, in this fashion she could see the signs of the combat printed visibly and terribly on his face.

"You fought with your hands! Oh, Miles, he has smashed you and broken you and driven you back to me. Is that it?"

"Do you think that is it?" he asked her, speaking at last.

"If it is, I'm lost! I'm lost!" sobbed the girl. "If you've failed, oh, nobody can help me, then!"

"Why are you so afraid of him?" he asked.

"Because he's . . . a devil!"

It was not quite the description that he would have given Jack Innis since their battle. At least Blondy was a fair and square fighter who disdained to take advantages. And now he determined to use the ruse that Innis had suggested.

"You don't have to fear Innis any longer," he said. "It was a hard fight. But Jack Innis will never trouble you again." He tried to tell himself that it was a mere flash of relief and that the glitter in her eyes was fear. But an instinct assured him that it was plain and brutal exultation.

"He's dead," she murmured. "Speak soft. Don't

let Dad know. He's always said that I'd get a man killed one day. Oh, Miles Ogden, what a hero you are. There isn't another man in the world like you. Tell me. Tell me everything about it."

"We fought until we closed. Then I got at him with my hands. And . . . he decided to leave this part of the country, Stella, and never come back again."

"Did he promise that?"

"Yes."

She drew back a little to stare into his face, towering above her.

He could see, against his will, that she was trembling with a fierce delight.

"That'll teach bullies! That'll teach brutes that they have to treat women with respect!" she cried to Ogden. "Oh, Miles, I . . . I hope that you . . . that you smashed him!"

He nodded, biting his lip.

"But have you any proof?" she asked with a sudden suspicion.

It was so pat with the arguments that Innis had advanced and his judgment of the girl that Ogden could not help sighing.

"Here," he said, "is the gun of Jack Innis. Do you know it?"

She almost snatched it out of his hand in her haste. "It's his gun!" she cried at last, clasping the revolver to her bosom. "Kiss me, Miles?"

He leaned mechanically; mechanically he touched his lips to hers, but he felt his very soul shrivel and wither in him. Then he held out his hand for the weapon.

She shook her head, saying: "You'll let me have this . . . for a souvenir, Miles."

"Look here," answered Ogden. "You have to remember that the losing of that gun meant the losing of all of the pride of Innis forever. He's a broken man, Stella. You don't want such a thing to remind you that he's ruined?"

"Don't I? Don't I?" cried Stella. "I'd like to have him torn to . . . but, oh, Miles, it doesn't seem possible that it's true."

"Stella," he said, "I've done what you want. Now I've come to ask you to do what you promised. Name the day for our marriage, dear. Nothing stood between us except big Jack Innis. Innis is no longer here to bother us."

Her eyes were suddenly abased to the floor. "Marriage?" she said. "Oh, Miles, we've hardly met one another. How can we set a day so early in our acquaintance?"

"Last night," Miles Ogden said gloomily, "you had no doubts."

"But you know"—Stella smiled—"there's a lot of difference between night and day. And . . . we're not going to be silly and rush at such important things, are we, Miles?"

His big head was bowed. "I'll take the gun again," he said huskily.

"Miles!"

He reached for the weapon and took it gently and firmly from her.

"You doubt me!" cried the girl, flaring with anger.

"Innis said it would be this way," Ogden answered, and, with no other farewell, he turned away from the house.

VII

He found Jack Innis, according to their prearranged plan, at Widow Creighton's house where he was a boarder. Freckles lay in on the bed with his head pillowed on a huge arm, smoking a pipe. He did not even turn his head when his companion entered.

"Well, mate," he said cheerily, "I'm sorry that things turned out bad for you."

"How do you know?" muttered Ogden.

"By the way you tramped along the deck. When a man goes up to stand watch, he walks pretty light. When he comes off, he's got lead in his feet. You got lead in your feet, old son."

Ogden threw the gun on the bed. Innis fumbled for it, found it, and shoved the weapon into the holster that was waiting for it.

"I'll never see her again," Ogden announced heavily, dropping into a chair.

"That's what you think now. Wait till you've had a chance to dream about her tonight. That'll change you back on the other side of the picture. I've swore that I'd never see her ag'in. I've swore it ten times. But here I am still in Oakwood. The worse she treats you, the harder it is for you to get clear of her. You think that you're goin' to pack up and vamoose, right now. You'll change your mind and wind up by stayin' here with me."

The spirit of prophecy assuredly had entered the brain of big Jack Innis. That night Ogden slept in the same room with his rival. In the morning they sat opposite one another with platters of ham and eggs in between.

"We can't both win her and we can't both marry her," said Innis. "But there ain't no good reason why we can't fight fair and square for her, Miles. Am I right?"

"Fair and square," Ogden repeated with a sigh, and they shook hands across the table.

They determined, consequently, to take alternate days for calling upon her, and they tossed a coin to begin with. Jack Innis won. His was to be the first encounter since the battle. He spent the rest of the day preparing for it, lying on the bed with raw meat clapped over each swollen eye and a cold towel about his mouth. In the evening, when he arose and looked at himself in the mirror, his features were still distorted by the battering that they had received, but he decided that he was presentable. He dressed himself as neatly as possible. Ogden had gone to the store and bought a shirt for his rival.

"And I saw a smooth-faced little rat there called Leicester Dennis," he told Innis. "He looked me over as cool as you please."

" 'You're Miles Ogden?' he says.

" 'I am,' I said.

" 'Well,' he said, 'I hope that you have better luck with the shirt than you had with your last fight.'

"I took a look at him. If he'd been forty pounds bigger, I'd have broken him in two. But he's small enough to know that he's safe. He takes advantage of being small, like a woman."

"I know him," said Freckles. "Someday I'll step on him and make a mud hole in the middle of the street."

So he donned the shirt and sallied forth. He found the girl beside her father on the verandah. She arose and expressed herself freely through the gloom of the end of the day.

"You're both nothin' but big cowards, John Innis," she told him. "I know all about it. You're both liars and cowards, and I hope that I never lay eyes on either of you again." With this, she flung into the house.

"Sit down, son," the sheriff said kindly. "Sit down and tell me why two honest-Injun men like you and Ogden are wastin' time over that bit of calico?"

"I dunno," Innis muttered sullenly. "It's because she's so damn' pretty, Sheriff. Can you figure out any better reason than that?"

"A lot better one, friend. The reason you both want her is because you can't have her. If she was free and easy to take, then neither of you'd be wantin' her for a minute."

"I dunno." Innis sighed.

"Well, forget about her for a minute and tell me about that time they marooned you down yonder in the South Seas. The one where the daughter of the chief thought you. . . ."

"*Sssh*," whispered Innis. "Dammit, Sheriff, she'll hear you in a minute."

"What if she did," said the wise sheriff. "D'you think that she wants a Sunday-school teacher for a husband? Go on, Freckles, and lemme hear that yarn."

It was an hour later when Innis rose from his chair and sauntered down the path. Going through the gate, he turned abruptly into the figure of a little man well-nigh a foot short of his own height. The collision, which he hardly felt, sent the other staggering and reeling away. The long arm of Innis shot out; the strong hand of Innis caught the little man and steadied him.

"You big, blunderin' fool!" snarled out the sharp voice of Leicester Dennis. "Can't you see where you're goin'?"

"Someday, son," said Innis, "I'll get so damn' blind that I'll put a foot down on you . . . in the dark. So long, and be a good little boy, Dennis."

The reception of Miles Ogden, the next day, was even more ferocious. She had no use for him, she told him plainly. He had broken her heart by deceiving her. She wanted nothing to do with him; she hoped that she'd never see him again. Ogden retreated in dismay.

"It's all up," he told Innis. "She's through with both of us forever."

"But," Innis said, setting his jaw, "I ain't through with her. I'll get her or bust. Run along if you want to. I stay on the job."

Which, of course, made Ogden stay to see in what way the battle might end. "Besides," said Innis, who was gathering wisdom partly from experience and partly from the lips of the sheriff, "she ain't the kind that can stand livin' alone. She's got to have her parties."

He was right. When the time of the next dance came, Stella succumbed. It was either Ogden or Innis for a partner, or no one at all. She went with Miles Ogden, and the giant so overawed her other admirers that only old Tom Shawmet dared to ask her to dance. The rest of the evening she alternated with Ogden and big Jack Innis, hating them with all her spiteful little heart every step they led her across the floor.

"Why don't your father do something?" old Tom asked her as they danced.

"He don't care!" sobbed the girl. "I think he likes to see me tortured and humiliated like this. I . . . I wish that someone would poison 'em."

So did half of the young men of Oakwood and the surrounding ranches. But none cared to step forward as the poisoner. Finally they decided that group action was permissible. There were twelve stalwart youths, picked men, who gathered together. On the way to Widow Creighton's house three of them lost their way or their courage and disappeared. Nine remained, and those nine laid in wait for Innis and Ogden and caught them when they came out for their evening stroll, according to their custom.

They caught the pair together, but it was like catching a pair of bears with bone-breaking power in the flip of either paw. The nine fought valiantly. In the first rushing assault, Innis broke the faces of two assailants, and then went down with three men clinging to his body. But Miles Ogden, uttering a shout like a giant gone berserker, picked up Larry Jones and flung him at the crowd. Larry's left leg was broken and three men were knocked down by that terrific blow. Then Ogden picked the assailants off the body of Innis, struck them, and pitched them into the garden loam.

After that, when Innis had dusted the dirt from his clothes, he and Ogden strolled off down the street, shoulder to shoulder, and left a swarming, struggling, groaning, pleading garden full of victims behind them. Five could walk; four could not. The good widow had the helpless carried into her front room and there she tended them. But they were all conveyed away before the terrible pair returned.

The older and wiser heads in the town consulted seriously upon this matter, but, after all, the two giants were so completely in the right, having been attacked by the others, that Oakwood had to pocket up its injuries and wait for another and a better day.

A fortnight rolled on; white winter dressed the mountains, although the days were still hot in the low-lying range about Oakwood. Still no one had found a proper plan for beguiling the two out of the town. On the hotel verandah bets were freely offered that Innis or Ogden would win the girl. Bets were also offered as to the length of time that would elapse before a gunfight with fatal consequences occurred between the pair.

It was at this time that the sheriff brought home odd news and delivered it at his board at the evening meal.

"Si Goodrich," he said, "has come in with a buckboard full of skins. It's going to be a mighty fine trapping season. Seems that they's a sort of a famine farther up north and a lot of good pelts are walkin' around farther south than they were ever seen before. Si swears that he seen a silver fox up near the headwaters of Kaska River right on the side of old Seminole Mountain. I said to Si . . . 'You was drinkin' hooch when you seen that.' 'Strike me dead,' he said, 'if I didn't see the varmint with my own eyes. I stayed a week longer'n I'd expected tryin' to catch it. But it's got brains, that fox has. It's twice as big as a red fox, and it's got twice as much brains.' If old Si could trap it, he says that he'd knock off trappin' for the rest of the winter. Well, he could afford to!"

"What's a silver fox?" asked Stella.

"A silver fox," said the sheriff, finishing his coffee noisily, "is something that's worth its weight in silver, doggone near. Yep, it's worth more'n its weight, sometimes."

She followed him out onto the verandah. "What does it look like?" she asked him.

"What?" yawned the sheriff.

"The silver fox, of course."

"Black, with a dustin' of silver hairs. The doggone finest fur that ever was seen. Back East where they can afford them things, they turn a handspring when they see a silver fox skin. But even them millionaires groan when they got to pay the price. What you askin' for?"

But Stella returned no answer. She was beginning to dream into the dark of the night, and a bright thought was growing in her mind.

VIII

The knock at the door was heavy enough to have announced the coming of a sheriff with all his posse of gunmen behind him, but when Miles Ogden opened the door, there stood in the threshold only the slender form of Leicester Dennis, wearing his highest stiff collar and his most purple tie.

"What do you wish?" asked Ogden.

"I have come with a message," Leicester Dennis announced. "Miss Cornish is willing to see you both . . . at once."

"She . . . ," began Miles Ogden, and then the lordly effrontery of the clerk's manner made him flush. "Do they give messages to monkeys in Oakwood?" he asked.

"Tell Miss Cornish," said Blondy Innis from the corner, "that our time is all took up this evening."

"Gentlemen," said Leicester Dennis, frowning his disapproval upon them, "are you making Miss Cornish a matter of jest?"

"What are you, little feller?" asked Blondy, rising leisurely upon one elbow. "Are you a man or a book?"

"What?" shrilled Dennis. "I'll tell Miss Cornish that you're a pair of ruffians and refuse to come."

"Hurry," said Blondy. "Here's a flying start for you." He had rolled from the bed to his feet at the last remark of the general merchandise clerk. Now he took Leicester Dennis by the collar, and, suspending him at arm's length, he carried Dennis to the front door of the house and thence kicked him off into the black space of the garden.

Then, shoulder to shoulder, Innis and Ogden strode up the street and reached the gate of the Cornish house just before a certain scampering little figure that was making for the same destination, choking and raging with shame and fury. They thrust Leicester Dennis from their way and went up the path with the heavy odor of the newly watered garden rank on either side of them. The quiet voice of the sheriff greeted them from the verandah.

"It's the first time that I ever seen one hook catch two fish. How d'you manage to do it, Stella?"

They heard an angry exclamation from Stella. Then she ran down the steps, and, meeting them, she gave them both a hand. Her laughter was like a light in the darkness—it made them see her. So she led them to the side of the house where they could speak together without danger of being overheard.

"Jack and Miles," she said, "here we are all tied up in a knot. Jack says that he wants to marry me . . . Miles says that he wants to marry me. I can't marry you both, can I?"

They waited in silence.

"There ain't a chance that I can please you both," said Stella. "And I've been trying to pick a choice. But it's hard to choose."

There was a groan from the two expectant suitors.

"If I like you, Jack, for one thing, I like Miles for another just as well. Besides, Miles forgave me after I broke my promise to him. And forgiveness counts a lot, Jack."

Jack Innis grunted.

"But I've thought of a way of leaving it up to chance," said the girl. "Si Goodrich saw a silver fox up Kaska River on the side of the old Seminole. Boys, the first one of you that brings me back the pelt of that fox, I marry. Is that fair?"

"Fair as can be," Miles Ogden agreed, the expert hunter and trapper,

"Hold on a minute!" cried Jack Innis, more sailor and cowpuncher than hunter. "Lemme think this here over, I dunno that I like the idea."

"Are you afraid," the scornful girl asked, "that Miles will beat you?"

"Damn Miles!" exploded Jack Innis. "Sideways, endways, or any way you want to take him, I ain't afraid of him!"

"Are you swearing in front of a lady, Innis?" Miles Ogden asked savagely.

"Hush!" cried the girl.

"Are you gonna teach me manners?" asked Jack Innis.

"One can't teach a wildcat parlor tricks, but one can at least throw it outdoors. Innis, you're a disgrace to yourself."

"Ogden, you act like you was safe in harbor, but I'm gonna show you that you're right out at sea in the middle of a. . . ."

Between them Stella Cornish flung herself. "Isn't it better to take it out on the fox than on each other?"

It was such good sense that they made a pause. In each, moreover, there were certain bruised spots that ached to the bone, recalling a battle that had been fought, after all, not so many weeks before. So they hesitated, hating one another like two wild animals, ready to rush and yet held back by the sight of the flashing tusks of each other.

"It's really better sense," Ogden said at the last. "We ought to do it, Jack."

"Maybe," said Innis. "You bein' a hunter by nacher and a trapper by trainin'. . . ."

"Innis, you know that I'm a lawyer by training."

"I was givin' you credit," said the sailor-cowpuncher, "for the bringin' up of a honest man. But leavin' that aside, I'll take you up. Ogden, anything from poker dice to catching silver foxes, I'll meet you fair and square and I'll beat you fair and square."

The girl had been turning from one to the other, anxiously. Now she said eagerly: "Shake hands on that, boys!"

Their great hands met and closed upon one another with a pressure that would have burst the bones of ordinary fingers. Thereat, Stella Cornish flung her arms around the neck of Jack Innis and kissed him roundly, and then offered the same favor to Miles Ogden before he had time to grow jealous.

They bade her good bye. They stopped at the verandah and bade the formidable sheriff *adieu*.

"What deviltry has my girl put you up to?" asked the wise sheriff.

At this, in the darkness, they both started. The prescience of the sheriff was sometimes a bit uncanny as at the present moment. They strode back to the Widow Creighton's, side-by-side, but their steps were long, and Jack Innis found himself straining to maintain the pace set by his huger companion. And all the way back to the house, not a word was said by one to the other.

At the house they prepared their separate packs. At the same instant they swung them upon their shoulders. At the same instant they started for the door. They hesitated, staring at one another with black faces, each unwilling to give way and let the other pass through first until Jack Innis, with a smile, stepped back and waved Ogden through ahead of him.

"The first step ain't the last step," Innis stated.

But there was no return for this courtesy. Miles Ogden shouldered through the doorway and strode off from the house.

Innis waited in the garden until the heavy beat of the heels of his late companion ceased to sound upon the hollow wooden sidewalk. Then he looked north and west where the lordly form of old Seminole rolled up head and shoulders above the nearer mountains, a great figure among the stars.

IX

A line of traps cannot be secured in a moment and set out in an hour. Although the hunters started at night, it was not until late the next day that they reached the village of Kaska, near the head of the river. There they bought traps of all conditions, and from Kaska they started out again. Innis was a full three hours behind his rival.

Three hours was a small matter in such a task, however. It was a day's march to the region where Si Goodrich had seen the silver fox. It was another labor of two days for Innis to select the sites for his traps. Even so, he was placing them largely in the dark. The rumors that had gone the rounds in Kaska town said nothing of the silver fox having been seen since Si Goodrich first had sight of it. Nevertheless, half a dozen ambitious hunters had already littered the sides of old Seminole with their traps. Ogden and Jack Innis were late arrivals in the chase.

It was gloomy work for Blondy. He was one who loved noise and companionship, whether in the forecastle or the cow camp. In the wretched lean-to that he constructed for himself, the hours were long as fate itself. After the warm sun of the plain far below, the mountain snows bit him to the bone with cold, and there were even times when he half felt inclined to give up the entire task and return to Oakwood to take his chance as he had taken it before. Even so, there would remain only one chance in ten that Miles Ogden might have the great luck to catch the fox.

Twice a day Innis walked the line of his traps. And twice a day he killed rabbits or starved coyotes that had been caught in the teeth of the steel jaws. In the first three days he caught as many red foxes. But what were red foxes to Innis. He disdained even to skin them, and returned sullenly back to his lean-to. On the fourth day a southeast wind drove an army of black clouds across the sky. On that day and for two days thereafter it snowed in a steady downpour, loading the limbs of the evergreens until they cracked. The snow turned to rain on the day following, and that night, the wind swinging to the north, the thermometer dropped a full thirty degrees.

The next morning Jack Innis looked across a scene coated with ice. The snow, melted at the surface by the warmer rain, had frozen again as smooth as glass. The tree trunks, the smallest twigs on the evergreens, the foliage itself, the shrubs and all their tiny branches, were all coated with thick, transparent coatings of ice. When the wind blew, there was a sound as of soft bells jingling through the forest as the icy boughs swung against one another. Everywhere there was a noise like the rustling of rain as the ice particles broke and dropped or floated to the ground.

No one could tell the beauty of that scene, for at mid-morning the last of the cloud was whipped from the sky by a changing wind, and the sun showed strongly across the mountains. Ten million brilliant mirrors gave back its light. The forest glittered like a thing made of diamonds, green-hearted diamonds. From the flare of the light thrown back from the snow, Innis had to shield his eyes by blackening the skin around them.

He made only half the round of the traps. The walking was far too difficult on that slippery surface, so he turned back toward the lean-to and reached it long before noon. Something was making off through the forest with much crackling through the shrubbery as he came up to the lean-to. Perhaps a stray timber wolf had come down to nose about among his possessions.

He entered the lean-to hastily and there he found that the worst of all wolves had indeed made him a visit. His supply of food, his reserve ammunition, saving for the bullets in his revolver and in his Winchester, he had kept buried under several immense rocks on the floor of the lean-to. He came back to find those rocks had been lifted and everything was taken out.

It was the work of the malice of Miles Ogden. There could be no doubt of that. It was only strange that Ogden should have descended to such low trickery—strangest of all that he should have fled from the coming of his rival—fled like a wolf through the forest. But when Innis remembered those bright, small eyes, like the eyes of a bird, he felt that, after all, anything was possible from his enemy.

He was out of his lean-to by this time. All the noise of the flight had died out long before. He looked about him to make out the probable course of the flight. To the left and behind him old Seminole sloped sharply up. But before him and to the right the ground swept down at a strong angle.

It was hardly probable that the fugitive would try to make away against the slope, particularly in such going as this. He was more apt to go downhill, and he would be sure to keep deep within the skirts of the forest. The woods, however, angled well away to the left. There was a much straighter and steeper course down the mountain to the bottom of the ravine below. That was the course that Innis selected. He went down that iced surface faster than a man could have run on the level, slipping and sliding down dizzy shoots, risking his neck a dozen times, but his fury made him blind to danger until he reached the level of the ravine with the mutter of the stream in his ear. Then he looked up and was appalled by the thing that he had just accomplished.

He hurried on down the ravine now, until he was at the edge of the woods; he had barely taken shelter behind a rock when the fugitive came in view. There could be no doubt that it was his man. He was running as well as he could over the icy surface of the ground, still turning his head to make sure that he was not pursued. But it was not Ogden, and that fact made Innis wonder.

It was a middle-aged fellow with a dirty growth of beard on his face, wearing a canvas coat whose fur-lined collar was turned up high about his head. At the sharp command of Innis, he stopped short and whirled about. His hands went up like a gesture of dismay, rather than surrender, when he saw the leveled rifle.

"You don't look happy, partner," said Innis, rising from behind the rock, still keeping the rifle on the mark. "Step up close and talk it over."

The other groaned. "Innis," he said in a voice made sharp with fear, "it ain't me that you want. Me, I'm just hired. It ain't me you want, Innis. I swear to heaven that it ain't. I got nothin' ag'in' you." He came forward with short, dragging steps as he spoke.

Innis grounded the butt of his Winchester and

dropped his hand to his revolver instead. He disdained this enemy too greatly to disarm him before proceeding deeper in the parley.

"You swiped my chuck," said Innis. "Where'd you put it?"

"You can get it easy, Innis."

"And the ammunition?"

"I . . . I just took that along. . . ."

"For luck, eh?"

"There ain't a bit lost. . . ." He removed the knapsack from his back.

"Put that back on. Just hike back up through the woods and show me where you put my stuff."

So the stranger led the way among the trees, walking slowly, keeping away from the trunks lest it should be suspected that he was trying to dodge into shelter from the man behind him. Now and again, a convulsive shudder ran through his body as though he felt the bullet tearing through his spine.

He brought Innis to a place hardly 100 feet from his lean-to. There, in the heart of a great, hollow-throated stump, eaten away with rot, and covered not only with the dust of the rot but with snow and ice, also, were the provisions. These he dragged forth and obediently bore them back to the lean-to. The knapsack full of the stolen ammunition he replaced at the same time. Then he faced his captor with a face working with terror.

"What you aim to do to me?" whined the thief.

"Suppose that I was to sink a slug in you and roll you down into the ravine?" asked Innis.

The other raised a dirty paw and fumbled at his throat as though the pressure of the collar were choking him.

"They'd swing you for murder, Innis," he mumbled.

"The river'd roll you along under the ice. If they found your bones in the spring, they'd be ground damn' fine, old son."

The captive licked his white lips. He could not speak for a time, but watched the face of Innis with enlarged eyes.

"But," went on Innis, "I dunno that I want to waste a bullet on you."

"I'm an old man, Innis," sighed the other. "And . . . I got a wife and three kids, Innis . . . and. . . ."

"A lot of good you are to them."

"I've had bad luck all my life, but I. . . ."

"Stranger," Innis stated, "if you tell me the whole truth, I dunno but what I might let you go. But it'll have to be the whole of the truth."

Radiance fell upon the face of the thief. He grew larger in that instant. "Miles Ogden done it!" he gasped out in his haste. "Ogden come to me and says . . . 'D'you want to get a supply of chuck and some ammunition for nothin'?'

" 'I ain't no thief,' I said to him."

"Hold on," broke in Innis. "Is that the truth?"

"Leastwise, that was what I thought. And when he said that it was robbin' you that he meant by it, I told him right straight that I wasn't so dog-gone ready to die as all that and. . . ."

"He give you some money, eh?"

"Fifty dollars. Money ain't nothin' to him. He's rollin' in it!"

"Then you come up and kept a watch on my camp."

"Yes, Mister Innis."

"You seen how long it took me to go the round of

the traps. When I started off this mornin', you figured that your time was come to get the stuff."

"You made a dog-gone fast trip," the thief said.

"I walked only half the trap line. Now, partner, tell me what else Ogden had planned ag'in' me."

The other looked wildly about him. "I dunno," he said faintly. "I'd like to tell you if I knowed. He didn't tell me no more."

Innis nodded. After all, it was strange that Ogden should have chosen such a rat of a man to do such important work.

"Where's Ogden's camp?" he asked sharply at last.

The other winced. "Mister Innis, if you was to miss up with him, he'd kill me sure."

"I ain't goin' to miss," Innis assured him bitterly. "I'm goin' to have it out with Ogden, damn his heart! One of the two of us ain't goin' to see the night come down . . . not on this here day."

The other shuddered. And yet there was a sort of savage pleasure in his eyes. Plainly he had small confidence that any human being could destroy the giant who had employed him and plainly he would be glad to see Jack Innis go down.

"It's around the mountain, about five miles north. You keep right on from here. You aim at them two peaks that are pretty near in line. You see 'em off there?"

"I see. The flat-headed mountain right behind the first?"

"That's it. Keep in a straight line for them. Then you ain't got a chance to miss his camp. He's got a tent stowed between two of the biggest pines right on the edge of the woods. There is no way that you can miss it."

"Now," said Innis, "where d'you aim to be goin'?

To cut in ahead of me and warn that skunk that I'm comin' for his hide?"

"Mister Innis, I'm goin' to drive straight for Kaska and stay there just long enough to say good bye to my friends, and then blaze away for some place pretty far east. When two gents like you and Ogden start trouble, there ain't no place for common folks in between you."

With that, he skulked away, and Innis, with a grin, watched him melt into the forest with no doubt that he would live up to the very letter of his promise.

X

There was only one course now left open with honor to Jack Innis, and that was to go headlong at his rival and destroy him or be himself destroyed. However, although he had entirely made up his mind that this was what must be accomplished and accomplished before the end of that day, there was no real hurry when it came to the actual work of facing and fighting big Miles Ogden.

It was now the most serious matter that had ever come into the life of Innis. He had fought before with many a man, but never with one he had so entirely tried in the first place as he had tried Miles Ogden. He knew that the man was without fear, that he would fight to the last ditch, and that until life was extinct in his body, he would be dangerous. He knew that in their first battle he had been saved from destruction merely by the chance interposition of that rock, which he was inclined to look upon as a stroke of Providence. Having been saved from destruction once, could he expect that heaven would still be kind to him a second time?

Moreover, this second battle would not be with the hands. Guns would decide it, and he had seen guns in the hands of big Miles Ogden. Sometimes he told himself that it was impossible that so huge and so bulky a man should be able to move so fast. But when he remembered how a revolver played lightning quick in the long, bony fingers of Ogden, and when he remembered, moreover, how straight the bullets flew when he touched the trigger, Innis could not help but sigh. Of all the battles of his life, this was to be the most perilous.

It should not be considered that he felt himself a whit inferior to big Miles Ogden when it came to the use of knife or of gun. Far from it. He was certain that he could hold up his end of the matter. If he were to die, he was doubly certain that Miles Ogden must die, also. But when he thought of Ogden, his size, his courage, his adroitness, he could not but admit that only a miracle could keep them both from perishing.

In a word, if there had been any way in which he could have avoided the battle, he would have welcomed the escape. But there was no way. His honor having been offended, it was his necessary duty to stand before Miles Ogden and tell him that he was a cur. It was his duty to draw his gun after that statement and do his best to murder the man. Otherwise, the story would leak out through the wretched vagabond who had been hired by Ogden to spike the guns of his bitterest rival. Such was the reasoning of Jack Innis as he sat before his lean-to and pondered the matter back and forth, his square chin resting upon his doubled right fist as upon a ledge of rock. But, having come to his conclusion, he began to look to his preparations for the journey.

Nothing was too minute for his eye. Nothing was too small a part of his outfit to receive less than his most careful attention. He considered, in the first place, that he had had a wretched and small breakfast. Now he cooked himself a hearty meal, ate it, and, lying down, banished all care from his mind by a great effort of the will. He wakened automatically at the end of an hour.

The afternoon was now well begun, but there was still plenty of time before the darkness should come. Moreover, the sky was still washed clean of clouds and the sun shone as brilliantly as in the morning, and so warmly that the ice in the trees was sending down a steady shower of rain.

His body was now well fed and rested. He next regarded his clothes. It would not do to risk having his arms bound around the armpits by the restraining stiffness of his heavy canvas coat. He accordingly threw that aside and put on, instead, a thick sweater that, as long as there was neither a fall of rain to wet him nor a stiff-blowing wind to drive the cold through his flesh, would keep him both warm and dry enough for the time being. And it would give him, above all, a perfect freedom in the use of every muscle in his powerful torso. If they came to a struggle hand to hand, that activity would tell. It would tell even more terribly if they were to fight in such a way that speed of hand and arm were to be decisive.

After this he considered his guns. He did not believe that the rifle would play the decisive part in the battle. They were almost certain to come to a speaking distance before they fought. He would have to explain his hostility, he presumed, and justify it by his accusation, before he attacked Ogden. And at short range certainly the rifle was helpless against the agility of a revolver.

Yet since there was a remote chance that the fight might take place at a distance, or even that big Ogden might avoid him and put off the issue, he was not able to leave that heavy weapon behind him. He went over his Winchester with the most painstaking care. He had the knotted brow of a scientist as he scanned the working parts. No soldier making ready for inspection, no soldier with black marks against his record, ever polished the inside of a gun barrel with more assiduity than did big Jack Innis as he made ready for his duel.

But after attention to his body, his clothes, and his rifle, after he had seen to the very edge of his hunting knife, there was the final and most important ceremony of all. He drew out a pair of revolvers. He held them in either hand and regarded them tenderly. They were not of the latest model. They were not of the lightest and the most convenient make. They were not dainty trifles; neither were they brilliantly polished jewels of the gunsmith's art. The wood of the handles was worn. Those finger groves had not been faintly impressed by the cunning precaution of the gun maker. They had been rubbed into existence by the instant friction of strong hands gripping that gun butt ever in the same place.

They were identical weapons, as anyone would have made sure, except that those faint finger groves were different. And the reason was that one was a right-hand gun and the other a left-hand gun. To the gunfighter there were marks upon each that were perceptible to the eye. To the gunfighter the half ounce less weight in the left-hand gun was perceptible to the touch, just as the slightly greater stiffness of the right-hand trigger was perceptible.

No one else in the world could have determined those finest of fine distinctions, but to Jack Innis they were all important. He had lived with those weapons all his life. They were, it might be said, his dear brothers, his tried and true companions who had stood by him through the thick and thin of a thousand perilous actions. When he was eight years old, he had been able to make those guns do conjurer's tricks for him. With them he had labored and practiced through the long years that followed. With those old Colts he had learned to shoot like lightning and straight as a string, so that in all his life he had met only one mate for him in speed and in accuracy, and that mate was big Miles Ogden with his long, bony hands. If indeed Ogden were a mate. That day, however, would furnish the proof. With the conscientious patience of an artist, he had labored two or three hours every day with his guns. When he rode along in the cow range, the guns were constantly in his fingers—those grooves were wearing deeper, the wood of the handles were growing blacker with dirt and perspiration and polishing smooth with friction. When he was alone, standing watch on the deck of the ship at sea, a revolver was the toy with which his fingers played as he walked back and forth.

He looked down upon the pair now with a strange happiness, as of a man beholding two dear friends who will not fail him in the time of need. They plied over his fingers as lightly as ever. They slipped from the holsters like the lash of a whip that is snapped. He dropped both guns into his pockets, and then kicked a tin can into the air. The tomato can rose to the height of a shallow arc. Before it fell, two guns spoke, and it was knocked spinning to a distance with a pair of holes punched through its sides.

All was well and all was ready. So, in the brightness of the afternoon he began his march toward the enemy. He covered the ground rapidly with his long stride, but still he was not going fast enough to suit his convenience. Now that he was started, his desire for battle gained impetus at every moment that passed. He began to hurry. Under the sweater perspiration rose. Still it was not fast enough, this pace that he was maintaining. He wanted to find the enemy at once before him and destroy the man while the hot mood was upon him.

So it was that he attempted a short cut down a glassy surface of ice before he was halfway through his journey. He had hardly started before he saw that he had made a rash attempt. A flow of water from the melting surface ice had been frozen solid again by a rising wind beneath the trees, and the result was that the whole face of the hill was as slick as grease. His feet went out from under him. At that, he fell flat and whirled upon his face, striking his hands and his body against the surface of the hill in order to check his impetus, but the very act of the fall had given a fresh violence to his speed and now he shot along as though on a toboggan. Twice he hurtled past sharp-toothed rocks that seemed to reach for him as he went past. And as he automatically shunted himself away from the second of these, a rock on the opposite side caught him. He felt the keen point of the stone tear his flesh like a dull knife ripping through rotten cloth. Then, his downward flight checked in this fashion, he was jerked into a whirling motion. His head struck a stone, and he fell into a soft thickness of dark.

XI

The shock with which he struck the bottom of the hill and the agony of his hurt leg wakened him from the brief mercy of that trance. He found himself in the heart of a small hollow. It was hardly fifty paces to the top of the hill down which he had just slid with such disastrous consequences. Over his head arose the mighty forms of the pine trees, shaking their heads against the sky. A little to one side a brook, too rapid of current to be frozen to death even in this bitter cold, went talking down the valley that was beginning here. And everything was shimmering and living with the brilliance of the sunshine that streamed through the ice crystals.

But the beauty of the place was a dead thing to poor Jack Innis. If he could live to appreciate the beauty of any other day he told himself that he would be a lucky fellow, for when he rose and strove to stand, the left leg, which had been injured, gave way beneath him like the worm-eaten cane of old man. He fell down upon his side again, and the agony of that second fall set him groaning.

When his nerves had ceased to some extent from leaping with that exquisite torture, he propped himself in a sitting position with one hand and with the other examined the extent of the wound. It was a thing to shock even such a hardy fellow as himself who had endured a hundred hurts before and seen a hundred injuries to others. But when there is no audience, even groaning is a poor language. He set his teeth and fought back the sickness that passed in waves across his brain. Then he started the work of bandaging.

It required an hour of unspeakable suffering before the work was done, but when it was at last completed his torment was hardly lessened. To stop the flow of the blood he had been forced to draw the bandages tight, and now the raw edges of the wound were crushed against one another, making a veritable hell of agony. A wave of hot thirst poured through him. But at least there was the brook to appease that appetite. As he crawled to it and buried his mouth in the tugging current, he thought vaguely of battlefields where thousands pour out their blood and feel that same hellish torment of thirst, but with nothing to comfort them better than a few warm drops in the bottom of the canteen or perhaps a wind laden thickly with dust raised by the trudging feet of some passing column. Compared with these, he was well off indeed.

Having refreshed himself with the water, his whole spirit rose somewhat. When he assayed the upslope, he found that he could not manage it, trailing his helpless leg behind him. The torture was simply too great for endurance. Neither could he lower himself along the course of the brook, for it was full of little precipices. There was nothing to do but remain where he was, light a fire to keep from freezing to death, and strive to attract attention by discharging his weapons from time to time.

The fire was the first matter. It was a bitter struggle before he was able to discover a bit of dry tinder. The melting snow or the rain had soaked all the fallen leaves, of course. But he managed with his great hunting knife to carve his way into the heart of a fallen tree. There was both dry rot and dry wood for the burning. And he welcomed it with a sigh of relief.

The tragedy was not revealed to him until he took out his matches, which he kept wrapped in a piece of oiled silk in such weather as this—a most necessary precaution and far better than any match safe for security from water. But he found that the silk had unrolled, and, as he sat in the snow bandaging his leg, the heat of his body had melted the snow that in turn had soaked through his coat pocket and drenched the matches. Their heads were a pulpy mass of red.

At this, he cast a despairing glance upward to the sun. It was sloped far, far toward the west. It was not his loss of blood or his position in the snow alone that had chilled him until he was trembling and numb-lipped with the cold; it was simply that there was less heat from the sun every moment he remained motionless, and there was, moreover, a rising wind that promised to become a big gale before long.

In such a position he had only one recourse, and that was to use the fallen, rotten trunk of the tree as a house. He had already made a breach in its side. This he now widened until there was room for him to drag his wretched body inside. And there he lay, wet, shuddering, but at least saved from the wind and from any fresh fall of water or snow, with the powdered, rotten wood that was placed around him not more than damp at the worst. It might even be, if he kept his hands and arms in motion from time to time and rubbed himself vigorously, that he would be able to last out the night until the sun of the next day brought him warmth again.

He told himself this resolutely, and shut from his mind the truer conviction that he had not a hope. Nothing that was not dressed in warm fur could hope to sleep in such a place through the bitterness of the winter night and live to see the light of the dawn again. How many a dawn he had seen, and yet never before had he looked upon them, particularly, as things of beauty. They were simply the moments when days of labor began. But now, to be free, to be able to labor, was enough and more than enough.

He thought of that fatal, pretty face of Stella Cornish that had been the mainspring of all of these disasters. She was not worth it, said the stubborn voice of instinct. She is worth a thousand times more, said the still stronger voice of stubborn self-will. It was better, after all, to die of cold than to die of folly. He would not admit the voice of instinct for an instant.

Jack Innis began to discharge the rifle. At first, at intervals of five minutes, he fired the weapon into the air. Then, feeling the intervals might be too long, he began to count to 100 between shots. In a short time he pulled his trigger upon an empty magazine. He had loaded his rifle and his revolvers. But he had not brought anything in his cartridge belt. Twenty-seven shots were enough to kill more than one man, but were they enough in this wilderness of mountains to attract a rescuer?

He started with his revolvers. How feeble, short,

and hoarse were those explosions compared with the sounds from the rifle. Besides, even if some hunter through the hills were to hear the explosions, would he know that it was a call for help? All mariners understand distress signals and answer them as they hope on a day of danger to be answered in turn. But what do landsmen know of such things? He who wandered within hearing of the guns might merely think that some hunter was practicing at a mark.

Innis groaned at the thought, but he kept on until there remained in his right-hand revolver only one shell. There he stopped, for when the end drew near and when the deadly drowsiness began to steal from his body into brain, when he began to yearn to draw one deep breath and then fall to sleep, he determined that he would end himself with a bullet.

With that determination he rested. As he rested he listened with all his heart. But there was no answering gun from the hills surrounding the hollow. There was no crackle of brush underfoot as some mountaineer hastened down to him. There was no distant hallooing.

The thick silence of the evening lay everywhere, that listening time of the day when the night has not yet come but is very near and all the world seems waiting for its approach. So the evening grew rosy with the setting sun, and so it changed to rich blues and purples, and Jack Innis, huddled in the log, with the icy cold stealing through his limbs and the agony of his wound turning into a half-delirious fever, told himself that he would wait until the complete night before he put an end to his misery. Certainly, in the condition in which he then was, he could not expect to live out half the night.

He fell into a delirious sleep. A monster flitted into the dream to haunt him, a shadow creature of giant size, with bright eyes and a red tongue lolling. It stood watching him with mingled cunning and malice, its head cocked upon one side. And the horror of it wakened Jack Innis.

His wide-opened eyes became conscious of the thick dusk that had poured through the woods. The monster of his vision had melted away, but in the middle of the hollow, one foot raised and its head cocked upon the side, was a shadowy little creature clad in a bushing fur and with a thick tail behind.

A fox, but a fox with a gray-black coat—surely there had never been anything like this before in the world. Then understanding rushed upon his mind. It was all true. This was the silver fox of which Si Goodrich had spoken, and now in his moment of destruction the beast had come to mock him and gloat over him. Vague, hideous Indian legends floated through his memory of animals that carry the souls of men and wizards transformed into four-footed things.

Automatically he raised the revolver in his stiff hand. The fox spat like a cat and wheeled away as he fired. Then it tumbled in the snow and rolled over and over.

It was dead, but there was no exultation in the heart of Jack Innis. He had wasted the bullet that he had reserved for himself. And of what use to him was the life that he had just snuffed out? Of what use to him was that rich pelt? A loafer wolf would probably tear it to bits before the body was cold and leave the snow sprinkled with tufts of long black fur, silvered with white threads.

He closed his eyes as the numb, delicious sense of

drowsiness rolled back upon him. A voice spoke in his dream. He opened his eyes and forced back his mind to consciousness in time to hear:

"Sounded from this way, I think."

A high-pitched, shrill, unpleasant voice. He tried to place it. Then, realizing that a human voice meant a rescue, perhaps, if rescue were possible, he shouted aloud.

There was a crushing of heavy feet through underbrush.

"Go easy! Go easy!" said the shrill voice. "It might be him decoying you. . . ."

A heavy bass made answer, a gloomily familiar voice: "That's the voice of a man in pain."

And into the clearing stepped the form of mighty Ogden.

"Look, by heaven!" cried Ogden. "The silver fox . . . still warm. That's what that shot was fired at. But why the devil doesn't the lucky hunter come out to claim his kill?"

To his side stole the form of a middle-aged man with a fur-lined collar of a canvas coat turned up high around his face—his face that was blackened with beard.

"Yonder," he breathed, "where the hole is tore in that rotten tree."

And Miles Ogden strode straight up to his enemy. He said with a sneer: "Are you too scared to fight, Jack?"

Innis found a voice oddly unlike his own. "I wasted my last bullet killing a fox for you to skin. Use a bullet on me, now, Ogden, and I'll be thankin' you. I'm ready for it."

"I ain't lookin' . . . I ain't hearin'," snarled out a voice of beastly venom and eagerness, as the thief turned his back and crouched down beside the silver fox.

But Miles Ogden leaned, and in his huge arms lifted the body of his enemy. "Jack," he said, "you're hurt."

"Hurryin'," Innis explained frankly and savagely, "to get at you, damn your heart!"

He saw the big head nodding above him in the dusk. "It was a yellow trick that I played you," said Miles Ogden. "It was the girl, Jack. I felt, somehow, that it was fate for me to lose her. So, I used dirty tactics to beat you. But now, old-timer, I see the straight of things. And the straight of things is that you mean a lot more to me than she could ever mean. You there . . . Steve! Start up a fire. Steady, Jack, we'll have you thawed out in a jiffy."

"Ogden," said the wounded man, "what might you be meaning by all this?"

"Why, Jack, I mean to try to make up for what I've done. You've killed the fox. I'll see that you get the pelt to Oakwood. I'll see that you get the full credit for it."

XII

How many weeks had passed since Miles Ogden and Jack Innis left Oakwood could be computed by the fact that the chill of the autumn had hardly deepened to winter when they departed and it was the thick of the cold season when two big men came back to town. One of them walked with a heavy limp in his left leg. Upon that side went Miles Ogden, his expression as dour as ever, his head carried as high, his eye as wickedly bright.

They said nothing until, in passing up the street to the heart of the town, they reached the house of the sheriff. There they paused.

"Are you goin' in with me, Miles?" Innis asked almost timidly.

"The devil, man," said Ogden. "Do you think that I'm afraid to face the music when I've lost the game? I hope, Jack, old-timer, that you'll see me pay up with a smile."

The great hand of Innis closed hard over the arm of his friend. So they turned in together through the gate.

"But why," Ogden asked as they went up the path together, "are all the folks out watching us and pointing and talking so hard?"

"Because they expected to see only one of us come back living," said Innis.

"Aye"—the larger man nodded—"they're like coyotes, aren't they?"

Innis paused halfway up the path.

"What's the matter?" asked his friend.

"I'm scared," said Innis frankly.

"To meet Stella?"

"That's it. Suppose she thinks that the wrong man won?"

"Why, Jack, there isn't a chance of that. Look at the face I wear. But you have a way with you that makes men and women both love you, old-timer."

So heartened, Innis went on, until they came to the verandah and went up to the front door. It was opened in answer to their knock by the sheriff himself. He cried out a hearty welcome at once.

"Well, lads," he said, "did you get tired of the wild-goose chase?"

"Did you think it was that?" asked Ogden, willing to draw out the man of the law.

"I didn't think. I knowed it, boys. Come in and sit down."

He ushered them to the best chairs in Mrs. Cornish's parlor. They put their muddy feet shamelessly on her clean rug.

"Think of you two young fools settin' out to find a silver fox on the side of old Seminole. Why, sons, most like there never was one, but old Si Goodrich saw a shadow on a coyote after he'd had a few shots of red-eye. He likes a bottle, old Si does. I recollect when I first met him. He was. . . ."

He lost interest in what he had been about to say. Jack Innis had been slowly unrolling a canvas-wrapped parcel, and, as he unwrapped it, a bit of dark fur began to appear, and then more and more. Until, finally, there was revealed on the lap of the sailor-cowpuncher a perfect pelt of a silver fox. The sheriff stood up with a gasp, and then he sat down again all as suddenly.

"Well," he said, "there ain't anything past a gent under thirty! Innis, did you get that all by yourself?"

Innis nodded, his half-frightened, half-happy eyes turning eagerly toward the door. "Maybe Stella is out?" he asked anxiously, blushing over her name.

"Maybe she is," the sheriff said gloomily.

"Maybe she'll be back home soon," said Innis.

"Maybe she will. Most like she'll be home too damn' soon!"

Something in this speech made Jack Innis rise

slowly from his chair. "I dunno what you're drivin' at, Sheriff," he said.

"I'm drivin'," said the sheriff, "at something that'll make you mighty swearin' mad at first. But afterward you'll thank your lucky stars that things turned out the way they did. Jack, Stella ain't here."

"Not here? Not home? Not . . . not in Oakwood?" gasped out Innis. "Maybe," he added faintly, "she's took a vacation, goin' East?"

"She thinks she's on a vacation," said the sheriff with a sort of malicious pleasure as he shrugged his shoulders. "Matter of fact, she's just gone to work for the first time in her life. Boys, she's married!"

It dropped Innis into his chair again. Miles Ogden gaped like one stunned.

"Who?" breathed Innis at last.

"Somebody that you can't kill. He's too damn' far beneath you, Jack. She up and run away with a skunk and married him right after you started out for old Seminole. It was just her way of gettin' rid of the two of you. The gent she married, Innis, is Leicester Dennis!"

After a great shock, a change of scenery is often recommended. No doctor took the case of Innis and Ogden in hand, but they prescribed for themselves, and, a month later, sitting two stalwart mustangs on the top of a low, sandy hill, they looked over a stretch of desert marked with Spanish dagger and the straying forms of a few lean cattle; to the south wound a dirty yellow streak across the landscape—the Río Grande.

Innis began to whistle, and his companion looked almost reproachfully at him.

"You seem a little gay, Jack?" he asked.

"I been thinkin'," Innis commented, "that maybe the sheriff knew her all along better'n we did. He had a longer chance, Miles."

Red Rock's Secret

Frederick Faust's saga of the hero Speedy began with "Tramp Magic", a six-part serial in *Western Story Magazine*, which appeared in the issues dated November 21, 1931 through December 26, 1932. As most of Faust's continuing characters, Speedy is a loner, little more than a youngster, able to outwit and outmaneuver even the deadliest of men without the use of a gun. He appeared in a total of nine stories. The serial has been reprinted by Leisure Books under the title *Speedy*. The first short story, "Speedy—Deputy", can be found in *Jokers Extra Wild*, followed by "Seven-Day Lawman" in *Flaming Fortune*, "Speedy's Mare" in *Peter Blue*, and "The Crystal Game" in *The Fugitive*. "Red Rock's Secret" was first published in the April 16, 1932 issue of *Western Story Magazine*.

I

Beyond the town lay a railway bridge, and under the bridge extended a flat-bottomed ravine filled with trees and brush. A small stream of water went winding through the pebbles and bare stones of the valley. It was an ideal spot for a tramp jungle, and, as soon as Jessica Fenton Wilson glanced at the cañon, she knew that she would have to take a look into it. For a month she had been at work over much country, and for a month her study had been among the tramps. They alone could give her, she felt, the information that she wanted so desperately.

So she jogged her mustang out from the town and pushed the nose of the horse over the edge of the ravine. It flinched, and then, with a snort of disgust, lowered its nose to smell at the sharp descent that its rider was asking it to make. She was looking, also, and deciding that, although somewhat risky, the trick might be turned safely enough. She was used to taking chances. So was the mustang, for that matter, since without further urging it gave a shake of its head and began to work down the slope.

Presently it was taking no more steps but, sitting down, with the front legs stiffly braced, the mustang was skidding down over the sand and loose gravel of the surface, while dust and stones swept behind in their wake or, loosening from the bank, gathered headway and leaped after them.

Halfway to the bottom of the slope, the mustang began to slew around to one side, and that was dangerous, of course. To fall sidewise, while traveling at that speed, would probably be death for horse and rider, so Jessica Wilson hurled her 130 pounds toward the other side of the horse, and had the secure satisfaction of feeling the sturdy little mustang straighten out under her.

They struck the bottom, the mustang staggering at the impact of the level ground, then it scampered hastily out of the way of the big stones that were galloping down the side of the slope after them, at full speed.

At a safe distance, Jessica Wilson turned and, dropping one hand behind her saddle, looked back and up to the towering slide. She could see now that she had gone at the thing too carelessly; it was only a wonder that she had not had a fall and a broken neck, perhaps. But, as it so happened, she was safe on the back of her mustang still, half glad of her escape, half gloomily wishing that it might have been her last ride on this earth—such was the melancholy that lay like a cold stone beside her heart.

Then she turned down the bottom of the ravine, jogging the pony toward the long, ugly, iron back of the railroad bridge that stretched above the tops of the trees. It made a pleasant and a wild place, this valley, with the irregular growth of tree and brush coming down on either hand under the solid wall of the cliffs and, sometimes, fine little meadows between the trees and the edges of the stone rubble, where the creek wandered.

In one of these meadows or, better still, laid back among the trees, she would probably find the jungle, if it existed at all in this ravine. After her month's intensive study of tramps, she made sure that they never would overlook such a good situation, with water, wood, and shelter provided, and with an open town waiting to be plundered hardly a mile away. Everything was exactly right, and the longer she considered the site, the more certain she was that she would find a jungle, and an occupied one at that.

So she was not in the least surprised when, through a narrow gap among the trees, she saw half a dozen forms lounging about an open fire that burned with very little smoke under a great laundry boiler. Over this boiler stood a ragged fellow with a stick in one hand, probing at the contents of the boiler with professional attention, and peering from under the shade of his hand into the steam that rolled up toward his face. There was such an air of authority about him that she decided he might be the very man in the world who could answer the question that lay heavily on her mind. So she pushed the mustang straight toward the gap among the trees.

It made her grow cold and tremble a bit in the saddle as she sent the horse forward. Tramps have an ugly reputation, generally deserved. Men who were real Westerners, she knew, would never harm her, but tramps. They lose all sectional virtues and take on all sectional vices. They may be simply harmless wanderers; they are probably more likely to be professional and seasoned criminals.

The weather-browned or reddened faces, all unshaven, that turned toward the girl and her horse as she came through the trees, made her feel that she was playing the fool. There were not six of them, but eight, and the more bad men in a crowd, the worse they are.

She had seen enough tramps, by this time, to recognize some of the types. Three of these were common specimens of the bundle-stiff, the men who put a stick over the shoulder, tie a bundle at the end of it, and so forge through the world looking for jobs that are easier, pay that is higher, and bunks that are softer. These fellows had their opened bundles beside them. For the bundle-stiff is a great housekeeper, and he is always at work with his sewing kit, darning, patching, mending, or he'll be washing at the edge of the creek—one of them was actually so employed at this moment—or in some way he'll occupy his hands, just as the old-fashioned housewife used to keep her fingers busy with her needle every instant that she was sitting down.

There was also a youngster of no more than seventeen or eighteen, dressed in clothes that had once been smart. He still possessed a certain air of grace in spite of a rent here and a stain there. He was a handsome youth, with a long, heavy forelock that hung down across his forehead. He threw back this lock with a graceful flourish of his head and looked out at Jessica Wilson with bold, bright eyes. Near him was a tall skeleton of a man, too old for this life on the road and too evil of face for any other sort of life. He sat embracing his knees, his cruel face thrust forward, his gray hair cropped close to an ugly skull. These, with the burly villain who was standing over the boiler, another rascal lying face down, and a third scrubbing clothes at the edge of the creek, made up the party. The sight of the man lying face down made her heart jump. For he might be the object of her quest.

With a hungry eye she measured the figure, and then shook her head a little. It could not be he.

She waved her hand in greeting. "Hello!" she said. "I thought I smelled mulligan stew as I came down the ravine. I had to follow my nose."

They muttered or waved greetings to her.

"Give her a hand-out, Smudge," said one of the bundle-stiffs to the cook.

"Would I be needing your advice on how to be polite?" asked the swarthy cook, giving the other tramp a look of scorn. Then he turned to the girl. "It's about ready to eat," he said. "We're only waiting for another couple of bunkies to come in before we start. Will you have a bite?"

"I will . . . and thanks," she said. Then she slid from the mustang, which dropped its head to crop the grass.

The cook, in the meantime, picked up a butcher knife and with it laid open a small loaf, one of a pyramid that reposed on the face of a newspaper nearby. Then he dipped a ladle through the cloud of steam and stirred the contents of the boiler. "What'll you have, ma'am?" he asked, putting on an air of attentive service. "We aim to please!"

"And how can you tell what's in the boiler without looking?" she asked curiously.

"I've got a sense of touch," said the cook solemnly. "Matter of fact, it developed so dog-gone much that some of my touches have got me into trouble. But I can feel the lip of this here ladle bump the side of a little new potato that's adrift down there, and now some beans are floating into it, and there's the drumstick of a chicken, or I'm mistaken."

"I'll try the drumstick, then," said the girl.

The ladle came instantly out of the pot, and the bread was covered with a portion of the stew, all reddened with the juice of canned tomatoes.

"There you are," said the cook. "And I'm calling you to mind that we're better than our promises. It's chicken breast, not a drumstick. There's more chicken down there, hiding, and some good, tender young veal, too. I'll have some out for you in another jiffy."

"Thanks," said the girl. "This looks good. It's neither breakfast nor lunch time, but the smell of this makes me hungry."

"You take on the road," the tramp said, grinning at her, "and every time the mulligan is ready, it's twelve o'clock noon. Good, ain't it?" He watched with sympathetic eyes of enjoyment as she tasted a corner of that great sandwich.

"Delicious," she affirmed. "I'd like to know the recipe."

"Why," said the cook, "that'd be hard to give you. It depends on the surroundin's, how I compose my mulligan. You take a town like that"—here he hooked his thumb in the direction of the village hidden behind the wall of the ravine—"and my mulligan is sure to be flavored with chicken, though I've seen other places where there ain't so much as a rooster's crow in the stew. Take it by and large, though, the more things you put in a mulligan, the better it is. And if you want to make it best of all, cook up the stew, then wait an hour for some of the boys to show up. That puts the sauce into it, I can tell you."

He grinned again, and she smiled back at him. She thought that she had never tasted anything half so good, and she was soon through with it, commenting: "This is a good place, isn't it?"

"Water and wood and the railroad handy. Sure it's a good place. It couldn't be much better."

"I've seen some jungles before," she said, "but none better."

"What would you be knowing about jungles?" asked the cook curiously.

"Why," she said, "I know the king of the tramp royals."

"Do you?" he asked, doubting.

"Yes, the king of 'em all," she insisted.

"And who might that be, that travels so light and so fast that he calls himself the king of the lot?" asked the cook.

"His name isn't likely to matter," said the girl. "He changes his name almost as often as he changes his coat. But, I'll show you his face, if you like."

"Carry his picture?" asked the cook, grinning again, but very differently.

"Yes, in my head," she said. "It's like this."

A smooth board from a cracker box lay on the ground near the fire, and, picking up a stick with a charred end, she began to draw, rapidly with fine, sweeping lines, a young man's face.

"You can draw, all right," said the cook. "But it looks to me like it's too pretty to be true. Didn't you get that out of a book?"

The other tramps had gathered around and stared in admiration at the skill with which she worked. It was, in fact, a face almost too beautiful to be manly, but with her final touches there appeared more strength about the chin and mouth. It was a sketch showing the shoulders of the man, as well, and his head was turned in an alert way with an expression of impatient happiness in the face.

"He's handsome enough," commented the girl as she stepped back and looked down at her work of art. "But he's not too handsome to be true."

"All right," said the youngster of the lot. "I kind of remember having had a look at that mug, somewhere. But I don't remember where."

"Anybody else recognize him?" the girl asked, keeping the hope and anxiety out of her voice as well as she could.

Nobody, however, seemed able to identify the face she had drawn, and her heart, which had risen high the moment before, sank again like a stone. She looked grimly and sadly about her. It would not do to pay even these men for the meal. "Thanks a lot for the mulligan," she said. "I never tasted anything better. Good bye, everybody."

They gave her a friendly chorus of farewell. The cook would have helped her into the saddle, but she swung up quickly before he reached her and rode off with another wave of her hand to them.

They were pleasant fellows enough, she was thinking, as she faced forward again. But not one of them so much as knew the face of the man she hunted, and despair came over her. It seemed that she would never come to the end of her trail.

A harsh voice hailed her from the rear. When she turned her head, she saw that it was the old man with the gray, cropped head, who was striding after her. She pulled up the mustang and awaited him, not altogether easy, there was so much evil in his face.

"That cinch is loose, ain't it?" he asked as be came up.

She dismounted and slid a finger under the girth. It was taut enough, even for mountain riding. The big fellow, however, began to fumble at the straps. As he worked, he said: "I wouldn't want 'em to think that I came here to talk to you about nothing special. Don't make no sign."

"I won't," she said.

"Every man there, I reckon, or most of 'em," said the man, "must've recognized that face you drawed. They wouldn't talk, but I reckon that it's all right for me to ask you what you want of Speedy."

II

She had turned her back toward the campfire and she was glad of it now, if it were important for her to conceal her expression from the rest of the tramps, for a flood of happiness and hope had swept over her as she heard the big man use this name.

"You know him?" she asked.

"The point is, do you know him, and how much?" asked the tramp.

She considered one instant, then, deciding that absolute frankness was her only means of drawing out the possible information that he could give her, she said: "I owe him my father's life. He made the man that I married."

The veteran straightened a little, thrusting out his jaw as though in anger, but still giving his attention to the purposeless untying of the straps. Then he said: "Made your husband, d'you say?"

"I say that, and I mean that," said the girl. "But it would take an hour to explain just what I mean by it, or all that Speedy did."

"I know," said the other. "The fact is, Speedy is likely to do a thing in one second that'll take you an hour to untie and get all straight again. He was a good friend to you, eh?"

"The best friend in the world."

"How long did you know him?"

"Three days."

"And then?"

"Then he disappeared without leaving any hint of an address with us."

"I reckon you know Speedy, all right," said the tall man. "That's the way that he acts. He camps where the hunting's good. When he stops seein' the big game, he barges along, and, most likely, he starts in the middle of the night. Besides, it ain't safe for him to remain in any one spot too long."

"Because he has so many enemies?" she asked.

"I reckon so. There's a hundred gents that would die for Speedy, but there's a thousand that would like to cut his throat. And someday it'll be cut, too!" He shook his head, half regretful, half savage. She waited and he blurted out: "You really want to find him, do you?"

"I want to find him. I have to find him."

"Humph," said the man, grunting, still very uncertain, it appeared, of what was the best thing to do in this case. Then he muttered: "Well, that's a pretty good gag, getting into a jungle and drawing Speedy's face. That shows you got nerve and brains, too. You been hunting Speedy long?"

"For a whole month. He never leaves an address behind him, you know." She smiled sadly, and sighed as she thought of the endless riding and the useless racking of her brain.

"He never leaves no address," agreed the tramp. "And yet I'll tell you what . . . I've seen him do a job and sign it, and the signature was wrote in red."

She exclaimed at that.

"It's true," her informant said, "but, all the same, I'd like to know where the right of this is . . . me to tell you where Speedy is, or not to."

"What harm could telling do?" she asked.

"I dunno," said the tramp. "It ain't for me to butt into Speedy's business, is all that I can say. It's for me and everybody else to keep hands off, so far as Speedy goes. But maybe I'll take the chance, and, if you find him, don't you be saying who sent you."

"I won't. Honest?" said the girl.

"Here's my hand on it."

"I can't shake your hand. They're watching yonder, and I been here too long, already."

"Why are they all afraid to mention Speedy's name?" asked the girl.

"Because," the tramp explained, "you never know whether you're gonna get a friend or an enemy of Speedy around the camp. I've seen guns smoke more'n once, just from bringin' up his name. But now, if you wanna know, I'll tell you. You go to San Lorenzo. Know where that is?"

"I know," she answered.

"There's a big new restaurant and pleasure place, sort of, started up down by the river. It's a greaser by name of Alonzo Martínez that runs it. In that restaurant, the last time that I was there, there was a scar-faced little peon that went around playin' a guitar that was slung around his neck, and shufflin' his feet. That little greaser, his name is Juan. That's the boy that can tell you where to find Speedy."

"San Lorenzo, Alonzo Martínez, Juan . . . I'll remember every name. And bless you for telling me," said the girl, the words coming straight from her heart.

"You find Juan, and he'll be able to find Speedy for you, all right, if he wants to. Whether he wants to or not, I can't say. He's a funny greaser, is what he is."

"Thanks," Jessica said. "I'll remember."

"Another thing . . . if you see Juan, it wouldn't do to mention Speedy's name so's any other person down there could hear it, or read it on your lips."

"I'll remember that, also," said the girl. "Is there any chance of this Juan having left San Lorenzo?"

"Every chance in the world," said the tramp. "Fact is you only got one chance in three of finding him. But that's the best that I can do."

He stood back from the horse, and she jumped eagerly into the saddle. Then, cautiously, she balled a $10 bill in the palm of her hand.

He saw the movement and shook his head sternly. "What kind of a thing d'you think that I am?" he asked her. "What kind of a fool to go and take money for talking about Speedy? No, you're welcome to what I've told you. If he really wants to find out who told you, you might as well knuckle down and tell him. He'd find out, anyway. You can say that Alkali Pete gave you the information."

"If you won't let me pay you, I can only thank you," Jessica said. "But it's more than gold that you're giving me when you tell me how to find him. Good bye, Alkali Pete."

"So long, ma'am," said the other.

He stepped back to give her free way, and she, with a cut of the quirt, started the mustang into full gallop, scattering the stones beside the creek noisily. Straight back toward the town she traveled, urging the horse all the way, with hope and fear weighing her down or lifting her as she rode.

San Lorenzo . . . Alonzo Martínez . . . Juan. The names went around and around in her head. She looked like one maddened by fear as she rushed the horse into the village and toward the railroad station.

III

The town of San Lorenzo lay in an elbow turn of the San Lorenzo River. Its soil was once Mexican, but the San Lorenzo followed an odd vagary and cut around the place. That was how it became an American town. However, it was American in little more than name. The mayor, the sheriff, the station agent, even, all possessed brown skins. San Lorenzo, with its narrow street, deep and soft in dust, its whitewashed adobe houses that squatted close to the ground, its idlers, its carelessness, its indifference to the present and dreamy confidence in the future, was typically Mexican.

There was only one big venture, only one big business in San Lorenzo, and that was the place of Martínez. It was a hotel, an inn, a saloon, a restaurant, and a store. Above all, the people loved to sit in the cool of the evening in the garden that Martínez had made under the trees along the river. There he would put out little round, iron-topped tables at which four people could sit if they nudged plate and glass close together. There he generally had music and some sort of special entertainment. In the center of the garden there was a little dancing floor that was weather-roughened and built in waves, but which, nevertheless, was well lighted and was always filled in fair weather.

This place of Martínez was celebrated. It brought Mexicans from many miles around. Now and then, a party of American cowpunchers or miners from the hills thirty miles away would come clattering into the place to find fun or fighting. They generally got both. Your Mexican is not always a good soldier, but he is one of the most dangerous single-handed fighters in the world. When his blood is up, his fear disappears.

This was the hotel to which Jessica Wilson went, as soon as she got off the train. She had left her horse a day distant, by the twistings and the changes of railroad that brought her to San Lorenzo from Alkali Pete. She carried with her a roll not of blankets, but of luggage, and a small roll it was, too, for that brown-faced girl knew as well as any man how to travel across country with no more than salt, matches, and a rifle by way of provisions.

When she came to the hotel, the clerk smiled at

her, found his smile freezing, and finally assigned a room to her. She went up and found it was at the rear of the hotel, in the least desirable part of the building. However, it had a good big window sunk through the enormous depth of the wall, and in addition there was an immensely deep and comfortable bed, with a feather mattress on top of it.

It was just before noon, and she was starving, so she went down as soon as she had washed her face and hands, and got a little round table under one of the huge trees.

The river ran almost at her feet, bubbling and rippling, the current setting well in toward the bank at this point. Round about under the trees there was a ragged effect of lawn, thriving where the trees shadowed it, scorched where the sun struck it in the middle of the day.

She ordered beans, hot beans—the hotter the better. She had tortillas, big and moist and gray, but delicious beyond all other food to the palate that has learned to appreciate Indian corn. She had roast kid that had been turned on a spit and thoroughly browned. When she finished her meal and her coffee, she felt that she never had dined more heartily or better in her life.

All through the meal, she was looking curiously about her for that small Mexican, that peon whose face was deformed by a scar—that lad who alone in the world could tell her where Speedy was to be found. It was not until she had finished her coffee that the entertainment began. It was not a whole orchestra—for the midday meal that would have been an extravagance, considering how few were the guests—but a single singer, who thrummed a guitar and sang a song of old Mexico in a soft, pleasant voice. She could not see him, for the moment, and she dared not start up to go looking for him. The last warning of Alkali Pete had been that she was not to mention aloud the name of the man she was hunting for. She must exercise the greatest caution.

The singer came nearer. Presently he was only on the other side of a vast cypress. She heard a husky-throated Mexican growl out a demand for another song of another sort. The song followed. And very well delivered it was. If there had been more volume to the voice, undoubtedly its quality would have brought this entertainer success on the stage. He sang with verve and with fire; she could fairly see him throw back his head and pour forth his spirit in song.

The singing ended.

"Catch this," said the Mexican.

There was a light *spat*, as though a heavy coin had landed in the flat of a palm.

Then Juan came into view around the trunk of the tree. He was exactly as Pete had described him; his face might have been quite handsome, poor lad, except that it was puckered and twisted by the grip of a big scar that deformed him. Nevertheless, he was not hideous. It was one of those transformations that are rather pitiful than disgusting. There was wistfulness in the puckering lines of his forehead and eagerness in his fine, dark eyes. His skin was very dark, almost blackish-brown, and that color obscured the fineness of his features. His legs were bare and the sinewy feet were slipped into the cheap sandals in which the peon always finds his greatest comfort. The guitar, as Alkali Pete had said, was suspended about his neck by a thick leather strap.

Juan, as he saw the girl, greeted her by taking off his big, cup-shaped straw hat and making a bow that showed her the back of his head and lean, athletic shoulders.

Would she hear a song? She would. What would she have? Why, anything that his fancy selected.

Instantly he was at it. She hardly heard the music, or listened to the romantic words of the ballad, that told of the loves and despairs of two unhappy ones long ago, for she was hastily scratching words in Spanish on a bit of paper, that asked: *Do you know Speedy? Can you bring me to him? Or bring him to me? I would give you a fine reward.*

As he finished the song, she smiled and held out a 25¢ piece. Along with it she dropped into his hand the wadded ball of paper.

That was discreet enough, surely, but how dexterous was the young man in closing his fingers over that paper ball, without the slightest hesitation. He went off; he sang again.

She, in the meantime, leaned back in her chair with her eyes closed, feeling that she was about to faint. For she had found the link that would bring her to Speedy, according to the solemn words of Alkali Pete. Juan could bring her to Speedy, if only the youth pleased to do so. Would he please? She should have given him more than a quarter. He would be disgusted and he would not trust her for the reward that she promised in the note.

She grew so sick at heart, thinking of this, that she went from the garden straight up to her room, and there she lay on the bed with her eyes closed, besieged by wretchedness. Sleep came to her at last, however. Her mind was active enough, but her body was inexpressibly weary, and presently slumber descended upon her.

When she awakened, the room was dark, and there was a light, scratching sound at the window.

"Don't be afraid," said a voice in Spanish. "It is Juan, *señora*."

She leaped from the bed and lighted the lamp. Her thoughts were spinning dizzily. It seemed to her that the scarred face of the youth, as he stood in the corner of the room, drifted this way and that before her eyes. How had he come? The door was locked still; the wall beneath the window was a sheer drop of two stories to the ground.

"You have asked for Speedy," said Juan.

"Yes, I heard that you could take me to him, Juan," said Jessica Wilson. "I have plenty of money to make it worthwhile. I'll give you part now, and part after I've found him. Are you sure that you can really take me to him?"

"Oh, yes," said the youth, and a painfully twisted smile came on his face. Then he added: "But who told you that I know him?"

"I don't think that I can tell you that," she answered.

"Then I don't know," said Juan. "Perhaps I can't take you. . . ."

"It was a big fellow with a cropped gray head of hair."

"Alkali Pete?" he asked.

"Yes."

"He talks, then?" Juan asked gloomily.

"I had a very hard time dragging it out of him. He's not a gossip, Juan. But about Speedy. . . ."

"Yes?"

"When do you think that I can see him?"

"Why, *señora* . . . now, if you please."

"Now?"

"Yes."

"This very moment?"

"Yes."

"Oh!" she exclaimed. "Take me to him instantly, Juan. I think he'll reward you, too, for being my friend."

A strange voice, pitched deeper, said to her: "Don't you know me, Jessica?"

She stared, bewildered. For the voice came from the youth. "Know you?" she gasped.

"I can't take off the scar . . . I don't dare wash off the stain, Jessica," he said. "But I thought that an old friend like you might know me again at the first glance."

"Speedy!" she cried, and ran to him with her hands flung out.

IV

Even in that moment of her emotion, she could not help noticing how deftly and surely he caught her two hands with his, with no uncertainty of gesture.

"It's been a month, Speedy," she told him breathlessly. "I've hunted half the world over, it seems to me. I still don't believe that it's you beneath that scarred face."

"You know that a little plaster and a little dye will

do a lot to a face," said Speedy. "Speak softly. These walls are thick, but there are some ears not far away that I don't want to hear the name of Speedy. Your husband's giving you trouble. What kind?"

"How did you know that he's giving me trouble?" she asked, half offended and also a little awed by his calm and detached manner.

"Nothing else would make you hunt a month to find me," Speedy replied. "Nothing but John and his welfare. Tell me about it."

"He's gone absolutely wild," said the girl. "That's the only way to put it."

"He's gone wild?" Speedy murmured.

He moved just a little, but, now, when she faced him, the light was on her. She knew that he was studying her expression as much as he was listening to her words, but that hardly mattered, considering that it was actually the eye of Speedy that watched her.

She had rehearsed the speech a hundred times; she knew exactly what she intended to say to him, but now the words evaporated. She simply stuttered: "He's left me, Speedy. That's all. And he'll never come back to me, I'm afraid."

He considered what she had said gravely. It seemed odd to her, in a way, that she should be confiding her troubles to a man who was hardly more than a youngster. On the other hand, there was in him a wisdom far beyond his years.

"John was willing to die for you," he said at last. "I suppose that he's just as fond of you, still. You have everything to give him, too. You have a good ranch that your father fixed up for you. And John likes the Western life. So what went wrong?"

She tried to find the right words again, and then

an inspiration came to her. "Would you be happy leading a life like that?" she asked.

He shrugged his shoulders. "I'm a queer fish," he replied. "Anybody ought to be happy with plenty of money, a pleasant life, and a wife he loves."

"Would you be happy if you had all those things?" she insisted.

He hesitated. "We're talking about John, not about me," he answered finally.

"Be honest, Speedy," she pleaded.

"No," he said at last. "No, I don't suppose that I'd be happy."

"Then tell me why."

"A ship isn't happy when it's always lying at anchor."

"I don't follow that."

He explained: "Well, I take it that some men are made for movement, and others are made to stay still and work in one spot."

"And you'd rather drift about than do anything else?" she asked anxiously.

"Not simply drift," he answered rather vaguely. "I don't mean that. I suppose that I'd be contented to stay in one place, if enough things were always happening."

She nodded at this. "That's the only way I can explain John and what he's done," she replied.

"Go on," he urged. "He simply left you one day?"

"He told me," Jessica explained, "that he couldn't be contented so long as the money that had bought the ranch came from father. He said that he wanted to go out and make his share, and prove that he was a man. Then he'd come back. Perhaps that's how he really convinced himself, honestly. But I know that other things were lying behind it."

"Such as what?"

"He'd lived a pretty sheltered, quiet life before he came West."

"Yes, that's true, from what he told me."

"He was always afraid that he lacked the courage of a real man."

"He said that. He was nervous about himself."

"Then," said Jessica Wilson, "that day came when you roused him and made him realize his own strength."

Speedy nodded and touched his face with a thoughtful hand.

"I know," said the girl. "He told me that you actually taunted him into fighting, and then let him knock you down, so as to raise his spirits."

"The old days don't matter," said Speedy. "The new ones are what count."

"The old ones explain the new ones," she replied. "At least, that's my theory. I know that after that day when he fought with Slade Bennett and killed him . . . after that day, John was changed. You know how changed he was."

"He'd found his self-confidence, that's all," Speedy said.

"Something more than that," she answered. "He'd gone all his life thinking that he was a coward, to put it brutally. After that day, he found that everything in life was dull, except the thing that you love, also."

"What's that?"

"Danger," said the girl.

Speedy moved a little farther back from her, staring fixedly into her eyes. "What do you mean by that?" he demanded brusquely.

"It's the truth," she insisted. "Nothing matters to

you, Speedy, except danger. That's the explanation of why you drift about the world with a hundred names and a hundred disguises. If you let yourself be known, everyone would be afraid of you, and danger would run away from you. And that's what you want to avoid. Why won't you carry a gun? Because that would make a fight too safe a thing for you. Oh, I realize what's in your mind. And now you've come to such a point that nothing pleases you, nothing excites you, except to be in a room with a half-mad gunman, he with a gun, and you with your bare hands."

"You'd make me out a monster," he protested.

"Answer me frankly, Speedy. Isn't it true?"

Instead of answering, he sighed and looked down for a moment toward the floor; so that he appeared to the girl, during this instant, as a mere inexperienced stripling. She had to force herself back into the realization that this was Speedy, the man of many names, of endless adventures.

Then he looked up. Even now, his answer was an oblique one. "You think that John has caught that sort of a fever?" he asked gravely.

"I don't think so. I know it," said the girl.

Speedy shook his head and sighed again. "Any signs when he was back at the ranch?" he asked.

"Not many. He was keeping himself in hand. Then there was the novelty of being married, I suppose. Besides that, he was busy working on the ranch, learning the ways of the range. But gradually I noticed that he was growing absentminded at the table, and in the evening he'd take to walking up and down the floor, forgetting to answer when I spoke to him. He dropped into the habit of taking rides through the night, also. It's a wild country up there, you know."

"I know," Speedy said gently, almost tenderly.

"But he'd ride out," Jessica Wilson said, "and, when he came back, the brush had torn his chaps, and his horse was always half dead the next morning."

Speedy nodded again. His expression was that of a physician who hears a list of interesting symptoms, but who will not commit himself to any expression of opinion until the last word has been heard.

The girl continued: "We had some pretty wild horses. There were seven or eight bad ones that father had picked up for a song and turned over to us . . . they came cheap because they were outlaws, and it was just one of father's rough jokes. But John took them seriously. He settled down to breaking those horses. He was smashed and battered to bits nearly every day. He should have broken every bone in his body, because he wasn't much of a rider, in the beginning. But he was at those wild demons every hour of the day. I don't know why he wasn't savaged."

"Because a horse knows when the rider isn't afraid," put in Speedy quietly.

"Perhaps that was it," she admitted. "At any rate, he worked for a month. The cowpunchers we had on the place used to laugh a good deal at first, but, when ten days had gone by, they laughed no longer. They were worried. So was I. Every day, John was out there in the corrals, fighting the horses. For two weeks he made no progress that we could see, and he was always covered with bruises and cuts. His head was in bandages. He could hardly walk. But all that month he was happy, laughing and singing about the place. At the end of two weeks, he rode one of those outlaws to a standstill. Thirty days after the start, he had every one of the lot in hand. It was a tremendous thing, considering that he was almost a green hand, to begin with. I can tell you that none of the cowpunchers was smiling at John by the end of that month. Then the horse-breaking ended, and I thanked heaven for it. But, after a few days, I almost wished that he were back at the work again, because his spirits were low every day, and he began that dreadful night riding again, like a prowling mountain lion. And always he was more and more silent.

"In the middle of this, we missed some cows. They'd been rustled. We located the trail and the pass in the hills that they'd been driven through, and John took three men and went off after them. Three days later, the other men came back. I'll never forget the sickness in my heart when I looked out the window and saw them coming, without John. But it turned out that they simply couldn't stay with him. On the trail he rode his horses into the ground. Then he took them on the lead and made another ten miles. In the middle of the night, he roused up the others, and struck out again. They were dead men in forty-eight hours and begged him to slow up, but the sign of the trail was growing fresher and fresher, and he wouldn't go any slower. A week later, he came back and he drove the cattle ahead of him. There was a bandaged man riding before him, herded along among the cows. That was one of the rustlers. The other rustler . . . there had been two, you see . . . would never ride again. He was dead. John had killed him, as he killed Slade Bennett . . . as he'll kill other men, until one day he's overmatched, or beaten by luck and is shot down and killed. Oh, Speedy," she ended, with a high-pitched cry of grief, "I know that he's like you. He caught the fever from you, and there's nothing in the world that will ever content him, except to fight, to fight against odds!"

Speedy went to her and separated the tense hands that she had gripped tightly together.

"Well," he said softly, "after that affair of the cattle rustlers, what happened? He sat about the house, growing more and more absent-minded again?"

Tears were still streaking down the face of the girl, but she nodded in agreement. "It was the same way," she said, "until one night he woke me up and stood by my bed, dressed for the road, with his hat in his hand, and a pack on his shoulders. He said that he was leaving the place for a while, and that he'd stay away until he was able to make a stake and not live the rest of his days on my father's charity."

"Did you say that there was a pack on his back?"

Yes. He wouldn't even take a horse from the place. He said that everything belonged to me, and from that time on he'd earn everything that he wore or ate or rode or used in any way."

"Did you beg him to stay?" Speedy asked.

"No," said the girl. "I just got up and put on a dressing gown. Then I went down to the front door with him and tried to keep smiling. I told him that what was best for him would have to be best for me, too." She put her hands over her face and shuddered, remembering that moment.

"You're the wisest girl that I ever knew," Speedy stated.

She snatched down her hands and stared at him. "And now, Speedy?" she breathed. "Will you help me?"

"You want me to find him and take him home?" he asked slowly.

"It isn't the finding him," answered Jessica Wilson. "I know where he is. And it isn't merely to bring him home. Oh, he's been back once or twice, just to drop in on me. He's written about his plans. He's always about to strike it lucky and come back for good. But I know in my heart that there's no lucky strike in the world so big that it will satisfy him. It isn't gold he wants, but danger. And who can cure him, Speedy, except the man who gave him the disease?" She came closer to him, as though that would make him feel more the force of her pleading.

"You want me to change his heart, Jessica. Is that it?" he asked.

"I want a miracle, Speedy," she confessed. "I'm sorry. I know that even you can't do it, probably. But I'm standing here and begging you to try. Will you?"

"I'll try," he said. "You'll tell me where he is. Yet, there's a little job that I'm trying to do here in San Lorenzo. Do you mind if I take a few days for that, before I start on the trail? I've almost run one quarry to the ground, and. . . ."

"Speedy, it's blood out of my heart, every minute you wait."

"Then I'll go," he answered instantly. "I'll start the moment you tell me where to find him."

V

When Speedy looked out through the door into the long, low room, he saw twenty men or more seated around the table. The cook had told him to go in and sit down with the rest of the logging crew. There were, in fact, extra places laid, and there seemed to be plenty of food left on the great platters, in spite of the heaps of beans, pale, soggy, boiled potatoes, and half-fried bacon that were constantly transferred to the plates. A boy went about the table with a bucket of steaming black coffee, and he was constantly employed in replenishing the empty cups.

The first glance at the crowd showed Speedy all these details of the picture; the second glance showed him John Wilson. He sat near the farther end of the table, talking and laughing with the men around him, a glowing spot of good cheer in the rather gloomy assemblage. For that camp was well above the frost line, and the bitterly cold air seeped in through the cracks of the door and the two windows. Four lanterns, bracketed against the walls, gave the light, and, since it shone from behind, every gesture made at the table was accompanied by a sweeping and distorted shadow.

At the end of the table nearest the door sat the boss, distinguished by a clean shirt and a felt hat pushed to the back of his head. Speedy paused by him.

"The doctor told me that I could sit in," he said.

The boss turned a burly face, blackened by a growth of whiskers, that was shaved, it appeared, no more than once a week—and the week was drawing toward the end. He did not use words, but surveyed Speedy with a glance that had in it neither surprise nor interest; only his eyes seemed to hold some contempt for the size of this man as he pointed toward an empty place with the heel of his table knife.

Speedy sat down. He was a good middle height, but he was dwarfed among these fellows. Mountain lumbermen are the biggest of the mountain breed. It requires a certain span of shoulders to swing an axe to the best effect.

However, there was a certain degree of hospitality shown by those nearest him. One large, grimy hand dragged a platter of beans nearer to him; another shoved forward a basin stacked with hot cornbread. He helped himself, with thanks, and began to eat, without so much as turning his head up or down the table. Too much curiosity is not expected of guests in the West. They should submit, first, to an inspection. After that, they may begin to look about. And Speedy knew the code.

At the same time, for all his apparently diligent attention to his plate and to nothing else, every face and form was imprinted on his mind and he weighed every man at the board with lightning glances. He had developed this faculty by training. It is not easy. It means photographing an image at a single glance of the eyes and holding the impression until it has been digested, analyzed, taken to bits, and put together again in the reasoning mind.

So, very quickly, he scanned the lot, and made sure that he had seen none of these men before, not one, except John Wilson. Keen as his memory was, he would hardly have remembered that man, except that he expected from the words of Jessica Wilson to find her husband here. For Wilson looked older; he was thin and brown of face now, and looked heavier and harder about the shoulders. Moreover, Speedy felt that he was something more than a mere semblance of hardy strength. Among all these mountaineer giants, he was dwarfed by none. A casual eye, even a most judicious one, might well have selected him as the best hand of the lot—not for sheer size, perhaps, but for the strength of spirit that shone out of his eyes. He seemed in the highest degree pleased with this world in which he found himself. His long years of higher education were not a load upon his shoulders that needed to be shaken off before he could meet these people upon their own ground. Speedy smiled to himself a little, but not altogether with pleasure.

He was to take this man in hand. He had given to Jessica Wilson his solemn promise that that was his task and that he would bend his best efforts toward accomplishing it. But, although he smiled, he could not help realizing that John Wilson was no longer what he had been at Council Flat, or again in the mining town. He was more. He was much more. He had nerve to match his bulk.

The source of his good nature began to appear presently, as the clatter of knives and forks grew less, and the men fell back upon their last cups of coffee, having mopped up plates full of molasses with chunks of the pone. In this comparative silence, the voices at the farther end of the table could be heard more clearly, and it was plain that John Wilson, whatever he had been doing before, was now badgering a certain low-browed Canuck who sat across from him. A dark mountain of a man was this fellow and, as he drank his coffee, with lowered head, he looked like a buffalo bull, about to charge. His nostrils expanded and quivered, while the cheerful voice of John Wilson continued with the pleasant narration of what he called a Sioux Indian story, which described how the Creator, having made men white and black, red and yellow, finally came to the making of Canucks, and selected for that purpose a certain sort of mud.

He got that far in the tale, with all eyes and many

sour grins of appreciation turned toward him, when the Canuck reached the limits of his patience. With a yell of rage he hurled his coffee cup across the table, half filled with the scalding liquid, and followed the cup with a leap at the throat of John Wilson.

Up rose John Wilson, with the gleam of a knife driving toward his own throat. But, as he rose, his up-darting hand struck the right arm of the Canuck to the side. With his other hand, he took him by the throat, and he drew the burly man straight across the top of that massive table, which shuddered from end to end.

Metal plates, cups, forks, knives, platters crashed on the floor, hurled by the kicking legs of the Canuck. But that was not what interested Speedy. He paid a little attention to the expert handwork of John Wilson. But he paid still closer interest to the face of the young man. Perfect and shining bliss was in the eyes of Wilson. It only brightened, as he avoided the second murderous upthrust of the knife. It glowed to a fire as, at last, he struck the Canadian senseless with a well-aimed stroke of the fist. Only one real blow had been struck, and the Canuck lay helplessly sprawling on the floor.

The boss came charging up. "Throw that cursed knife artist out of the camp!" he roared. "Kick him out, and throw his pack after him. If I catch him here in the morning . . . I'll hang him to the first tree. Shorty, make out his time and pay him off, hear me?"

"Yeah, I hear you," said Shorty.

"And now for you," continued the boss. He whirled on his heel, and faced big John Wilson. He was big himself, that boss; he was fully as big as the man he now faced, but there was a subtle difference between them that was not entirely a matter of the difference in years. John Wilson, let us say, looked like a wolf that is kept lean and fit by the struggle for life in the mountain desert. The boss was rather a cage-fed animal.

"And what for me?" asked Wilson.

"I'm through with you," said the boss. "It ain't the first time that you've started pandemonium popping around here. You've picked out three of the best men I've got, and you've had a fight with every one of 'em. You don't know one end of an axe from another. I'll have no more of you. I'm gonna throw you out!"

"Throw me out?" asked John Wilson.

"I'll throw you out, if I gotta have guns to do it!" shouted the maddened boss.

"Well, let's see," said Wilson. He stepped a little forward, and ran his eyes over the crowd of men. "Guns or no guns, d'you know what I think?" he said to the boss finally.

"What d'you think, you pup?" shouted the boss.

"I think," said Wilson, "guns or no guns, you haven't got enough men here to throw me out."

"By thunder and fire, I'll teach you, then!" roared the boss.

"Will you?" said Wilson. "I don't know about that." He walked to the corner of the room and held out a cup to the frightened little roustabout that carried the coffee bucket. "Fill this, kid," he ordered.

"Throw a ladle of it in his face, you little fool!" cried the boss.

But the coffee was not thrown into the face of big John Wilson. It was merely poured until the cup was full.

The fallen Canadian was now getting to his feet. He stood up, staggering, his eyes still glassy. One hand he pressed against his jaw, as though he feared that the bone might be broken. Perhaps that was the case. A heavy blow it had been, according to the ideas of Speedy.

He, very calmly, saw and took good note that John Wilson held the coffee cup in his left hand as he deliberately sipped its contents, and then he looked up and down the rows of scowling faces that were turned toward him.

"Guns or no guns," said John Wilson, "you won't throw me out of your camp, Weatherby. You haven't enough men to do it, and they're not the right kind."

A shout of anger broke from several throats, and now Speedy leaned forward in the intensity of his interest. His own eyes glowed yellow as the eyes of a hunting lion. He saw the same light in the eyes of John Wilson, as the man faced these enemies. It was joy, the sheer joy of battle that burned in them. He was actually smiling with irrepressible pleasure, as he surveyed the others.

They were ready to rush him. They were ready to grip him with their hands, pierce him with their knives, and yet he stood his ground and taunted them. But that right hand that was draped so carelessly upon his hip did not intend to occupy itself with either fist blows or a knife handle. Something better than that was surely in its reach.

VI

It might be that John Wilson was armed, but, no doubt, there were other guns in that rough crowd, although they were not drawn. Speedy could tell the reason. It was simply because the man so openly asked for trouble that he did not get it. He sipped at that cup of coffee still, and dared them all with his eyes.

The boss showed himself a man of sense, for he called out suddenly: "There'll be no blood on this here floor . . . nobody go near that ruffian! Wilson, you might've showed more sense than this."

"I'm ready to be fired, chief," John Wilson said. "I simply don't want to be thrown out. It's a cold night, and I don't want to be marched out into it."

"Then stay in the bunkhouse tonight," said the boss. "I'm not gonna have gunfighting around here. And I'll tell you this, Wilson, one of these days you're gonna find yourself in a jail or else hanging from a rope collar off the branch of a tree. And I don't care much which thing happens to you. Shorty, make out Wilson's time, will you?"

"Never was gladder to make out anybody's time since I came here," Shorty commented with a snarl.

"What's the matter with you, Shorty?" asked Wilson. "When did I step on your toes?"

"You've stepped on toes all around," said Shorty. "You're a bully, is what you are."

"Picking on little boys like this?" Wilson asked, gesturing toward the crowd.

"It ain't size that counts in a fight," said Shorty. "And you damn' well know it. What would your size count, if a little chunk of a hundred and sixty pound middle-weight champeen out of the ring came and jumped you? You're a bully, Wilson, and every bully gets his in the long run."

"That may be," Wilson said, shrugging his heavy shoulders. "I'll go and sleep on that, and I'll leave you boys tomorrow morning. So long."

He waved his hand at them and strode toward the

door. Sullenly they gave way before him. One man made a move as though to throw himself at the back of the big fellow, but he was held by a companion.

"Gun plays are no good," said the lumberjack with the restraining hands. "We ain't gonna start anything like that here."

John Wilson stepped out through the door, to go to the bunkhouse. Behind him a subdued muttering broke out. Then one man said loudly: "If I had a gun, I wouldn't mind stacking up ag'in' him."

"Aw, you're a fool, and a loud-mouthed fool," declared another brutally. "You shoot off your face sooner than you would a gun. Take my word and leave Wilson alone, unless you wanna get salted down with lead."

More talk was following as Speedy slipped from the crowd through the door and stepped into the open night.

It was cold and crystal clear. The sweetness of the air, after the smoky, steaming atmosphere of the bunkhouse, sank to the bottom of his lungs at every breath, and so for a moment he forgot the purpose for which he had made this journey, forgot Jessica Wilson and her husband, forgot his own strange life, and lost himself in the tingling cold and beauty of the mountain night.

His glance ran up the tall, arrowy forms of the pines to the stars they pointed toward, and beyond the trees he looked at the great mountains, blocking out the lighted sky in immense wedges of shadow. The snowy peaks, here and there, glistened faintly, so that some of those summits looked like the crests of enormous waves that come rolling, sleek and dark, out of the night to overwhelm a ship.

A shudder of increasing cold went through him.

Then he stepped on and pushed open the door of the bunkhouse. It was built long and low, like the dining room, but larger. There was a stove toward either end, each reddening with the fire that burned in it. But even that double source of heat hardly expelled the chill from the room. It was lighted, similarly, by two smoky lanterns that filled the place with dim shadows.

Wilson, when the door was thrust open, was halfway down the room, arranging the blankets of his bunk, and he turned like a flash, as though to face danger. Speedy walked straight toward him, and saw the frown of Wilson turn into curious wonder. Then a cry came from the lips of the big man.

"Speedy!" He ran to meet him, and Speedy smiled and waved his hand in greeting, before he gripped the big fingers of his friend. "Speedy, where did you drop from?"

"Out of the sky, where all good people come from," said Speedy. "I've just been watching you jam things up in the dining room."

"Hold on! Were you in there?"

"I was eating near the boss."

"The mischief you were. I didn't see you."

"You weren't seeing faces . . . you were only seeing your own ideas," Speedy declared.

"I guess I made a fool of myself," John Wilson said, frowning. "You know, Speedy, I got some smoke in the brain, sort of. . . ." He paused a moment, entangled in his words.

"You got fire in the brain, and that's different," answered Speedy.

"Fire?" repeated Wilson.

"Who wants to live like a log?" Speedy asked

rather sharply. "I don't, for one, and I'm glad to see that you don't, either, John."

"You take it that way?" asked Wilson.

"Of course, I do. That was worthwhile . . . to stand up there and tell the lot of 'em to go to the old boy. That was filling your hand with something worthwhile, I'd say."

"Well, I'm relieved that you take it that way, Speedy," said John Wilson. "But, then, I might have known that you would. That's why you drift around. Trying to find something worth mixing with. But what brought you up here, Speedy? You didn't see Jessica, did you?"

"Jessica?" said the other. "Look here, John, why should I see Jessica?"

"I didn't know. Only, you see, Speedy, I'm trying to make a decent stake for myself. Tired of living on her father's charity. That's what it amounted to."

"You're right," Speedy said cheerfully. "I don't blame you. You cut loose, did you, to make your own pile?"

"That's it," answered Wilson.

"It's the only thing for a self-respecting man to do," Speedy stated gravely. "I think a lot more of you for it, John."

"Do you?" Wilson murmured, and he smiled with pleasure and relief.

"And," Speedy continued, "perhaps, if you're really on the loose, we can travel together for a while."

Wilson exclaimed loudly with pleasure. "Son," he said, "there's nothing in the world that I'd like so well! Will you go on with me tomorrow morning?"

"I can't wait that long," Speedy said. "Sorry, but I've got to stir my stumps."

"Hold on! Start out in the middle of a cold night like this?"

"It's not very cold," Speedy advised. "I've seen nights a lot worse. Oh, don't worry about the cold, old fellow. You might get a nip of frost in a foot or a hand, but that's nothing."

John Wilson cleared his throat and then sighed. "Well, Speedy," he said less enthusiastically, "I'm with you, if you say the word. We'll start now."

"Roll your blankets, then. Have you got a horse?"

"Yes, I've got a horse picketed out in the field behind the stable."

"Saddle it up, then. I'll be ready in ten minutes, and meet you in front of the cook house. Is that a go?"

"Only, Speedy, what's the terrible rush . . . and the night's like ice!"

"It's a long story, old man," Speedy said. "But the chief thing is that, if I don't keep lively on this trail, I'm likely to be dead on it. You understand?"

"You're followed?"

"Yes."

"By who?"

"Later on I'll tell you. Are you starting with me? Mind you, John, if you ride with me, the way may be a little rough. But if it's excitement you want. . . ."

"I'll meet you in front of the cook house in ten minutes," Wilson said curtly.

Speedy stepped out again into the night.

VII

All was by no means clear in the mind of Speedy at this time. His scheme was still a vague one, and, although it took on more color as he considered it, he only knew that he might cure John Wilson by an overdose of what he now longed for.

Danger, the hunger for danger, was what now possessed the very soul of Wilson. It was, therefore, Speedy's task to eradicate that appetite. How he would go about the business, he did not know. But he saw the need of it.

What the foreman of the lumber camp had told John Wilson was undoubtedly true. He would either end with a rope around his neck and his feet dancing on thin air, or else he would find himself in jail. A man cannot hunt trouble, west of the Mississippi, without eventually finding more than he can digest. Furthermore, John Wilson carried a gun, and knew only too well how to use it. It might even be that he was developing into something of a bully.

But to the swift mind of Speedy the plan came, even while he was pulling up the cinches. What he conceived was enough to make even his own steady nerves jump. Part would be fact and part would be fancy, in what he said to his companion. But already he was composing the speech when he rode the mustang out under the light of the stars and joined big John Wilson in front of the dining cabin.

He had not even had a goal for this midnight journey, in the beginning. He had merely felt that, from the first, it would be well to make the days that Wilson spent with him as arduous as possible. For himself, he could sleep in the saddle, closing one eye at a time, as it were. Or he could lie down on a bare rock, relaxing utterly for an hour, and then rise refreshed. Heat, cold, thirst, hunger he had endured so many times that they were his familiars. It would be very strange if Wilson, in spite of his bulk and muscle, could endure the same strains. He must be worn down. When the crisis came, it must be intense enough fairly to overstrain every nerve.

There was another and a grimmer side of the question. Once entered through the door of this adventure that Speedy had conceived, could they escape with their lives? That question he could not answer. He dismissed it, finally and characteristically, with a shrug of his shoulders.

In the meantime, they were riding farther up the pass, the horses stumbling in the deep ruts that the logging carts had dug into the ground. A moon had joined the stars, and the light that it poured down through the pass was like a ghostly spray. They were cold to the bone. John Wilson was shuddering with the bitter weather. But he made no complaint, merely thrusting forward his head in a way that did not entirely please Speedy. He would have been more at ease if he had only seen signs of weakness in his friend.

They reached the height of the pass. Before them extended a broken country of rough mountains, ragged ravines, and a mighty forest sweeping up to the high line where timber failed and the lofty peaks went up in lonely nakedness against the sky.

"Over there," Speedy said, waving his hand northwest. "That's where we go."

"All right," said Wilson, his voice half stifled because his teeth were locked by the cold. "And what do we find there?"

"Dupray," said Speedy.

"Dupray?" Wilson repeated. "Who's he?"

"Charley Dupray. You've heard of him."

"I've heard of Satan, too. What do we want with Charley Dupray?"

"His scalp, that's all," Speedy answered calmly.

Wilson was shocked, but he merely grunted. "Go on, Speedy," he then said. "Do a little talking, will you? You want Dupray's scalp. That's all right, but won't you want a regiment of the regular Army to get the scalp of Dupray?"

"Maybe," Speedy said. "But that's the fun of it, John."

Wilson cleared his throat, preparatory to speaking, but he did not speak.

Speedy was pleased. "I'll tell you a yarn, John," he said.

"Go ahead."

"I used to know," continued Speedy, "an old trapper by the name of Eric Langton. He trapped in the mountains, not such a long distance from here. He was a fine old man of about sixty. Straight as a rod . . . strong as a mountain lion. I used to drop in on him, now and then. One time, when I needed to lay up for a while, I went to visit old Langton, and spent three weeks with him. I would have stayed longer, but, at the end of three weeks when I came back from hunting, one evening I found that the fire hadn't been lighted in the stove, and supper wasn't ready. The cabin was dark. I lighted the lantern, and then I saw Langton lying in a corner, with his head propped up against some stove wood, and both hands clasped over his breast. There was blood all over the floor. His eyes were open, but they were glazed. I thought that he was dead, but when I leaned over him, he blinked a little and his lips moved. They were blue-gray, those lips of his. He should have been dead hours before, but there was too much will in him to let him die until I'd come back, and he'd had a chance to tell me his story."

"Go on," John Wilson said when Speedy paused. "This yarn of yours is as cold as the night air. But go on. I've got a chill already so deep that anything you say won't make me any worse."

"Well," said Speedy, "I saw that he was so far gone that I didn't even dare to give him a drink of whiskey to brace him up. There was no use trying to bandage the wound, either. His poor old hands were pressed over it, and still the blood was leaking out gradually, and his life with it. You understand?"

"I understand," Wilson said hoarsely. "What scoundrel would have hurt a harmless old fellow like him?"

"Pretty harmless and pretty old," agreed Speedy. "I simply squatted by him, and put my ear against his lip. He made a faint whispering sound. But it was simply breath . . . no articulation in it. Then it occurred to me that perhaps he'd be able to write. I grabbed a piece of paper and put it on a magazine in front of him, then I pushed a pencil into his hand. The blood ran down off his hand onto the paper. But he was able to scratch six shaking letters on the paper before the pencil dropped out of his fingers and his head fell over on his shoulder. He was dead."

"Poor old chap," Wilson said, shaking his head.

"I picked up the paper," Speedy continued, "and saw that the six letters, all wabbling and running downhill, made up the name, Dupray, and from that minute I knew that I'd never be able to rest, really, till I'd got back at Dupray."

"Would Dupray go out and murder an old man like that for nothing?" asked Wilson.

"Not Dupray himself, but one of the hungry dogs that works with him. And that puts the fault back on Dupray again, in a way. However, you can see that it wasn't an easy job."

"Getting at Dupray? I should say not. A job for a crazy man, Speedy. Really, just a job for a crazy man. Dupray always has a dozen first-class gunmen around him, hasn't he?"

"Of course, he has," agreed Speedy very cheerfully. "And I've always known that it was too much for any one man to turn the trick. I had to have help. Not a bunch of men to try to find Dupray's gang ... numbers will never locate a fox like that ... but one good man to guard my back. You understand? When I saw you stand up before that gang of big lumbermen, I knew that I'd found my man at last. For the first time, I'd found a man who might go through the fire with me. Tell me, John, am I right?"

Wilson did not answer at once. But then, resolutely thrusting out his head, with his jaw set, he muttered: "Speedy, I owe something a lot more than life to you. And I'll never say no to you while there's life in my body."

VIII

Never did a man hear an answer that was at once so pleasing and so displeasing. It conveyed to Speedy every suggestion of personal devotion; it also showed heroic determination, more almost than Speedy desired to find. He was, in fact, silent for a moment after Wilson had spoken. Then he said: "I'm thanking you for that, John. I can't ask for more than that."

"Don't thank me for words," John Wilson said abruptly. "Words are cheap and easy enough. Wait till I've actually done something for you, instead of merely talking about it."

"All right," Speedy said, nodding his head. He pressed his feet into the stirrups and tightened the grip of his knees against the barrel of the mustang. Then he drew in a great breath of the cold, pure air. He was wondering where in all the world one could find more perfect manhood, than in his own country of the far West. His respect for John Wilson swelled in his heart, yet his trouble increased, also. He wanted to find a strain of weakness in the man— and that strain would not, it seemed, appear.

As they rode on down the broken, winding trail, John Wilson asked: "You never got up against Dupray before this, Speedy?"

"Never got up against him?" repeated Speedy, his mind not particularly intent on the words he was speaking. "Why, John, I've had a few run-ins with the Dupray people. They operate on a pretty big scale and I've had run-ins with them, well enough."

"Anything bad?"

"Well, I don't know what you'd call bad," murmured Speedy. "The worst was with Lee Purvis, I suppose."

"I don't think I ever heard of Lee Purvis."

"Not many people had, even when Lee was alive," Speedy said. "He didn't wish to be known. There never was a man who cared less to crowd his way into print and pictures. Oh, no, Lee was a modest sort of a fellow, but he was wonderful, too."

"Wonderful about what?"

"About precious stones. Diamonds, emeralds, rubies, sapphires, pearls. He knew all about 'em, including how to get them without digging them out of a mine."

"Jewel thief, you mean?"

"It's hard," said Speedy, "to call an artist like Lee Purvis a plain thief. No, he wasn't exactly a thief, though he did a good deal of stealing. I suppose that all of his thefts, added together, would have been worth a couple of millions. He had the brains for the business and he used his brains all the time. It was a pretty sad year that didn't see Lee Purvis on the long end of some hundred or two hundred thousand dollar deal." He broke off speaking and threw his head back slightly. He seemed to be drinking in the beauty of that night sky, or the great lift and heave of the mountains, or perhaps he was dreaming about the glorious exploits of Lee Purvis in the past.

Said his companion: "Go on, Speedy . . . don't cut me off short like this. How did you get interested in the game?"

"Why," Speedy said, "that was when Lee stole the Windover jewels. I knew Tom Windover, and his whole share of the inheritance was in the stones.

Above half a million of 'em ... the biggest haul that Lee Purvis had ever made. Tom was a pretty sick man, at that time. He had a couple of youngsters. His ranch wasn't paying very well. When the jewels were stolen, it looked pretty hopeless for him. I saw him, about that time, and he told me all about the stones. So I started off on the trail."

"And got 'em, eh?" said Wilson.

"The trouble was," Speedy went on, "that Lee Purvis was hooked up with Dupray in that deal. Dupray had engineered a lot of the hard parts, and Purvis, when I got on his trail, was streaking it for the mountains to get the loot to Dupray and make a fair division with him. When I started catching up with Lee, a lot of hurdles were pushed across my path, and Dupray's gang was putting them there."

"Hurdles like gunmen in the way, eh?" commented the other.

"Yes, that and other things," said Speedy. "It was quite a job, and it would take me too long to tell you everything that happened. But finally I got my hands on the stuff. Then they chased me, pretty closely, too, John. Finally they killed the horse that I was riding, drove me into the rocks, and cornered me on the edge of a ravine with a thousand feet of cliff dropping away behind my back."

"Go on!" pleaded his friend as Speedy paused to shake his head at the recollection.

"Well," he said, "I lay there for three days, without food or water, frying in the sun. But on the third night, a thunderstorm rolled over the mountains and darkened the moon for me. So I started to climb down the rocks. Dupray's fellows, with Lee Purvis among 'em, seemed to guess that I might try that trick, so they lined up along the cliff, after rushing my rock nest and finding the bird gone. They fired at me by the lightning flashes and nicked me a couple of times, but not enough to stop me from climbing . . . then, as they saw that I was getting away, Lee Purvis got nervous and began to follow me. Of course, the rocks were slippery with the rain water, and Lee had a fall that ended him, poor fellow.

"I found him at the bottom of the cliff when I got down into the ravine below. He was lying on his back, with his face turned up toward the lightning, looking as peaceful as a child. Poor Lee. There was an artist for you, partner. But, as I was saying, that was the worst run-in that I ever had with Dupray and his men. Dupray was there with them, that night. And he never could forget the thing. It lingered in his mind, and he's always promised a tidy little fortune to any of his men who can snag me and show him the proof that I'm gone. There's only one proof that will really satisfy him, however."

"What's that?"

"My head," said Speedy.

Wilson shuddered. "Look here, Speedy," he said, "you don't mean to say that you'll try to break in on Dupray's gang, when half of them know you by sight, do you?"

"It's not the old Speedy that they'll be seeing, though," he said. "I expect to change my face, old son."

"You're going to trust to a disguise, among those expert crooks?" exclaimed John Wilson.

"Well, why not? With a patch of plaster to make a scar on my face, for instance, and a little stain to turn me into a Mexican."

Wilson threw up his hands. "A made-up scar, you say? Anybody could see through such a disguise as that."

"I know what you mean," answered Speedy. "The fact is that most patch scars are clumsy affairs. But I've worked for years to make mine correct. Sun and water won't wash it off, John. And the hand can't detect any rough edges. I've worked on showing the red seam of a fresh scar or the white pucker of an old one. I know how the skin gathers along the edge of the cut, and I think that I can deceive even a physician. At least, I have deceived 'em a good many times."

"But Dupray and his men, they're experts, Speedy. You surely wouldn't trust to a disguise."

The growth of horror in his companion began to please Speedy more and more.

"Disguises are considered cheap things by most crooks," he said in explanation of his plans. "They're not used because, once the disguise is detected, it's the prison at once for the fool underneath the mask. Things like false beards and mustaches are generally very bad, I admit. But let me tell you, partner, that I can put on a false beard so real that it will stand shaving, and still seem to show the natural skin underneath. I can put on a beard so strongly fastened that you could drag me around a room with one hand sunk in the tangles of it. That happened to me once, as a matter of fact."

"You were dragged around a room by your false beard?" exclaimed Wilson.

"Yes, and I had to submit to it," Speedy stated. "Because if I had manhandled the fellow, I'd have disproved what I was trying to make clear, that I was a decrepit, bedridden invalid. I had to take the hauling about and the beating and kicking. And I howled till my throat cracked." He laughed cheerfully at the memory.

"What happened to the people who did that to you, Speedy?" asked John Wilson grimly.

"As a matter of fact, they didn't have much luck in the end," answered Speedy. He went on cheerfully: "Trust me, John. I'll fool the Dupray gang, now that I have you to go along with me. You'll be the boss, and I'll be the servant . . . your peon. How's that?"

"How am I to pass myself off, so that we can get at the Dupray outfit? And what are we to do when we get there?" asked Wilson.

"I'll tell you," Speedy began. "I know a little village in the mountains, yonder, and in that village there's a small inn. In the inn's yard there's a garden, and that garden runs back to a wall built against the rubble and loose stones of the hillside . . . built as far back as the *conquistadores*, in the centuries when they were spilled across this part of the world. There's an old iron door, they say, set into the side of that wall . . . beyond the wall, in those old days, there used to be a passage of some sort dug into the heart of the mountain. At least, there's a bell still fastened over the arch of the gate, and people in the village say, if any man dares to ring that bell just at sunset, a lot of strange things will be sure to happen to him."

"That sounds like a lot of nonsense to me," said the other calmly.

"It may sound like a lot of nonsense," Speedy said, "but my idea is that that bell and that door are the way to enter the Dupray gang . . . if they want to take you in."

"And I'm to ring that bell at sunset?" queried Wilson.

"You'll have the nerve to do it, I know," the other said.

"I'll try it, I suppose," muttered Wilson.

"All that happens," Speedy said, "is that they give you a few tests, I suppose . . . courage, marksmanship, and that sort of thing."

"*Humph*," said John Wilson. "And if I get through, what about you?"

"Why," Speedy said, "you're a gentleman so used to having service that wherever you go, your servant will have to go, also."

IX

The town of Red Rock was a queer hodge-podge, similar to others appearing in some sections of the Southwest. It had been an Indian stronghold in the old days; there were still remains of the rude stone walls at the top of the big hill that overlooked the place. Then it had become a Spanish possession, and the Spaniards had built a stone blockhouse on the same hill, but inside the old Indian wall. The ruins of the fort made a picturesque gesture against the sky to the eyes of those coming into the valley for the first time.

The town of Red Rock, which was both American and Mexican, lay down in the valley itself, and it was composed equally of Mexican adobe houses and American frame ones. For your true Western American does not feel that a house is a house unless it is built of boards. Although stone may be at hand, although adobe bricks are cheaply made and usually will outlast the timber ten times over, although the thin boards may be a mere shell through which the heat of summer simmers and through which the winds of winter blow, entering by a thousand crevices made by the warping of the timbers, still a house is not a house unless it is built of wood. As for adobe houses, commodious as they may be, cool in summer and secure against every winter tempest, the Westerner feels that they are little better than caves in the ground. So Red Rock was a combination, and it rambled and scrambled over the floor of the little, narrow valley at its will.

In Red Rock, the arrival of every stranger was an event, at least to the children. So now they came out to stare at the two riders, for it was not every day that they had a chance to look at a master so magnificent or a servant so deformed.

Big John Wilson rode on a splendid chestnut half-bred gelding that carried itself like a king, and, although his clothes were ordinary enough, clothes did not matter particularly in Red Rock, unless it were a Mexican *caballero* who was wearing them. And John Wilson looked like a man who has extracted much good from this world and who expects to get yet more before the end of his days. His manner, his bearing, his great size, the quality of his horse were enough to fill the eyes of the gamins of Red Rock. But after an admiring glance at him, they turned their attention to Speedy, who rode to the rear.

He was disguised as Jessica Wilson had seen him

in San Lorenzo; that is to say, his skin was darkened, his forelock fell down to his eyes, a ragged straw hat, much crumpled as though it had been trampled in the road, was on his head, ragged trousers covered his legs only to the knees and his thin brown shanks descended to worn sandals. He rode humped over a little, like one who has spent most of his life on foot, rather than in the saddle, as was customary in that part of the world.

He was entirely without pride, for his head was bent forward on his neck, so that the motion of the horse made it work back and forth, very like the swaying movement of the head and neck of a chicken as it walks. But his face was the chief attraction. There was a scar, it appeared, that began near the left eye and curved down the side of the face, ending quite close to the back of the jaw. It was a great scar and an old one. One could tell its age by the whiteness of the seam. And it pulled on the skin, which appeared polished and sleek over the cheek bone and, puckering down the sides of the scar, drew the ear a bit forward and exercised a considerable pull upon the eye and the mouth. All of the talking had to be, almost perforce, upon that side of the face, and the eye was like the eye of a Chinaman.

A rabble of the youngsters formed behind the mustang of Speedy, hooting and shouting. Deformities are ridiculous to boys when they are young enough and wild enough. So they ran at the heels of the mustang, until the horse put down its head and kicked out. This rejoiced them all the more, although they would rather have tormented the rider than the horse he rode upon, so they scattered forward, and danced and pranced beside Speedy while they poked their fun at him and twisted their faces into hideous contortions in imitation of the deformity.

He paid no attention.

Presently one of them picked up a stone out of the dust and threw it with a good aim, fully at the head of the rearward rider. A slim brown hand flashed up, caught the stone in full flight, and caused it to disappear. And still Speedy appeared to pay no heed.

There was a yell of surprise at this accident or exhibition of skill. Again and again, the stones were thrown at Speedy, but all, in exactly the same manner, were caught out of the air by the same flashing brown hands; and still he kept his head straight forward and looked as stupid as ever. It was very plain that this was a game and that he enjoyed it.

A big lout of fifteen caught up a stone that filled his fist, and it not only had sufficient weight to crack a skull with even a glancing blow, but there was great strength in the arm of the boy. However, an odd thing happened just as he was poising the rock. The hand of Speedy flicked out and a sizable pebble that he had caught a few minutes before was flung with unerring aim. It cracked against one of the shins of the big youth with such force that he let out a yelp, like a dog when a careless or a mischievous foot steps on its tail. The rock dropped from the boy's hand. He began to dance about on one foot, holding the hurt place of the injured shin with both hands, and his cruel young companions, like so many wolves, yelled and roared with laughter at his bad luck. They broke off their yelling, however, and the hurt lad forgot his pain and came limping after the rider of the mustang, gaping, and then shouting with joy. For a miracle was happening.

Out of the agile hands of Speedy a fountain of

stones was rising. They danced in the light of the afternoon sun, and they fell into his hands only to rise again. They formed varying shapes and designs. They flowed in an arch. They spouted high and fell to right and left, and presently the speed of the hands was so great that they disappeared from the eye, like the whirring wings of a hummingbird, and only the stones remained, darting up through the air as though they were endowed with the will and the freedom of flight.

Tremendous shouts of applause followed this exhibition, which continued until they drew up in front of the old inn.

There they dismounted, and the stones disappeared in the pocket of Speedy as he hurried forward to hold the head of his master's horse. There he stood patiently, looking straight before him. But the lads knew, now, that he was at least something more than a fool, and they kept at a distance, making a wide circle around him.

"Are you a circus?" one of them asked, as big John Wilson strode into the entrance of the inn.

"I'm not even a peg of a circus tent," Speedy answered, speaking very good, slangy Mexican.

They whooped at his answer. They pressed closer. They wanted to know if he could juggle knives, swallow fire, eat snakes. They poured out their questions, until a servant came out from the inn at a dog-trot, to say that the master had found a room and that he would show the way to the stable.

There was a patio, with the stable on one side of it, the inn on the other side, and Speedy soon saw the two horses put up and feed of wretched, sunburned hay pitched into the manger. Then he was led into the hotel and showed the room that Wilson had selected.

For Wilson there was a bed. For the servant, a pair of sheepskins were thrown on the floor. They would serve as both bed and covering. No, there was a straw pallet, brought at Wilson's insistence, and the big sheepskins, skins of the fine mountain sheep, were stretched over it. Water was brought for the washing of hands. Supper, it appeared, would be ready just after sunset. Then they were left alone.

Their window looked over the garden at the back of the inn, and from that window big John Wilson stared at the arch of the doorway in the wall. This wall held back the earth and rock that otherwise would have caved in from the hillside to the very door of the inn. The face of the door was dark; it looked the iron that Speedy had declared it to be. Above it, with a rope of cloth hanging down under it, was a large bell.

Wilson continued to stare. The garden was empty, except for one elderly man who sat on a bench in the sun with something to drink in a glass beside him while he read his newspaper with his wide-brimmed straw hat tilted back to keep out the slant rays.

Speedy was busily working, laying out the pack of Wilson, when the latter said: "Don't carry on that nonsense of being a servant, Speedy, when we're alone."

"It's better to keep inside the part, whether there's an eye looking at you or not," Speedy advised him.

"Tell me one thing," said Wilson.

"Yes?"

"Why did you do the juggling? What was that for, Speedy? Won't it call too much attention to you?"

"People, pretty soon," Speedy explained, "may start asking why you insist on having me with you, even when you're on the other side of that iron door. Well, they might as well know that I have a pair of hands and know how to do a few things with them. It will save you from a lot of explanations, perhaps. Besides, it amused me."

"It will be sunset in an hour or more," said Wilson, "and that's the time for us to ring the bell, isn't it?"

"Yes, of course."

"Then we'd better put our heads together and do some planning," suggested Wilson.

"There's nothing to plan," said Speedy. "We've talked everything over once, and, if we talk it over again, we'll only confuse ourselves. I'm going to have a nap."

Instantly he was stretched out on the pallet of straw, with a sheepskin over him and his eyes closed.

X

Wilson, regarding him rather grimly, made sure that his companion was actually asleep. His eyes were not only closed, but, ten seconds afterward, his chest was rising and falling with a gentle regularity. The whole of the slender body was relaxed and Wilson looked down on the smaller man with both awe and wonder. He knew what strength was locked up in it, but, as he looked at the slender outlines of the man, what he remembered about him now seemed incredible. Then he went back to the window and remained there, his elbows resting on the deep casement, staring at the iron door for some minutes.

Nothing had changed in the garden; the man sat on the same bench. Nothing had altered about him, not even in the crossing of his legs, except that the red liquid in the glass had diminished.

Wilson went back to his own bed and sat down on the edge of it. The whole thing seemed to him very like an elaborate jest. Beyond a doubt, there was nothing behind that door but the solid wall of the hillside. Perhaps there never had been. Perhaps the whole matter was a fairy tale invented by the active imagination of Speedy for his diversion and to put an edge on his nerves. At least one thing was certain—Speedy was capable of any hoax, no matter how gigantic.

He drew out his revolver, cleaned it carefully, reloaded it, and then looked to the big, long-bladed hunting knife that he carried. Even with both of those tried weapons, he could not feel secure, and yet Speedy, with empty hands, with nothing but the strength of his slender body, was prepared to face the danger.

Suppose, in spite of the disguise, that they should recognize him. Suppose that someone looked hard at the right profile, disregarding the left, and in spite of the darkness of the skin recognized something of the fine features of this strange youth? Men who had once seen Speedy in action were not likely to forget any of his features for a long time. These ideas were crowding through the mind of Wilson when a light hand fell on his shoulder.

He leaped to his feet. He barely kept himself from shouting aloud, and there he found Speedy, standing beside him, with the grotesquely distorted face and grave eyes.

"It is time, *señor*," Speedy said.

"How did you get off that pallet without making the straw in it crackle?" asked Wilson, breathing hard from the shock he had had.

"Patience and prayer," Speedy said soberly, "accomplish many things. Otherwise, I cannot tell how it was done, *señor*."

Wilson muttered something to himself, clapped his hat on his head, and gave it a jerk to bring it well down over his eyes.

Through the casement, he saw that the garden wall was red-gold in the sunset light, and the bell above the iron door was gilded likewise. He was not sixty seconds, perhaps, from the strangest adventure that he had ever met, and the most dangerous. But, squaring his shoulders and drawing in a deep breath, Wilson made a sign of his hand and nodded.

"We'll start, Speedy," he said.

Then he strode first through the door, the perfect picture of a master, down the stairs, and through the short corridor into the garden.

The man with the newspaper lowered it, looked at them, folded the paper, and looked again. A second drink seemed to have been brought to him, for the glass was half full again. He sipped, detached a cigarette from one of the little bundles of handmade ones that were tied to the brim of his straw hat, and lighted it. Through a cloud of thin smoke, he continued to observe the two strangers.

Wilson stopped before him. "What does that door open on, *amigo?*" he asked.

The man with the straw hat shook his head.

"Well," Wilson said, "I've heard that there's really something behind it."

"Perhaps, *señor*," said the Mexican. "One never knows. The gold that a man hunts for may all the while be in the rocks on which he has built his house. As for me, I know nothing."

"What's the bell for that hangs over it?" asked John Wilson.

"As for me, *señor*," said the other, "I was raised well and taught to answer all the questions whose answers I know. As for those I do not know, I give you my regrets, *señor*, and commend you to heaven . . . with your servant." He took off his hat, as he spoke, and revealed a thatch of thick, iron-gray hair on his head.

But John Wilson had an idea, and a very shrewd one, that the bow of the Mexican was chiefly to cover a leering smile, some traces of which still showed in his face as he straightened himself again.

Once more Wilson looked at the door before him, and then strode straight up to it. There was no doorknob to it. It looked rather like a heavy panel inset among the rocks. He shrugged his shoulders and suddenly laid his hand on the rag of worn, rotting rope extending from the bell. It was barely within reaching distance. As he gripped it, a sharp cry from the inn went through him like the edge of a knife. He jerked his head over his shoulder and saw first the distorted face and the calm eyes of Speedy, and, beyond Speedy, there was the dim image of a woman's figure disappearing from the dark arch of the window of the very room that they had just left. His blood went cold and his brain grew dizzy. However, his hand was already on the rope, and now he jerked it down.

The bell was cracked; moreover, the clapper was

layered about with thick, red rust, and the result of the strong tug was merely a dull, unmusical, toneless reverberation that sounded like hollow mockery to the ear of John Wilson. He made a step back from the iron panel.

"This is all nonsense, Speedy," he said.

"Well, perhaps it is," muttered Speedy, "but that name. . . ."

A shudder went through Wilson as he realized that he had used the forbidden name that would reveal the identity of Speedy in case an ear were pressed close to the inside of that doorway.

"I'll try again," Wilson said gloomily. "But it seems to me just a lot of rot." He stepped forward, grasped the rope, and then the voice of Speedy stopped him.

"If there is nothing but the hillside to hear, *señor*, why should we wake up the stone with our noise."

To Wilson, it seemed that this was either some elaborate hint that he could not understand, or else it was sheerest nonsense.

Then suddenly, soundlessly, as though upon well-oiled hinges, the door opened. Jet black darkness was within that doorway, and whoever had opened it was invisible.

"Well?" John Wilson said. It seemed to him that a dim echo of his own voice came back to him, but he could not be sure. He turned his head and saw that the man of the straw hat had disappeared, leaving his half-finished glass of wine, if wine it were. A sudden sense of chilly mystery swept over the soul of John Wilson.

"Well, Pedro," he said, "there's the door open, at last. And nothing to see inside."

"*Señor*," said Speedy, "you observe that we are no longer inside it, do you not?"

"I observe," Wilson started to say angrily, and then he remembered that, after all, it was not a real servant who stood at his heels, but one whose hints were orders. He settled his hat more firmly on his head and strode through the doorway.

Instantly it clanged heavily behind him!

XI

Wilson, in the darkness, had out his gun instantly. He stepped back, put his shoulders against the cold of the iron door, and stared into the swimming blackness before his eyes. But there was nothing to be seen, no light whatever, except the red gleams that his own excited imagination called up. He strode forward a few steps and bumped his head on the low ceiling of the passage. His elbows touched the sides of the tunnel—rough pebbles and dirt that brushed away and fell rattling about his feet.

Then a sudden, powerful sense of stifling came on him. His heart raced; he choked. So he stood for a moment with bent head, convincing himself that the sensations were merely the result of an overstrong imagination. If Speedy were only there to take charge, to tell him what to do. But what could even Speedy suggest at a time like this? He could not help wondering, again, if Speedy had not planned the whole affair as a great jest.

He started forward again, keeping one hand raised above his head to ward off another collision, and worked gradually on until he thought he heard the light *crunch* of a footfall on the gravel path behind him. He tried to turn, but his shoulders were wedged in tightly. A light flashed, with a little ringing sound of metal, as though the shutter of a bull's-eye lantern had been pushed back, and at the same instant a blow crushed against the back of his head. He pitched forward into more utter darkness.

When he opened his eyes, flames were whirling before them. The flames cleared to the penetrating brightness of sunlight. No, it was only the dull glow of a lantern that fell upon his face.

And then a voice said above him: "He's coming around."

He tried to move his hands, but found that the wrists were bound stiffly together with rope that cut painfully into his skin. He was lying, he discovered, in a small shack. The air was warmed by a fire in a small cooking stove on top of which a pot steamed. There was the fragrance of coffee through the place. Instantly it made him hungry, so hungry that he forgot the pain in his head. That pain, oddly enough, was not at the base of the skull where the blow had fallen, but straight across his forehead, just above the eyes.

He lay on a damp, earthen floor. Seated on a stool beside him was a man in a blue flannel shirt with a cartridge belt strapped around his hips and a Colt in a leather holster weighting it down at one side. He was a broad chunk of a man, nursing a short-stemmed pipe in a hand that had a blue anchor printed across the back of it, the anchor chain disappearing up the sleeve of the shirt.

"He's comin' around, Bones," said the watcher.

"Let him come, Sid," said the other.

John Wilson turned his head. On the other side of

the shack was the second speaker, Bones, tall and gaunt enough to warrant the use of that nickname. There was always a smile on his face, owing to the outthrust of a large pair of upper teeth, but the wrinkles around the eyes and the gleam of the eyes themselves gave no hint of good nature. He worked with rapid, deft fingers at the construction of a horsehair braid that might become, later on, part of a bridle, perhaps. His shirt was blue flannel, like Sid's, but he had added to it the surprising decoration of a red necktie.

"You can sit up, brother," Sid said to Wilson.

The prisoner raised himself, hitched about, and put his back against the wall. "This is better," he announced calmly.

"Want anything?" asked Sid.

"No," Wilson answered, still perfectly calm. "A new head, maybe. That's all."

"That's the trouble with Bones," commented Sid. "Always thinks that the other gent has a head made of iron, like his own. That's the trouble with you, Bones."

"Aw, shut your face," Bones said, yawning. "What made you ring the bell, brother?"

"Curiosity," said Wilson.

"And what else?"

"Nothing to tell you."

"No?"

"No," Wilson said steadily.

"I got half a mind to sock you again," Bones said, pausing in his work for the first time and looking steadily at the captive.

Wilson answered nothing.

"Whacha expect to see when the door opened and you went into the tunnel?" asked Sid, as Bones industriously resumed the braiding of the horsehair.

"Well," Wilson said, "I expected to see Dupray."

Sid rose, went to the stove, poured out some coffee into a cup, and sipped it.

"Cool, ain't he?" he asked of Bones.

"Yeah, he's cool," Bones agreed, without looking up.

"He's all-fired cool," said Sid, insisting on the point, "is what he is. I dunno but what he's cool enough to do."

"What you know don't matter," suggested Bones.

"Aw, leave off sticking pins and needles in everybody," Sid said. "This bird, he's cool, is what he is. What's your name, brother?"

"That's for Dupray," said Wilson.

"Listen to him," said Sid. "Listen at him, will you? All right, son. You're gonna talk to Dupray. Maybe you'll wish that you hadn't talked before you're through, though. Here comes the chief now, I guess."

A footfall came up to the door of the cabin and a little man with a pale, round face entered. He looked like a cross between a half-breed Chinaman and a frog. To increase the strangeness of his face, he was wearing a skullcap of black silk that appeared when he took off his hat. He paused as he entered, and looked at the prisoner.

"That's the one, eh?" he remarked.

Neither Bones nor Sid answered this question. The newcomer sat down on the edge of the center table and folded his hands in his lap. His hands were as small and sleek as the hands of a woman. Like Chinamen of high caste, he wore his fingernails very long.

As he looked down at the prisoner, he said: "You never saw me before, did you?"

"No," said Wilson.

"Who are you, then?"

"I'll tell you when I find out who you are," Wilson told him.

Sid observed again: "He's cool, Charley. Look at how cool he is, and with his head all busted by Bones, a minute ago."

"Shut up," commanded the other. He added, to Wilson: "Who do you think I am?"

"I think you're Charley Dupray."

"Suppose I am."

"If you are, I'll talk."

"I'm Dupray," said the little man. "Who are you?"

"I'm John Wilson."

"Wilson, or was it Smith that you said, or Jones, or Brown?" asked Dupray.

His eyes were slits, the pupils shifting almost out of sight when they moved up and down. He was the ugliest piece of flesh that ever had been called a man, it seemed to Wilson.

"My name is Wilson," said the captive.

" 'Wilson, that's all,' " quoted Sid with a grin.

Dupray turned his round, frog-like head toward his man, and Sid stepped a little to the side, as though to get away from the impact of that glance.

"Your name is Wilson, then," Dupray concluded, nodding his round head as he looked back at the man on the floor.

"Yes," said John Wilson.

"What brought you up here?"

"I was looking for something to do."

"What?"

"Quick money," Wilson said.

"That's it, is it?"

"Yes."

"Going to get your quick money out of me?"

"You'll point the way for me."

"Will I?"

"Yes," said Wilson.

"Cool, that's what he is. He's cool as a cucumber," murmured Sid, his admiration increasing, although his voice was much lowered.

"What makes you think that I'll use you?" said Dupray.

"You can't afford to turn me down," said Wilson.

"No?"

"You can't afford to. I'm the stuff that you want," said the captive.

"What do I want?"

"You want steady nerves . . . I've got 'em. You want a good rider . . . I'm that. You want a good shot . . . I'll stand up to the best."

"You've got a lingo, anyway," declared Dupray. "Where did you hear about me?"

"All over the range."

"Where did you hear about the iron door and the bell?"

"From Speedy," Wilson stated.

The foolish words had dropped from his lips involuntarily. His hair lifted on his scalp. His eyes, however, he controlled, keeping them calm and fixed steadily on the face of the other.

The name Speedy, however, had caused an instant sensation. Bones leaped to his feet; Sid, with an exclamation, actually snatched out a revolver. Even the frog face of Dupray wrinkled all over with hate and with malice as he heard the word.

"Speedy's a friend of yours, is he?" asked Dupray.

"He used to be," Wilson answered.

"What made him a friend?"

"He pulled me out of a hole once."

"How was that?"

"I was having some trouble with a fellow called Slade Bennett."

"You knew Slade Bennett?" Dupray asked, his eyes gleaming again.

"Yes. Pretty well, but not for long."

"How did you come to know him?"

"By fighting him."

"With your hands?"

"No, with guns."

"He dropped you, eh?"

"No, I killed him," said the prisoner.

"He killed Slade Bennett," breathed Bones. Only gradually the tall, skinny fellow reseated himself, his eyes round as they stared at the captive.

"You say you killed Bennett. I remember, now, it was a man named Wilson that killed Slade. Slade was my friend." Dupray paused for an answer.

Wilson merely shrugged his shoulders, as though words were not necessary. He added: "Well, Bennett picked the fight. But that doesn't matter. I'm glad I bumped him off."

For the first time, Dupray smiled a little. And the expression did not make his face more attractive. "You killed my friend, Bennett . . . Speedy sent you up here . . . and still you think you can have a place with me?" he asked.

"If I didn't think that," said Wilson, "why would I have come?"

Even the inhuman, cold eyes of Dupray were opened a little by the blunt shock of this question. "Because you're a fool, perhaps," he said.

"Because," Wilson said, "I didn't think you were fool enough to have a man like me tapped on the head by way of introduction to your crowd. But I'm going to come in, Dupray, and I'm going to bring my servant in with me."

XII

Dupray, with the tip of a pale-red tongue, moistened his lips, and all the time he looked at Wilson with eyes as thoughtful as those of a cat when it considers a helpless mouse. "Bluff won't work up here," he said, shaking his head at last.

"Do you call this a bluff?" asked Wilson. And he lifted his bound hands.

"Cool, that's what he is," came the whisper of Sid. "Damn cool, I call it."

"Speedy," Dupray said. "How long have you known him?"

"I knew him for three days," Wilson said. "Afterward, he got tired of me."

"What made him tired?"

"He didn't like the way I treated my wife."

"How did you treat her?"

"I left her."

"Why?"

"I couldn't stand the ranch life. Riding herd and that sort of business, it was nothing for me."

"What sort of work do you think you'd have with me?" demanded Dupray.

"Work with something more to it than cows and one day like the other day."

"You intend to go back to her?" asked Dupray.

"Why should I go back to her?" asked Wilson. "The ranch and the ranch life will be just the same when I go back."

"This rot about the servant," Dupray said. "You think that I'd take in a greaser, a common peon, to ride with me?"

"He's not common, and he's not exactly a greaser. He's got a lot of white blood in him."

"Has he?"

"Yes, he has."

"And what makes you think that you can come in here with a body servant?" Dupray asked, tilting his head a little to one side.

"Because you'll want me . . . and because I'm used to having somebody to look after me."

"He's got a nerve, is what he's got," Bones said. "A servant, eh?"

"What can this greaser do . . . what's his name?"

"Pedro."

"What can he do, then?"

"Cook, make a patch, sew on buttons, clean knives and guns, cut up game, roll cigarettes."

"You can't roll your own, eh?" Dupray said, sneering.

"Pedro can roll 'em better," Wilson stated.

"I'm going to take in Pedro so that you won't have to roll your own? What else can the fool do?"

It was plain that Dupray was much irritated. "He can do anything that he's needed for," Wilson said. "Including putting a knife in anybody's throat."

"Oh, he's a knife expert, is he?"

"He is. He can stand five paces off and hit a mark half an inch wide with a knife."

"He can't," Dupray contradicted.

"He can, though," argued Wilson. He cast back in his mind. At five paces, a line half an inch long dwindles so that it looks hardly more than a pencil stroke. Was it possible that Speedy could actually hurl a knife and strike it? He felt that he had overshot the mark a good deal in making this boast. But Speedy could accomplish almost anything to which he set his hand.

"Suppose that I believe you," Dupray said, "and you bring in the peon, Pedro, and let him try his hand at hitting a half-inch mark at five paces." He grinned with sudden, irrepressible malice as he made the suggestion.

"Well?" Wilson said.

"If he can do that two times out of three, even," Dupray said, "then I'll believe the other lies that you've been telling me, and I'll take you into the band, let you have this Pedro to take care of you like a baby in the cradle, if you wish. But if . . . ," and he paused, and was lost a moment in thought. "But," he repeated, "if he fails, I'll cut his throat before your eyes and cut yours afterward. That's all. Bones, go get the greaser."

He turned his back on the prisoner at this and, sitting down close beside the stove, he held out his gray hands to the warmth of it, although already the room was quite hot. More than ever, he seemed to big John Wilson a mere cold-blooded creature and not human at all.

This was the Dupray of whom, along the latter part of the journey, Speedy had told such strange tales. This was the Dupray who could speak a dozen languages, forge any man's handwriting after a few moments' study of a specimen, ride any horse that walked, endure privations that would kill a dozen others, shoot like a heaven-inspired lightning flash, outwit the cleverest, read the very mind of a combination lock. This was the man who had made fortune after fortune and piled up treasure that, it was said, he never spent—a bloodless miser, who increased his store and gloried only in money for the sake of money. This was the great Dupray, who now crouched before the stove, almost hugging it with his arms.

Well, this was a strange world, it seemed to John Wilson. There was Speedy, who looked like a too-handsome stripling, good for nothing but charming to the ladies, with the soul of a demon and the cunning of a cougar.

Suppose, then, that Bones tried to bring Speedy. Bones would simply die on the way, and perhaps Speedy, before long, would be prowling about the cabin, bent on extricating his friend. For upon the perfect faith of Speedy, whatever else might be true of him, upon his absolute loyalty to a friend in need, Wilson knew that he could depend.

For his own part, he was still a little dizzy after the ordeal that he had passed through, facing the frog-like features of Dupray, and the wild pulsation of his heart was only gradually beginning to subside.

The minutes passed. Not a person in the cabin moved except Sid, who occasionally, as he stood at the open door, turned and glanced at the captive, then gave his attention once more to the outdoors.

Finally he said: "All right. They're here."

"Both?" Dupray asked.

"Both," said Sid.

He stepped back from the door, and through it

came Speedy; as he stood blinking a little at the lantern light, he saw Wilson.

"*¡El señor!*" he cried, and, throwing out his hands, he leaped for Wilson.

Sid, without a word, struck that leaping figure solidly on the side of the head and knocked Speedy flat on the floor.

Dupray had regarded the whole scene over his shoulder, unconcerned. "That's all right, Sid," he said. "Pick the fool up. Draw a half inch line on the door, Bones. Half an inch wide and a foot long."

It was done. Speedy was picked up from the floor, and, as he stood with his hands to his head, Wilson said: "There's no trouble, Pedro. It's only a little test that's to be given you, and I know you can do it. Stand across the cabin floor . . . and throw a knife into a half-inch mark."

"Ah," Speedy said, shaking his head, "that is not a wide mark, *señor*."

Dupray had turned his back on the scene once more. His hands continued to hover over the hot surface of the stove.

He said: "Pedro, you'll hit that mark, or else I'll have your throat cut first, and your master's throat cut second. Do you understand me?"

"The good saints!" gasped Speedy.

"You'll find Satan more used to this sort of a place," Dupray remarked. "Are you ready?" Still he did not turn his head, but faced the stove.

"*¿Señor?*" Speedy pleaded, holding out pathetic hands to Wilson.

Wilson wondered at him, the subtlety and the depth of the acting, the pathos of that heartbreaking and frightened voice, with the chattering of the teeth at the end of the word. "Pedro," he stated, "it is true. You hit the mark two times out of three, or else. . . ." He paused. The pause said more than words. And the heart of John Wilson fell like a stone.

Bones was marking off the five paces, while Speedy cried out, wringing his slender brown-stained hands: "Ah, but you step too far. The paces are altogether too long."

"He said five paces. He didn't say how long them paces was to be," Bones snapped, and grinned. Still grinning, and then nervously licking his ever-dry upper lip, the tall man stood by, a gun in his hand.

Speedy held up both hands to the ceiling as though to call the saints to witness this injustice. As a matter of fact, it was not fifteen feet, but nearer to twenty where he took his post, near the farther wall of the cabin. Three hunting knives were stuck into a log beside him, ready to his hand.

One moment Speedy murmured, as though repeating a prayer, his eyes closed, his fragile body wavering a little from side to side. Then, with a quick catch of his breath, he caught up one of the knives and balanced it carefully in the palm of his hand.

There was a partial mist before the eyes of Wilson. It might be that in practice, with nothing depending upon it, Speedy could perform the difficult feat, but surely no human being in the world could do the thing with the chilly eyes of death itself fixed upon him. But now he was standing with his toe on the mark, and his eyes fixed burningly on the target.

"Put the lantern nearer to the line," he commanded briefly, huskily.

The order was obeyed in silence.

Then, swiftly, the brown hand went back, and the knife slithered out of the palm, struck the door with a distinct shock, and was fixed there, humming like a bee.

Bones leaped to the spot with one bound.

"A miss!" he shouted. "He missed it by a full inch!"

XIII

Fear became in John Wilson an electric thing that caused the heart to contract, and suddenly a tingling rush of cold enveloped his forehead and shot into the roots of his hair then down, sweeping through his hands and out to the fingertips.

Speedy, in the meantime, had groaned aloud and again threw up his brown hands to implore luck.

It was interesting to note the behavior of the others. Sid took on an air of real concern and looked with an anxious frown toward the target that Pedro had failed to hit, but Bones was openly exulting, even laughing a little, as he looked toward the frozen face of John Wilson. Strangest of all was the behavior of the great Dupray, for he had not turned his head for a single instant, but continued to extend his hands over the stove.

He merely said: "He has two more chances to make his hits. Then we'll do something about it, if he misses."

Vaguely John Wilson wondered what would happen. When Pedro missed, the others could not realize that they would have on their hands not a frightened Mexican, but Speedy himself, raging among them at close quarters. Perhaps he would try to knock over the lantern, first of all, and then to liberate the prisoner and put a weapon in his hand. But what good would that be, when the force of the ropes had numbed the arms of Wilson almost to the elbow?

At any rate, there was Speedy, balancing the second knife in his hand and giving a little cry as he hurled it, far harder than the first.

Bones did not advance so eagerly this time. He merely leaned a little forward, and growled: "Well, he had some luck, that time. He split the middle of the line."

"He's getting the range, perhaps," Dupray suggested. Still the man did not turn his head, but now he began to rub his cold hands together and feverishly hold them out toward the warmth once more. His whole concern was apparently more to warm his hands than any interest in the death of two men, which was about to be decided by the next cast of a knife.

Swiftly Speedy picked the third knife from the wall and nursed it for a moment in his cunning right hand, narrowing his eyes toward the mark. Again the hand quickly jerked back, and John Wilson closed his eyes.

He heard the *thud* of the knife; he heard the *hum* of it as it quivered in the wood, and then, as that humming died out, there was silence. That silence seemed to endure for centuries. John Wilson strove to open his eyes, but he could not. He was seeing, in his imagination, the long, skinny hand of Bones reaching for the throat of Speedy, and Dupray still at the stove with his back turned, but mysteriously aware of all that was happening.

Then said the voice of Bones in a gasp: "Damn, he's cut the mark again. There it is, right on the edge of the mark, but in it, all right."

John Wilson opened his eyes and took a breath. He had been almost stifled during the preceding moments. Then he saw that Speedy was picking the three knives out of the door and laying them carefully upon the center table.

At this, Dupray turned suddenly from before the stove, strode quickly around the table, and, coming up to Speedy, laid the muzzle of a revolver against his breast. His left hand fell upon the shoulder of Pedro, and his eyes were fastened upon him.

"Who are you?" Dupray asked in English.

"Pedro, *señor*," Speedy answered.

"You lie!" Dupray accused.

The eyes of Speedy opened. He looked, as if wondering at this strange talk, toward John Wilson.

Wilson bit his lip—so much had that eloquent glance tempted him to speak. But he very well understood, in his heart, that the look was no more than a gesture, with no meaning behind it. It was Speedy who would have to speak the final words in this matter.

"You lie," Dupray repeated insistently. "You're no more a Mexican than I am. You're acting a part. You're no more afraid than I am. You're not shaking. You're steady as a rock."

Wilson, staring with horror, saw the truth so rapidly revealed.

Speedy said: "Why should I be afraid, *señor*, since two of the three knives hit the mark?"

"Bah," Dupray said, and thrust him away.

Speedy staggered, seemed to lose balance, and fell back heavily, his shoulders against the wall.

Dupray followed him a single step. His head thrust out. There was a suggestion of malicious cruelty in his whole attitude. But suddenly he snapped his fingers and went hastily back to the stove, over which he extended his hands once more. "I have to take chances on everything," he said, no longer regarding Speedy, now cowering against the door, under the leveled gun of Bones. "I take a chance on you, Wilson. You have nerve enough, and, if you're able to do as much as a man, as Pedro's able to do as a servant, you'll be worth my while. Bones, set him free. Fix him up with a bunk, blankets, anything he wants. I'll see him again in the morning. We ride to-morrow, you know, and we may try the pair of them together on the trip."

He left the stove and went to the door as he spoke. Stepping out into the night without any other farewell, he said, without turning his head: "You can tell them where we ride." He was gone, even the last words dying out as he continued straight ahead into the darkness.

Bones, for a moment, stared toward the opened doorway, then, with a grunt and a shrug of his shoulders, he approached Wilson and cut the rope that held his hands.

Wilson stood up.

"How are you feeling, partner?" asked Sid.

"Hungry," Wilson answered, although that was not the readiest word to his lips.

"Bones, you're the cook," said Sid.

"No, no," said Wilson. "There's Pedro here. A good cook. Pedro," he added in Mexican, "food for the three of us, and enough scraps left over for you, too, at the end."

Speedy made a gesture of assent and hurried to explore the larder. He found the usual supplies: bacon, white flour, cornmeal, a few potatoes, old, withered onions, some cans of tomatoes, one of plum jam. There was coffee, of course, in plenty. Straightway he began to busy himself with the food, and, as he worked, the strains of an old Mexican song filled his throat and floated softly through the room.

"Shut up that noise!" Bones cried angrily.

John Wilson raised one finger. "He sings to please me," he informed Bones.

"And who in the mischief are you but a damn' recruit?" exclaimed Bones, his smile hardening about his buckteeth.

"Why," John Wilson said, "from this time on, I'm as good as anybody you know, except Dupray. And what about you, Bones? What are you good for?"

Speedy, turning an instant from his cookery, observed the pair of them—Wilson obviously resenting that blow in the dark that had struck him down, and ready enough to fight on account of it, and Bones equally determined not to give ground.

It both raised and depressed the heart of Speedy. If anything were to quell the spirit of John Wilson, what he had just been through seemed enough to have lowered his courage, at least. Instead of that, he seemed as aggressive as ever, and his eyes were filled with fire as he stared at the tall, thin form of Bones.

"Gentlemen," Speedy interrupted cheerfully, "when the flood comes, the lion lies down by the lamb, and the bird sleeps safely on the same branch with the serpent. Are we not all friends, now that we are all together?"

Wilson and Bones continued to glare at one another, but Sid pressed in between them.

"Steady," Sid soothed. "You boys don't want to make trouble. You've had trouble enough for one night, Wilson. And you, Bones, know what the chief does when anybody starts a fight in camp. Back up, the pair of you."

"I'll back up when there's somebody able to make me back up," declared Bones. "I'll have more air, in the meantime, while I wait for another day." So saying, he stalked out of the cabin.

XIV

Never were the cunning fingers of Speedy more expert and rapid than in the preparation of that meal. Sid and the new recruit, John Wilson, talked together while Speedy cut the rashers of bacon, making them translucently thin. Then he was mixing cornmeal with flour for frying, and, after the bacon had become crisp, a shower of transparent slices of potatoes fell into the same pan. In no time at all, the meal was served—a place for Sid, a place for John Wilson, while Speedy served them, eating a covert mouthful now and then, it appeared, while he was returning to the stove for one thing or another.

They ate, and Sid talked over the meal. It was his second supper that night, but his appetite was good. It was, he said, something worthwhile to eat food prepared like this, and for his part he could understand why Wilson carried a servant about with him on his travels. Sid would try the same thing, one day, but where was one to find another Mexican like Pedro?

"They're born like Pedro, not made that way," Wilson commented dryly. Then he wanted to know where they were to ride the next day, and Sid told them briefly.

It was a simple job. The stage to Red Rock from Cumberland was bringing over a heavy shipment of gold bullion. The point for the hold-up had been picked out. The driver of the stage was a green hand. The guard was a known fool and probably a coward. Sid missed his guess if a single shot would have to be fired, beyond a salvo to bring the stage to a halt. They would soon gut the coach, and take whatever was worthwhile from the passengers.

"But," Sid added, "that ain't what bothers me. It's a dead-easy job, but we oughta leave things alone, as close to home as the Red Rock stage. Everybody'll know that we had a hand in the work. And what we want around our own front yard is peace and quiet and good neighbors. It gets folks stirred up . . . stage robberies do . . . when they know the gents that've been robbed. I dunno why it is, but it always gets people mad. But the way with Charley Dupray is that he can't go and leave his hand off of bullion. Solid gold and solid silver, that's what makes his mouth water. Them things . . . and jewels. He's got a fortune on him all the time in unset diamonds and emeralds, and things like that. I've seen him pour half a dozen rubies into the palm of his hand and set for an hour, staring at 'em and loving 'em. He's that kind of a gent. It's his weakness. He don't drink. He don't foller the ladies. It's only the real stuff that bothers him . . . the gold, the silver, and the jewels.

"I seen a time when we went and raided a mine and we got about a ton and a half of silver. Well, take it any way that you want to, silver ain't worth much. It's a weight, that's all it is. And we had to have a whole string of pack mules to take the stuff away.

But I tell you what, I see the chief pattin' and strokin' that bar silver like every bar was a cat that was purring. That's why he wants to go after the Red Rock stage. There's been more money aboard it lots of times, but not in gold bullion. It's the real metal that he goes drunk on."

"So that's what we're in on tomorrow?" John Wilson said.

That's what you're in on," answered the other, nodding. "Pedro, gimme another slab of them fried potatoes, will you?"

"Is that the moon rising?" asked Wilson.

"That's her, all right."

"She looks like a forest fire," said Wilson. "I'll have a look at her."

"Go ahead," answered Sid. "I'll hold down the fried potatoes while you're away."

Wilson got up and stepped through the door and a little distance into the dark so that he could see to full advantage the rising of the moon in the throat of the pass, soaring slowly up among the great pine trees. By that increasing light he could also see in outline, at least, the nature of the nearer setting. It was plainly the wreckage of an old mining camp, the cabins sitting in a huge, irregular circle, half lost among brush and saplings of twenty years' growth. In one or two of these, feeble lights glimmered and these, no doubt, were the quarters of the band of Dupray. Strongly as the mountains fenced in the hollow in which the old camp lay, even more strongly, Wilson felt, he and Speedy were enclosed in the hand of the bandit leader. What gain could come to them, he could not dream.

It even began to seem to him that love for danger, of which Speedy had spoken to him, might be a mania in the man so strong that he could not help throwing himself headlong into the most diabolical trouble, blindly hoping and trusting that he would afterward be able to break out again. Certainly there had been something insanely headlong in the whole procedure of Speedy in this matter. So, breathing deeply of the purity of the pine-scented air, Wilson struggled vaguely with the whole problem and decided that on the ride tomorrow he must certainly strive to break away.

He was still standing in the brush, watching the rising of the moon as it detached itself at last from the tops of the trees and suddenly floated a great distance into the blue-black of the sky, putting out the stars that swarmed like fireflies, when a man came stepping past him to the door of the cabin he had just left.

"Is the chief in there?" asked the stranger, as he came to the open door.

"He's over in the main shack, I guess," the voice of Sid answered dimly, from the interior.

At once the other turned and tramped away, the brush crackling like burning firewood about his feet. It was not long before a light touch plucked at the sleeve of Wilson.

He turned with a great start, and the voice of Speedy murmured: "Did you see him?"

"The stranger? Yes."

"Not a stranger," Speedy advised. "It was the old man from the garden, the fellow with the glass of wine. And he means us, by this trip, I think."

"How could he mean us?" Wilson whispered.

"What else would bring him here in such a hurry, with his eyes sticking out of his head?" Speedy asked. "Remember, we left horses and luggage back there at the hotel. They have light fingers and sharp eyes. They may have been able to put two and two together and make a million about us. Hurry. We'll follow him and see what he does."

The form of the stranger was already a mere dark blur in the distance, heading toward one of the lighted cabins, as they began the pursuit.

"Step in my tracks," Speedy muttered over his shoulder.

Wilson, obeying, found to his bewilderment that he was making no noise whatever, but weaving silently back and forth through the brush.

"What about Sid, left alone in there?" asked Wilson. "He'll grow suspicious."

"There are plenty of fried potatoes to keep Sid from thinking of anything else for quite a time to come," Speedy said. "Don't worry about him. Our worries all lie ahead of us, just now. Unless I'm very far wrong, we'll have our hands full before you've counted a hundred twice."

They saw the shadow of the stranger pause in front of the dimly lighted doorway of one of the cabins, and then the man entered. Speedy increased his pace, and in a moment they were standing at a window. It had been boarded over to keep out winter wind, or the cold breezes of the mountain night, but there were plenty of cracks through which they were able to look into the interior.

They saw three men playing cards at a table. One of them was no other than their new acquaintance, Bones. To the side of the table, just rising from a bunk and throwing back his blankets, was the great Dupray, and in front of him stood the stranger—the old man of the garden behind the inn, the newspaper, and the glass of wine, with the broad-brimmed straw hat in his hand and the thatch of splotchy gray hair.

Dupray was saying: "I told you never to come up here till you were sent for, or until you had news, and real news. What do you mean by it?"

"*Señor*," said the other, "I have news, indeed."

A horse whinnied loudly, at this moment, from the shed behind the cabin.

When the noise died down, the messenger was saying: "This is the truth that we found, *señor*. The small boys in the street saw the man with the scarred face juggle eight stones at once like a performer in a circus. When we examined the luggage that the two left behind them in the hotel, we found in the little bundle that belonged to the man of the scarred face some new strings for a guitar. Do you understand, *señor*?"

"A juggler who plays a guitar? Well, what of that?" asked Dupray.

"Is there not a saying," the old man said, bowing a little, "that the north wind can give the sky a hundred faces and that Speedy can assume even more?"

"Speedy!" exclaimed Dupray, going back a step. Then he added rapidly: "A man who can juggle, plays a guitar, and can throw a knife into a half-inch mark from a distance of twenty feet . . . who dares come up into my camp with another man and who is cooler than his master . . . Speedy! A thousand demons. I've grown old and blind. Speedy *is* in the camp." He turned on the three who were rising with stupefied faces from the table while a shower of cards fell to the floor. "Get out and at him!" exclaimed Dupray. "Gather around the cabin. But go like wildcats stalking a mountain lion. He has ears that hear everything and a wit that understands everything. Get out of the shack and surround that cabin. I'm coming with you. Quick! Quick! Don't make a move until I've joined you. Walk on eggs and hold your breath. Don't even whisper. Speedy! Oh, if I can only put a knife in his heart tonight, I'll die happy tomorrow. If I can fry the snake over a fire this evening, let me burn forever afterward."

As he spoke, that impassive face contorted to a dreadful mask, and he raised his right hand to register the vow or the threat, whichever it might be called.

The other three hastily left the place, but even their first steps they took cautiously and stealthily, as though from the first moment they were proceeding against a terrible and almost invincible power. They cleared from the front door of the cabin, and slowly crossed the brush tangles toward the light that, in the distance, marked the cabin where Speedy and his companion were supposed to be.

Two things filled the mind of Wilson, along with wonder that Speedy did not instantly give the signal for them to flee. The first was the sight of Dupray removing a little chamois sack from a vest pocket and attaching it to a buckskin thong that was looped around his neck. The second was that at his ear there was a faint sound of music that made him think that he was turning mad. Then he realized that in fact Speedy was humming, under his breath, the last Mexican tune that Wilson had heard him sing.

"To the door," Speedy murmured. "Softly . . . softly." As he spoke, he led the way, and they passed rapidly, noiselessly around the corner of the building. At the door Speedy crouched. Running steps came toward them from the interior of the shack. A shadow swept across the threshold. The body of Dupray followed. Then Speedy leaped, as a cat springs, out of the darkness of the ground, and struck Dupray helpless with a blow.

XV

There was not a groan, not a sound. There was only the dim flurry of Speedy's hands as, with flying fingers, he wound cord around the hands of his captive and inserted the gag between his teeth. Then he stood up and drew Dupray, also, to his feet.

"Carry him, John," he said to Wilson. "He's heavier than you think, but not too heavy for those shoulders of yours. Steady, now, and in two minutes we're away."

"This way," Wilson urged. "Don't go back toward the danger of. . . ."

"This way," Speedy answered with a dangerous purr in his excited voice. "Are you stopping to argue with me . . . now?"

Wilson followed, humbled and overawed, while Speedy led the way rapidly around the side of the house and to the shed behind it, from which the neighing had been heard.

"The moon, the cursed light of the moon," Speedy muttered, fumbling at the latch of the shed. "That makes everything twice as difficult. Twice, at least."

The door opened under his hands, and he entered, with Wilson following in haste to get out of the increasing flood of the silver light that might already have betrayed them if careful eyes had looked back in that direction.

In the hollow cup of his hands, Speedy shielded the match that he had lighted, but allowed sufficient radiance to escape to show the line of sleek-backed horses that stood in a long row before them—a full score of priceless mounts, hot-blooded every one of them, as John Wilson could have sworn. Two, at the nearer end, were saddled, one of the pair lying, the other still munching in his manger.

"Good," murmured Speedy. "Now we have it, John. You never thought, Dupray, that somebody outside your gang would ever thank you for keeping horses saddled and ready?"

Feverish impatience ate up the heart of Wilson. "Do we take those horses, Speedy?" he asked. "Or do we ride with this Dupray, too? What are we to do with him?"

"We're to take him back to law and order, John," Speedy declared, already throwing a saddle on the back of the next horse in line. "Hold him fast. We. . . ."

He had slid the bridle over the head of the tall horse and was drawing up the cinches, when the ears of John Wilson were split by a blood-curdling shriek from the throat of his captive:

"Help! This way! Help! The stables!"

The first yell so startled him that it was not until he had allowed those six words to escape that he clapped his hand over the mouth of the other. His hand was promptly bitten to the bone. He snatched it back and struck the face of Dupray brutally. He was rewarded by feeling the body go limp in his arms. He kicked open the door behind him and flung the limp weight over the saddle on the back of one horse, while he himself sprang into a second saddle.

Before them an uproar of shouting had broken out. Someone fired a revolver three times, the shots blending.

As Wilson mounted, he was aware of shadows running toward them through the moonlight. A volley of bullets hummed through the air above them, about them. And there was the voice of Speedy, calling: "Spur, John, spur!"

So they rushed down the hollow, neck to neck, Wilson on one side of the limp body of the outlaw, and Speedy on the other.

At the throat of the ravine, the tumult was dying out behind them. The firing had ceased, for a thick screen of trees and brush, quite shut them from the sight of the gang. Then they halted long enough to right their captive in his saddle. As he recovered consciousness, he made an effort, sat up straight, and cursed them with a low breath.

But Speedy was already tying the feet of Dupray into the stirrups. It was the best way to make sure of his careful riding. He might try to throw himself to the ground in the midst of the pursuit, otherwise. That maneuver he would never attempt, however, if it meant being dragged along the ground under the trampling hoofs of the horse.

When they had their captive secure, gagged once more, lest he should guide the pursuit by a yell at the critical moment, they rode on again, but not at full speed. There were two things against that, Speedy said. In the first place they did not know the trail perfectly. In the second place, nothing saps the strength and wind of a horse so much as to run it suddenly at full speed before it has a chance to grow warm with work, particularly in the cold of mountain air. And what cold it was.

As they climbed the next hill, they saw the pass stretching before them and rode down it with a long, swinging canter that turned the air into a rapidly flowing river of ice water, numbing them from head to foot. The very vitals of John Wilson turned into a lump of ice finally, as the voice of Speedy made him look back. He could see a dozen dark forms of riders streaming over the ridge of the hill behind, in sharp pursuit.

But still Speedy would not allow them to ride at full speed.

"They're catching up with us, Speedy!" shouted Wilson. "Do you see?"

The last frantic question was like a bullet kicking up the dust of the road before them.

"Pull down to a trot for this grade," was the calm command of Speedy in answer.

Wilson, overcome by a wave of horror and awe, obeyed in spite of himself.

All the rest had been nothing, absolutely nothing. Not the blackness inside the tunnel of the iron door, nor the cold questions Dupray had put to him, nor the frightful moment when Speedy was striking at the mark for both their sakes, nor the blood-chilling instant when, in the stable, the voice of Dupray had screeched for help so close at hand—none of those moments was of any weight, to Wilson, compared with the time they spent trotting their horses up that grade, while a host of yelling demons flogged and spurred their frantic horses after them, and Dupray rode with his head turned, fiercely devouring that hope. No, nothing else was of the slightest account.

Was he a man who loved danger? Never, if danger meant zest gained by an experience such as this. An utter sickness came over Wilson, and then a blind, rioting panic. He hardly knew what he was doing as he put the spurs into the tender flanks of his horse. Not until the dark crown of the hill rose like the crest of a wave between him and the pursuit, not until that moment did he realize that he had abandoned a tried comrade in the hour of need. But what need was there for loitering at the jaws of death, as Speedy had chosen perversely to do?

He pulled back to a hand gallop, and then saw Speedy and the form of Dupray beside him, swing over the crest, still at a trot, and then break into a swift gallop down the incline. Behind them, hardly a moment away, came the others, charging. And every rider of them was firing as he came!

Well, they were shooting from very irregular firing platforms for one thing, and at swiftly moving targets for another, and there was only the treacherous light of the moon to show them their prize. Yet it seemed wonderful to Wilson, nevertheless, most wonderful that Speedy had dared to toy with the danger as long as this, letting it close in on him to such a degree. That it was partly generalship, as well as mere love of peril, was obvious, however, in almost the same moment, for those eager riders in pursuit had driven their horses frantic, had burned them up in the first mile, and winded them most of all in rushing the steep grade of the hill.

For now, suddenly, they began to fall behind. They left off shooting. They were devoting all their efforts to flogging and spurring their spent horses to a greater effort. Well, how can men, suddenly alarmed in the middle of the night, be expected to remember calmly that a horse that can journey 100 miles between sunrise and sunset, may also be exhausted by one single mile of sprinting?

Speedy drew alongside, and still he was keeping his horse well in hand. The moon struck on the face of Dupray and showed the silent agony that contorted it as he gave up the last hope.

Out of the shame and the bitterness of his heart, Wilson cried out: "Speedy, forgive me if you can!"

"Forgive you?" Speedy called cheerfully. "Why, man, everybody loses his head once in a lifetime, at least. Besides, I may have drawn it a bit fine. I thought their hands would be too cold for straight shooting off a galloping horse."

XVI

They were through the pass and had got down in the valley, with the wide lowlands spread before them and San Lorenzo marked in white on the horizon, their road winding pleasantly over an easy, level plain. Wilson rode at the side of the frog-faced man; Speedy was in the rear, as always. But now he rode up and said to his friend:

"Look here, John. I didn't show you these." He picked from his pocket a small chamois sack.

"This is what Dupray tied under his shirt. I took it away from him while we were scuffling around. And it's no wonder that he preferred to wear the stuff nearest to his heart." As he spoke, he turned the little sack upside down, and out of the open mouth of it streamed a shower of blood-red flame.

At least, so it seemed as it first caught the eye. Then Wilson saw the rubies heaped high on the palm of Speedy, the sunlight weltering, ebbing, and flaring as he moved his hand.

"Just in case Charley Dupray should find himself shipwrecked on a desert island," Speedy murmured. "This would fill his eye and his dull moments . . . it would fill the eye of any jeweler in the world, too. What a necklace this would make, John. Yes, for the Queen of England, or Missus van Rockheimer. Look at this big fat one with the bright face. How would that do as a pendant, or to put into the business end of a king's scepter, eh?"

"It's a beauty," John Wilson agreed, nodding his head.

"Not very many in the world better than this, are there, Charley?" Speedy asked.

The criminal turned his head, looked at the great stone for a moment, and then jerked his eyes away again, as though he could not endure to see the stone in another hand. "I'll tell you this, Speedy," Dupray said, "I can take you to a place where you'll find enough jewels to make that heap in your hand look like nothing at all. You could have the lot of 'em . . . all the jewels and all of the hard cash." He passed the pale, pink tip of his tongue over his bloodless lips. It was like the rapid flicker of the tongue of a snake. He shuddered, in spite of the heat of the sun. "I'd turn over the whole thing to you two fellows. You'd be rich for life, and your children after you. That's what you'd be. Rich forever! And that means great and famous, or better than great and famous. People turn into aristocrats in this world after they've had money in the family for ten years. All they need to do is to set up a racing stable, buy an oil painting or two, entertain the queen of Bulmania, and keep a box at the opera. Ten years of that, and you're an aristocrat. Well, you'll have enough money to split it two ways. And still you'll both be made.

"Oh, very well, very well. You can shake your head, Speedy, and smile at me," went on Dupray, "but the fact is that I can show you fifty-pound bars of gold. You understand? Fifty-pound ingots of massy gold. You know how they talk in the fairy tales about the massy gold? The poets are full of it, too. Well, I can show you the massy gold and masses of it, too. I can make yellow fire dance in front of your eyes, young men. I can show you a sight that few men in this world ever have seen. I tell you, I've heaped up wealth, and I've heaped up wealth, and it all lies there, ready to the hand. None of this rot about putting it in ships and buildings and land for me. Nothing but wealth that appeals to your hands and your eyes. You can back up the dray and carry off the load, except that one dray will never hold it all."

His lips parted. A frightful pallor deepened on his face and his forehead was beaded with sweat. "I tell you what, Speedy, I'll pay you everything in the treasure, if you'll let me have my life and that one ruby."

"Do you mean that?" asked Speedy.

"It's not that the stone is worth so very much money," Dupray said. "That isn't it, man. It's only that I'm used to that ruby. You understand? My eye's used to it . . . my eye loves it. The way a mother loves the face of her youngster, not because it's the prettiest face in the world, but because it's her child. That's the way that I love that ruby. You're a sensitive man, Speedy, or I couldn't talk to you like this. But you'll understand me when I speak to you like this, straight out of the heart. I drench the pair of you with wealth, and, in exchange, you give me nothing but my freedom and that one stone."

"Charley," Speedy said, "why didn't you make us an offer long ago, before we got down into the plain?"

"Because," Dupray explained, "I knew that you never intended to take me to the jail, really. Of course, I knew that nobody would turn me in when he had a chance to get my money. I was waiting for you to name your price. That was all. But, now that we've got as close to San Lorenzo as this, I see that you are going to hold me up for the whole lot."

"Suppose that we put you in prison, in spite of your treasures," said Speedy. "Suppose we jail you, and let your treasure rot, eh?"

The frog-face grew white, and the eyes shut for an instant. Then they opened and Dupray said: "You've got half a million, say, in that handful. You fools, how many other handfuls do you think I have? I can dip in and choose where I wish. Rubies? Yes. What about yellow topaz, though? Yellow as golden fire. Then there's a great flat-headed sapphire that would make you think of a lake in the mountains and. . . ."

He stopped suddenly, for he found that the eye of Speedy was resting upon him with infinite pity and mercy and understanding as well, yet there was inexorable justice waiting in that eye, also.

"You mean to run me in, then, and let the stuff go to waste?" Dupray asked.

"If you had all the money in the world . . . if that mountain were one diamond, and you owned it all," Speedy said, "I wouldn't turn you loose. Because I know you, Dupray, and you're not a man, but an evil spirit. You look like a ghoul, and you are one. You're the only man I ever knew that I could hate with my whole heart. There's no kindness, gentleness, good faith, or anything human about you. You're going to prison, and you'll walk out of that place to hang . . . unless the mob tears down the walls to get at you first."

He said this so calmly that big John Wilson could hardly give credence to his ears. But he realized, then, that Speedy was inexorable in his determination. He realized, too, that money was no real temptation to this strange man.

But no smile came on the face of Speedy until they had seen the steel door of a cell close on Dupray, leaving that hideous frog-face in the shadow. Not once had Dupray spoken since Speedy had given him his answer. But hatred spoke in his silence more clearly than in his talk.

They went from the jail to the hotel.

"I'm ashamed to face Jessica," John Wilson said. "When I look back, I feel that I've been a dog. I don't dare to face her, Speedy."

"Why should you feel that way?" Speedy asked. "You told her that you wanted to go out and make a fortune for yourself, and you've done that. I've an idea that none of those rubies . . . except maybe the big fellow, there . . . can be identified, and so they'll belong to you and me, old son. And your half ought to be eighty or a hundred thousand. That's something of a fortune, isn't it? That'll enable you to hold your head up and look your father-in-law in the face, no matter how rich he may be."

"It's true," Wilson said. "But there's more than money to give her."

"What?" Speedy asked curiously.

"A new idea," Wilson stated. "I can give her that.

Because I was rather a restless fellow, when you found me, Speedy, but I left all that restlessness back there in the moonlight on the slope of that hill, where you kept the horses at a trot, with all those demons galloping up behind us." He shivered, then shrugged his shoulders to get rid of the memory.

"Go out into the garden. She'll be down by the river at this time of day," Speedy said as they turned into the entrance of the hotel.

He himself followed on more slowly. He was still within the shadow of the garden gate when he heard a girl's voice cry out joyously. And in that joyous cry Speedy himself could find a measure of reward and of thankfulness.

About the Author

Max Brand is the best-known pen name of Frederick Faust, creator of Dr. Kildare, Destry, and many other fictional characters popular with readers and viewers worldwide. Faust wrote for a variety of audiences in many genres. His enormous output, totaling approximately 30,000,000 words or the equivalent of 530 ordinary books, covered nearly every field: crime, fantasy, historical romance, espionage, Westerns, science fiction, adventure, animal stories, love, war, and fashionable society, big business and big medicine. Eighty motion pictures have been based on his work along with many radio and television programs. For good measure he also published four volumes of poetry. Perhaps no other author has reached more people in more different ways.

Born in Seattle in 1892, orphaned early, Faust

grew up in the rural San Joaquin Valley of California. At Berkeley he became a student rebel and one-man literary movement, contributing prodigiously to all campus publications. Denied a degree because of unconventional conduct, he embarked on a series of adventures culminating in New York City where, after a period of near starvation, he received simultaneous recognition as a serious poet and successful author of fiction. Later, he traveled widely, making his home in New York, then in Florence, and finally in Los Angeles.

Once the United States entered the Second World War, Faust abandoned his lucrative writing career and his work as a screenwriter to serve as a war correspondent with the infantry in Italy, despite his fifty-one years and a bad heart. He was killed during a night attack on a hilltop village held by the German army. New books based on magazine serials or unpublished manuscripts or restored versions continue to appear so that, alive or dead, he has averaged a new book every four months for seventy-five years. Beyond this, some work by him is newly reprinted every week of every year in one or another format somewhere in the world. A great deal more about this author and his work can be found in *The Max Brand Companion* (Greenwood Press, 1997) edited by Jon Tuska and Vicki Piekarski.

Additional Copyright Information

HEADING WEST
Western Stories
NOEL M. LOOMIS

Noel M. Loomis creates characters so real it's hard to believe they're fiction, and these nine stories vividly demonstrate his brilliant storytelling talent. Within this volume, you'll meet Big Blue Buckley, who proves it takes a "Tough *Hombre*" to build a railroad in the 1880s and "The St. Louis Salesman" who struggles with the harsh terrain of the Texas prairie. Most poignant of all is the dying Comanche warrior passing on the ways of his people in "Grandfather Out of the Past," a tale that won Loomis the prestigious Spur Award. Each story sweeps you back in time to the Old West as it really was.

ISBN 10: 0-8439-5897-9
ISBN 13: 978-0-8439-5897-3

To order a book or to request a catalog call:
1-800-481-9191
This book is also available at your local bookstore, or you can check out our Web site **www.dorchesterpub.com** where you can look up your favorite authors, read excerpts, or glance at our discussion forum to see what people have to say about your favorite books.

MAX BRAND®

Luck

Pierre Ryder is not your average Jesuit missionary. He's able to ride the meanest horse, run for miles without tiring, and put a bullet in just about any target. But now he's on a mission of vengeance to find the man who killed his father. The journey will test his endurance to its utmost—and so will the extraordinary woman he meets along the way. Jacqueline "Jack" Boone has all the curves of a lady but can shoot better than most men. In the epic tradition of *Riders of the Purple Sage*, their story is one for the ages.

AVAILABLE MARCH 2008!

ISBN 13: 978-0-8439-5875-1

LOUIS L'AMOUR
Grub Line Rider

Louis L'Amour is one of the most popular and honored authors of the past hundred years. Millions of readers have thrilled to his tales of courage and adventure, tales that have transported them to the Old West and brought to life that exciting era of American history. Here, collected together in paperback for the first time, are seven of L'Amour's finest stories, all carefully restored to their original magazine publication versions.

Whether he's writing about a cattle town in Montana ("Black Rock Coffin Makers"), a posse pursuit across the desert ("Desert Death Song"), a young gunfighter ("Ride, You Tonto Riders"), or a violent battle to defend a homestead ("Grub Line Rider"), L'Amour's powerful presentation of the American West is always vibrant and compelling. This volume represents a golden opportunity to experience these stories as Louis L'Amour originally intended them to be read.

AVAILABLE MARCH 2008!

ISBN 13: 978-0-8439-6065-5

To order a book or to request a catalog call:
1-800-481-9191
This book is also available at your local bookstore, or you can check out our Web site **www.dorchesterpub.com** where you can look up your favorite authors, read excerpts, or glance at our discussion forum to see what people have to say about your favorite books.